ADVENTURES IN TIME AND SPACE

DARINGLY IMAGINATIVE STORIES BY THE WORLD'S
GREATEST SCIENCE-FICTION WRITERS!

•

– A dying lunatic takes a private trip to the Moon.

•

– A robot mother invades the earth from another
world and begins to lay her deadly eggs.

•

– A desperate man reaches into the future and
discovers that time is a murderous circle.

•

– A god-obsessed assassin kills a beautiful visitor
from outer space and triggers a strange revenge.

•
SELECTIONS FROM
ADVENTURES
IN
TIME
AND
SPACE
•
Edited by
RAYMOND J. HEALY
and
J. FRANCIS McCOMAS

BANTAM BOOKS
TORONTO · NEW YORK · LONDON

Selections from
ADVENTURES IN TIME AND SPACE
A Bantam Book / published by arrangement with
Random House, Inc.

PRINTING HISTORY

Random House edition published August 1946

2nd printing ... September 1946	4th printing ...... August 1950
3rd printing .... February 1947	5th printing ...... August 1951
6th printing .... July 1952	

Modern Library Giant edition published November 1957

2nd printing ... November 1957	6th printing .... June 1961
3rd printing ...... March 1958	7th printing .... May 1962
4th printing .... June 1958	8th printing ...... August 1963
5th printing ... September 1959	9th printing ..... October 1964

Bantam edition published January 1966

ACKNOWLEDGMENTS

For permission to reprint copyrighted material the following acknowledgments are gratefully made to:

Street & Smith, Inc., publishers of ASTOUNDING STORIES, *and to the Editors of that magazine for the following stories:*

"Requiem" by Robert A. Heinlein, "Black Destroyer" by A. E. Van Vogt, "Time Locker" by Lewis Padgett, "Mechanical Mice" by Maurice A. Hugi, "As Never Was" by P. Schuyler Miller, "Quietus" by Ross Rocklynne, "Farewell to the Master" by Harry Bates, copyright, Street & Smith Publications, Inc., 1939, 1940, 1942, 1943.

Robert Moore Williams, author, for "Robot's Return," from ASTOUNDING STORIES, *copyright, Street & Smith Publications, Inc., 1938.*

Bantam Books are published by Bantam Books, Inc., a subsidiary of Grosset & Dunlap, Inc. Its trade-mark, consisting of the words "Bantam Books" and the portrayal of a bantam, is registered in the United States Patent Office and in other countries. Marca Registrada. Bantam Books, Inc., 271 Madison Avenue, New York, N. Y. 10016.

PRINTED IN THE UNITED STATES OF AMERICA

CONTENTS

REQUIEM / by Robert A. Heinlein

One wonders how Columbus might have felt if circumstances had left him standing on the dock, watching his tiny fleet sail westward without him. Robert Heinlein has envisioned the man who made space travel possible forced by ill-health to stand earthbound and watch the first rocket ship, his ship, soar out through space to the moon. The story of the frustrated pioneer is a rare combination of realistic detail and poignant charm.

ON A HIGH HILL in Samoa there is a grave. Inscribed on the marker are these words:

> "Under the wide and starry sky
> Dig my grave and let me lie.
> Glad did I live and gladly die
> And I lay me down with a will!
>
> "This be the verse you grave for me:
> Here he lies where he longed to be,
> Home is the sailor, home from the sea,
> And the hunter home from the hill."

These lines appear another place—scrawled on a shipping tag from a compressed-air container, and pinned to the ground with a knife.

It was not much of a fair, as fairs go. The trotting races didn't promise much excitement, even though several entries claimed the blood of the immortal Dan Patch. The tents and concession booths barely covered the circus grounds, and the pitchmen seemed discouraged.

D. D. Harriman's chauffeur could not see any reason for stopping. They were due in Kansas City for a directors'

1

meeting; that is to say, Harriman was. The chauffeur had private reasons for promptness, reasons involving a certain party on Eighteenth Street. But the boss not only stopped; he hung around. He didn't seem much interested in the racetrack or sideshows, though.

Bunting and a canvas arch made the entrance to a large inclosure beyond the racetrack. Red and gold letters announced:

> This way to the
> *MOON ROCKET! ! ! !*
> See it in actual flight!
> Public Demonstration Flights
> TWICE DAILY
> This is the ACTUAL TYPE used by the
> First Men to Reach the *MOON! !*
> *YOU* can ride in it! !—$25

A boy, nine or ten years old, hung around the entrance and stared at the posters.

"Want to see the ship, son?"

The kid's eyes shone. "Gee, mister, I sure would."

"So would I. Come on."

Harriman paid out fifty cents for two pink tickets which entitled him and the boy to enter the inclosure and examine the rocketship. The kid ran on ahead with a single-minded preoccupation of boyhood. Harriman looked over the stubby curved lines of the ovoid body. He noted with a professional eye that she was a single-jet type with fractional controls around her midriff. He squinted through his glasses at the name painted in gold on the carnival red of the body, *Carefree*. He paid another quarter to enter the control cabin.

When his eyes had adjusted to the gloom caused by the strong ray filters of the ports, he let them rest lovingly on the keys of the console and the semi-circle of dials above. Each beloved gadget was in its proper place. He knew them —graven in his heart.

While he mused over the instrument board, with the warm liquid of content soaking through his body, the pilot entered and touched his arm.

"Sorry, sir. We've got to cast loose for the flight."

"Eh?" Harriman started, then looked at the speaker. Handsome devil, with a good skull and strong shoulders—reckless eyes and a self-indulgent mouth, but a firm chin. "Oh, excuse me, captain."

"Quite all right."

"Oh, I say, captain . . . er . . . uh—"

"McIntyre."

"Captain McIntyre, could you take a passenger this trip?" The old man leaned eagerly toward him.

"Why, yes, if you wish. Come along with me." He ushered Harriman into a shed marked "Office" which stood near the gate. "Passenger for a check-over, doc."

Harriman permitted the medico to run a stethoscope over his thin chest and to strap a rubber bandage around his arm. Presently the doctor unstrapped it, glanced at McIntyre, and shook his head.

"No go, doc?"

"That's right, captain."

Harriman looked from face to face, his disappointment plain to see. "You won't take me?"

The doctor shrugged his shoulders. "I couldn't even guarantee that you would live through the take-off. You see, sir," he continued, not unkindly, "it's not only that your heart condition makes heavy acceleration dangerous, but at your age bones are brittle, highly calcified, and easily broken in the shock of take-off. Rocketry is a young man's game."

McIntyre added: "Sorry, sir. I'd like to, but the Bates County Fair Association pays the doctor here to see to it that I don't take up anyone who might be hurt by the acceleration."

The old man's shoulders drooped miserably. "I rather expected it."

"Sorry, sir." McIntyre turned to go, but Harriman followed him out.

"Excuse me, captain—"

"Yes?"

"Could you and your . . . uh . . . engineer have dinner with me after your flight?"

The pilot looked at him quizzically. "I don't see why not. Thanks."

"Captain McIntyre, it is difficult for me to see why anyone would quit the Earth-Moon run," said Harriman a few hours later. Fried chicken and hot biscuits in a private dining room of the best hotel the little town of Butler afforded, three-star Hennessey and Corona Coronas had produced a friendly atmosphere in which three men could talk freely.

"Well, I didn't like it."

"Aw, don't give him that, Mac—you know damn well it was Rule G that got you." McIntyre's mechanic poured himself another brandy as he spoke.

McIntyre looked sullen. "Well, what if I did take a couple o' drinks? Anyhow, I could have squared that—it was the damn persnickety regulations that got me fed up. Who are you to talk? Smuggler!"

"Sure, I smuggled! Who wouldn't—with all those beautiful rocks just aching to be taken back to Earth? I had a diamond once as big as— But if I hadn't been caught I'd be in Luna City tonight. And so would you, you drunken blaster—with the boys buying us drinks and the girls smiling and making suggestions—" He put his face down and began to weep quietly.

McIntyre shook him. "He's drunk."

"Never mind." Harriman interposed a hand. "Tell me, are you really satisfied not to be on the run any more?"

McIntyre chewed his lip. "No—he's right, of course. This barnstorming isn't what it's all cracked up to be. We've been hopping junk at every pumpkin doin's up and down the Mississippi Valley—sleeping in tourist camps, and eating at greaseburners. Half the time the sheriff has an attachment on the ship, the other half the Society for the Prevention of Something or Other gets an injunction to keep us on the ground. It's no sort of a life for a rocket man."

"Would it help any for you to get to the Moon?"

"Well—yes. I couldn't get back on the Earth-Moon run, but if I was in Luna City, I would get a job hopping ore for the company—they're always short of rocket pilots for that, and they wouldn't mind my record. If I kept my nose clean, they might even put me back on the run, in time."

Harriman fiddled with a spoon, then looked up. "Would you young gentlemen be open to a business proposition?"

"Perhaps. What is it?"

"You own the *Carefree?*"

"Yeah. That is, Charlie and I do—barring a couple of liens against her. What about it?"

"I want to charter her—for you and Charlie to take me to the Moon!"

Charlie sat up with a jerk. "D'joo hear what he said, Mac? He wants us to fly that old heap to the Moon!"

McIntyre shook his head. "Can't do it, Mr. Harriman. The old boat's worn out. We don't even use standard juice in her—just gasoline and liquid air. Charlie spends all of his time tinkering with her at that. She's going to blow up some day."

"Say, Mr. Harriman," put in Charlie, "what's the matter with getting an excursion permit and going in a company ship?"

"No, son," the old man replied, "I can't do that. You know the conditions under which Congress granted the company a monopoly on lunar exploitation—no one to enter space who was not physically qualified to stand up under it. Company to take full responsibility for the safety and health of all citizens beyond the stratosphere. The official reason for granting the franchise was to stop the enormous loss of life that occurred during the first few years of rocket travel."

"And you can't pass the physical exam?"

Harriman shook his head.

"Well, what the hell—if you can afford to hire us, why don't you just bribe yourself a brace of company docs? It's been done before."

Harriman smiled ruefully. "I know it has, Charlie, but it won't work for me. You see, I'm a little too prominent. My full name is Delos D. Harriman."

"What? You are old D. D.? But, hell's bells, you own a big slice of the company yourself; you ought to be able to do anything you like, rules or no rules."

"That is not an unusual opinion, son, but it is incorrect. Rich men aren't more free than other men; they are less free—a good deal less free. I tried to do what you suggest, but the other directors would not permit me. They are afraid of losing their franchise. It costs them a good deal in—uh—political contact expenses to retain it, as it is."

"Well, I'll be a— Can you tie that, Mac? A guy with lots of dough, and he can't spend it the way he wants to."

McIntyre did not answer, but waited for Harriman to continue.

"Captain McIntyre, if you had a ship, would you take me?"
McIntyre rubbed his chin. "It's against the law."

"I'd make it worth your while."

"Sure, he would, Mr. Harriman. Of course you would, Mac. Luna City! Oh, baby!"

"Why do you want to go to the Moon so badly, Mr. Harriman?"

"Captain, it's the one thing I've really wanted to do all my life—ever since I was a boy. I don't know whether I can explain it to you or not. You young fellows have grown up to rocket travel the way I grew up to aviation. I'm a great deal older than you are; maybe fifty years older. When I was a kid practically nobody believed that men would ever reach the Moon. You've seen rockets all your lives, and the first to reach the Moon got there before you were old enough to vote. When I was a boy they laughed at the idea.

"But I believed—I believed. I read Verne and Wells and Smith, and I believed that we could do it—that we *would* do it. I set my heart on being one of the men to walk the surface of the Moon, to see her other side, and to look back on the face of the Earth, hanging in the sky.

"I used to go without my lunches to pay my dues in the American Rocket Society, because I wanted to believe that I was helping to bring the day nearer when we would reach the Moon. I was already an old man when that day arrived. I've lived longer than I should, but I would not let myself die—I will not!—until I have set foot on the Moon."

McIntyre stood up and put out his hand. "You find a ship, Mr. Harriman, I'll drive 'er."

"Atta boy, Mac! I told you he would, Mr. Harriman."

Harriman mused and dozed during the hour's run to the north into Kansas City, dozed in the light, troubled sleep of old age. Incidents out of a long life ran through his mind in vagrant dreams. There was that time—oh, yes, 1910—a little boy on a warm spring night. "What's that, daddy?"

"That's Halley's comet, sonny."

"Where did it come from?"

"I don't know, son. From way out in the sky somewhere."

"It's *beyootiful*, daddy. I want to touch it."

" 'Fraid not, son."

"Delos, do you mean to stand there and tell me you put the money we had saved for the house into that crazy rocket company?"

"Now, Charlotte, please! It's not crazy; it's a sound business investment. Some day soon rockets will fill the sky. Ships and trains will be obsolete. Look what happened to the men that had the foresight to invest in Henry Ford."

"We've been all over this before."

"Charlotte, the day will come when men will rise up off the Earth and visit the Moon, even the planets. This is the beginning."

"Must you shout?"

"I'm sorry, but you—"

"I feel a headache coming on. Please try to be a little quiet when you come to bed."

He hadn't gone to bed. He had sat out on the veranda all night long, watching the full Moon move across the sky. There would be the devil to pay in the morning, the devil and a thin-lipped silence. But he'd stick by his guns. He'd given in on most things, but not on this. The night was his. Tonight he'd be alone with his old friend. He searched her face. Where was Mare Crisium? Funny, he couldn't make it out. He used to be able to see it plainly when he was a boy. Probably needed new glasses—this constant office work wasn't good for his eyes.

But he didn't need to see; he knew where they all were: Crisium, Mare Fecunditatis, Mare Tranquillitatis—that one had a satisfying roll!—the Appenines, the Carpathians, old Tycho with its mysterious rays.

Two hundred and forty thousand miles—ten times around the Earth. Surely men could bridge a little gap like that. Why, he could almost reach out and touch it, nodding there behind the elm trees.

Not that he could help to do it. He hadn't the education.

"Son, I want to have a little serious talk with you."

"Yes, mother."

"I know you had hoped to go to college next year"— Hoped! He had lived for it. The University of Chicago to study under Moulton, then on to the Yerkes Observatory to work under the eye of Dr. Frost himself—"and I had hoped so, too. But with your father gone, and the girls growing up, it's harder to make ends meet. You've been a good boy, and worked hard to help out. I know you'll understand."

"Yes, mother."

"Extra! Extra! Stratosphere Rocket Reaches Paris. Read aaaaalllllll about 't." The thin little man in the bifocals snatched at the paper and hurried back to the office.

"Look at this, A. J."

"Huh? Hm-m-m, interesting, but what of it?"

"Can't you see? The next stage is to the Moon!"

"God, but you're a sucker, Delos. The trouble with you is, you read too many of those trashy magazines. Now, I caught my boy reading one of 'em just last week and dressed him down proper. Your folks should have done you the same favor."

Harriman squared his narrow, middle-aged shoulders. "They will so reach the Moon!"

His partner laughed. "Have it your own way. If baby wants the moon, papa will bring it home for him. But you stick to your discounts and commissions; that's where the money is."

The big car droned down the Paseo, and turned off on Armour Boulevard. Old Harriman stirred uneasily in his sleep and muttered to himself.

"But, Mr. Harriman—" The young man with the note-book was plainly perturbed. The old man grunted.

"You heard me. Sell 'em. I want every share I own realized in cash as rapidly as possible; Spaceways, Space-ways Provisioning Co., Artemis Mines, Luna City Recreations, the whole lot of them."

"It will depress the market. You won't realize the full value of your holdings."

"Don't you think I know that? I can afford it."

"What about the shares you had earmarked for Tycho Observatory and for the Harriman Scholarships?"

"Oh, yes. Don't sell those. Set up a trust. Should have done it long ago. Tell Mr. Kamens to draw up the papers. He knows what I want."

The interoffice 'visor flashed into life. "The gentlemen are here, Mr. Harriman."

"Send 'em in. That's all, Ashley. Get busy." Ashley went

out as McIntyre and Charlie entered. Harriman got up and trotted forward to greet them.

"Come in, boys, come in. I'm so glad to see you. Sit down. Have a cigar."

"Mighty pleased to see you, Mr. Harriman," acknowledged Charlie. "In fact, you might say we need to see you."

"Some trouble, gentlemen?" Harriman glanced from face to face. McIntyre answered him.

"You still mean that about a job for us, Mr. Harriman?"

"Mean it? Certainly, I do. You're not backing out on me?"

"Not at all. We need that job now. You see, the *Carefree* is lying in the middle of the Osage River, with her jet split clear back to the injector."

"Dear me! You weren't hurt?"

"No, aside from sprains and bruises. We jumped."

Charlie chortled. "I caught a catfish with my bare teeth."

In short order they got down to business. "You two will have to buy a ship for me. I can't do it openly; my colleagues would figure out what I mean to do and stop me. I'll supply you with all the cash you need. You go out and locate some sort of a ship that can be refitted for the trip. Work up some good story about how you are buying it for some playboy as a stratosphere yacht, or that you plan to try to establish an Arctic-Antarctic tourist route. Anything as long as no one suspects that she is being outfitted for space flight.

"Then, after the department of transport licenses her for strato flight, you move to a piece of desert out West— I'll find a likely parcel of land and buy it—and then I'll join you. Then we'll install the extra fuel tanks, change the injectors and timers and so forth, to fit her for the hop. How about it?"

McIntyre looked dubious. "It'll take a lot of doing. Charlie, do you think you can accomplish that change-over without a dockyard and shops?"

"Me? Sure, I can—with your thick-fingered help. Just give me the tools and materials I want, and don't hurry me too much. Of course, it won't be fancy—"

"Nobody wants it to be fancy. I just want a ship that won't blow when I start slapping the keys."

"It won't blow, Mac."

"That's what you thought about the *Carefree*."

"That ain't fair, Mac. I ask you, Mr. Harriman—that heap

was junk, and we knew it. This'll be different. We're going to spend some dough and do it right. Ain't we, Mr. Harriman?"

Harriman patted him on the shoulder. "Certainly we are, Charlie. You can have all the money you want. That's the least of our worries. Now, do the salaries and bonuses I mentioned suit you? I don't want you to be short."

"—as you know, my clients are his nearest relatives and have his interests at heart. We contend that Mr. Harriman's conduct for the past several weeks, as shown by the evidence here adduced, gives clear indication that a mind once brilliant in the world of finance has become senile. It is, therefore, with the deepest regret that we pray this honorable court, if it pleases, to declare Mr. Harriman incompetent and to assign a conservator to protect his financial interests and those of his future heirs and assigns." The attorney sat down, pleased with himself.

Mr. Kamens took the floor. "May it please the court—if my esteemed friend is *quite* through—I suggest that in his last few words my opponent gave away his entire thesis. 'The financial interests of future heirs and assigns.' It is evident that the petitioners believe that my client should conduct his affairs in such a fashion as to insure that his nieces and nephews, and their issue, will be supported in unearned luxury for the rest of their lives. My client's wife has passed on; he has no children. It is admitted that he has provided generously for his sisters and their children in times past, and that he has established annuities for such near kin as are without means of support.

"But now, like vultures—worse than vultures, for they are not content to let him die in peace—they would prevent my client from enjoying his wealth in whatever manner best suits him for the few remaining years of his life. It is true that he has sold his holdings; is it strange that an elderly man should wish to retire? It is true that he suffered some paper losses in liquidation. 'The value of a thing is what that thing will bring.' He was retiring and demanded cash. Is there anything strange about that?

"It is admitted that he refused to discuss his actions with his so-loving kinfolk. What law, or principle, requires a man to consult with his nephews on anything?

"Therefore, we pray that this court will confirm my client

in his right to do what he likes with his own, deny this petition, and send these meddlers about their business."

The judge took off his spectacles and polished them thoughtfully.

"Mr. Kamens, this court has as high a regard for individual liberty as you have, and you may rest assured that any action taken will be solely in the interests of your client. Nevertheless, men do grow old, men do become senile, and in such cases must be protected.

"I shall take this matter under advisement until tomorrow. Court is adjourned."

From the Kansas City *Star:*

ECCENTRIC MILLIONAIRE DISAPPEARS

—failed to appear for the adjourned hearing. The bailiffs returned from a search of places usually frequented by Harriman with the report that he had not been seen since the previous day. A bench warrant under contempt proceedings has been issued and—

A desert sunset is a better stimulant for the appetite than a hot dance orchestra. Charlie testified to this by polishing off the last of the ham gravy with a piece of bread. Harriman handed each of the younger men cigars and took one himself.

"My doctor claims that these weeds are bad for my heart condition," Harriman remarked as he lighted his, "but I've felt so much better since I joined you boys here on the ranch that I am inclined to doubt him." He exhaled a cloud of blue-gray smoke and resumed. "I don't think a man's health depends so much on what he does as on whether he wants to do it. I'm doing what I want to do."

"That's all a man can ask of life," agreed McIntyre.

"How does the work look now, boys?"

"My end's in pretty good shape," Charlie answered. "We finished the second pressure tests on the new tanks and the fuel lines today. The ground tests are all done, except the calibration runs. Those won't take long—just the four hours to make the runs if I don't run into some bugs. How about you, Mac?"

McIntyre ticked them off on his fingers. "Food supplies

and water on board. Three vacuum suits, a spare, and service kits. Medical supplies. The buggy already had all the standard equipment for strato flight. The late lunar ephemerides haven't arrived as yet."

"When do you expect them?"

"Any time—they should be here now. Not that it matters. This guff about how hard it is to navigate from here to the Moon is hokum to impress the public. After all, you can see your destination—it's not like ocean navigation. Gimme a sextant and a good stadimeter and I'll set you down any place on the Moon you like—without opening an almanac or a star table—just from a general knowledge of the relative speeds involved."

"Never mind the personal build-up, Columbus," Charlie told him. "We'll admit you can hit the floor with your hat. The general idea is, you're ready to go now. Is that right?"

"That's it."

"That being the case, I *could* run those tests tonight. I'm getting jumpy—things have been going too smoothly. If you'll give me a hand, we ought to be in bed by midnight."

"O. K. When I finish this cigar."

They smoked in silence for a while, each thinking about the coming trip and what it meant to him. Old Harriman tried to repress the excitement that possessed him at the prospect of immediate realization of his lifelong dream.

"Mr. Harriman—"

"Eh? What is it, Charlie?"

"How does a guy go about getting rich, like you did?"

"Getting rich? I can't say; I never tried to get rich. I never wanted to be rich, or well known, or anything like that."

"Huh?"

"No, I just wanted to live a long time and see it all happen. I wasn't unusual; there were lots of boys like me—radio hams, they were, and telescope builders, and airplane amateurs. We had science clubs, and basement laboratories, and science-fiction leagues—the kind of boys that thought there was more romance in one issue of the *Electrical Experimenter* than in all the books Dumas ever wrote. We didn't want to be one of Horatio Alger's get-rich heroes, either; we wanted to build spaceships. Well, some of us did."

"Gosh, Pop, you make it sound exciting."

"It was exciting, Charlie. This has been a wonderful, romantic century, for all of its bad points. And it's grown more wonderful and more exciting every year. No, I didn't want to be rich; I just wanted to live long enough to see men rise up to the stars, and, if God was good to me, to go as far as the Moon myself." He carefully deposited an inch of white ash in a saucer. "It has been a good life. I haven't any complaints."

McIntyre pushed back his chair. "Come on, Charlie, if you're ready."

"O. K."

They all got up. Harriman started to speak, then grabbed at his chest, his face a dead gray-white.

"Catch him, Mac!"

"Where's his medicine?"

"In his vest pocket."

They eased him over to a couch, broke a small glass capsule in a handkerchief, and held it under his nose. The volatile released by the capsule seemed to bring a little color into his face. They did what little they could for him, then waited for him to regain consciousness.

Charlie broke the uneasy silence. "Mac, we ain't going through with this."

"Why not?"

"It's murder. He'll never stand up under the initial acceleration."

"Maybe not, but it's what he wants to do. You heard him."

"But we oughtn't to let him."

"Why not? It's neither your business nor the business of this damn paternalistic government to tell a man not to risk his life doing what he really wants to do."

"All the same, I don't feel right about it. He's such a swell old duck."

"Then what d'yuh want to do with him—send him back to Kansas City so those old harpies can shut him up in a laughing academy till he dies of a broken heart?"

"N-no-o-o—not that."

"Get out there, and make your set-up for those test runs. I'll be along."

A wide-tired desert runabout rolled into the ranch-yard gate the next morning and stopped in front of the house. A heavy-set man with a firm, but kindly, face climbed out and spoke to McIntyre, who approached to meet him.

"You James McIntyre?"

"What about it?"

"I'm the deputy Federal marshal hereabouts. I got a warrant for your arrest."

"What's the charge?"

"Conspiracy to violate the Space Precautionary Act."

Charlie joined the pair. "What's up, Mac?"

The deputy answered. "You'd be Charles Cummings, I guess. Warrant here for you. Got one for a man named Harriman, too, and a court order to put seals on your spaceship."

"We've no spaceship."

"What d'yuh keep in that big shed?"

"Strato yacht."

"So? Well, I'll put seals on her until a spaceship comes along. Where's Harriman?"

"Right in there." Charlie obliged by pointing, ignoring McIntyre's scowl.

The deputy turned his head. Charlie couldn't have missed the button by a fraction of an inch, for the deputy collapsed quietly to the ground. Charlie stood over him, rubbing his knuckles and mourning.

"That's the finger I broke playing shortstop. I'm always hurting that finger."

"Get Pop into the cabin," Mac cut him short, "and strap him into his hammock."

"Aye, aye, skipper."

They taxied on the auxiliary motor out of the hangar, turned, and started out across the desert plain to find elbow room for the take-off. McIntyre saw the deputy from his starboard conning port. He was staring disconsolately after them.

McIntyre fastened his safety belt, settled his corset, and spoke into the engine-room speaking tube. "All set, Charlie?"

"All set, skipper. But you can't raise ship yet, Mac. *She ain't named!*"

"No time for your superstitions!"

Harriman's thin voice reached them. "Call her the *Lunatic*. It's the only appropriate name!"

McIntyre settled his head into the pads, punched two keys, then three more in rapid succession, and the *Lunatic* raised ground.

"How are you, Pop?"

Charlie searched the old man's face anxiously. Harriman

licked his lips and managed to speak. "Doing fine, son. Couldn't be better."

"The acceleration won't be so bad from here on. I'll unstrap you so you can wiggle around a little. But I think you'd better stay in the hammock." He tugged at buckles. Harriman partially repressed a groan.

"What is it, Pop?"

"Nothing. Nothing at all. Just go easy on that side."

Charlie ran his fingers over the old man's side with the sure, delicate touch of a mechanic. "You ain't foolin' me none, Pop. But there isn't much I can do until we ground."

"Charlie—"

"Yes, Pop?"

"Can't I move to a port? I want to watch the Earth."

"Ain't nothin to see yet; the blast hides it. As soon as we build up enough speed to coast up to the change-over point, I'll move you. Tell you what; I'll give you a sleepy pill, and then wake you when we cut the jets."

"No!"

"Huh?"

"I'll stay awake."

"Just as you say, Pop."

Charlie fought his way up to the nose of the ship, and braced himself on the gimbals of the pilot's chair. McIntyre questioned him with his eyes.

"Yeah, he's alive all right," Charlie told him, "but he's in bad shape."

"How bad?"

"Couple of cracked ribs, anyhow. I don't know what else. I don't know whether he'll last out the trip, Mac. His heart was pounding something awful."

"He'll last, Charlie. He's tough."

"Tough? He's delicate as a canary."

"I don't mean that. He's tough way down inside—where it counts."

"Just the same, you'd better set her down awful easy if you want to ground with a full complement aboard."

"I will. I'll make one full swing around the Moon and ease her in on an involute approach curve. We've got enough fuel, I think."

When they commenced to coast in a free orbit, Charlie unslung the hammock and moved Harriman, hammock and all, to a side port. McIntyre turned the ship about a transverse axis so that the tail pointed toward the Sun, then gave a short blast on two tangential jets opposed in couple to cause the ship to spin slowly about her longitudinal axis, and thereby create a slight artificial gravity. The initial weightlessness when coasting commenced had knotted the old man with the characteristic nausea of free flight, and the pilot wished to save his passenger as much discomfort as possible.

But Harriman was not concerned with the condition of his stomach.

There it was, all as he had imagined it so many times. The Moon swung majestically past the viewport, twice as wide as he had ever seen it before, all of her familiar features cameo-clear. She gave way to the Earth as the ship continued its slow swing, the Earth itself, as he had envisioned her, appearing like a noble moon, eight times as wide as the Moon appears to the Earthbound, and more luscious, more sensuously beautiful than the silver Moon could be. It was sunset near the Atlantic seaboard—the line of shadow ran down Hudson Bay, slashed through the eastern coast line of North America, touched Cuba, and obscured the eastern bulge of South America. He savored the mellow blue of the Pacific Ocean, felt the texture of the soft green and brown of the continents, admired the blue-white cold of the polar caps. Canada and the great Northwest were obscured by cloud, a vast low-pressure area that spread across the continent. It shone with an even more satisfactory dazzling white than the polar caps.

As the ship swung slowly around, Earth would pass from view, and the stars would march across the port—the same stars he had always known, but steady, brighter, and unwinking against a screen of perfect, live black. Then the Moon would swim into view again to claim his thoughts.

He was serenely happy in a fashion not given to most men, even in a long lifetime. He felt as if he were every man who had ever lived, and looked up at the stars, and longed.

At least once he must have fallen into deep sleep, or possibly delirium, for he came to with a start, thinking that his wife, Charlotte, was calling to him. "Delos!" the voice had said. "Delos! Come in from there! You'll catch your death of cold in that night air."

Poor Charlotte! She had been a good wife to him, a good

wife. He was quite sure that her only regret in dying had been her fear that he would not take proper care of himself. It had not been her fault that she had not shared his dream and his need.

Charlie rigged the hammock in such a fashion that Harriman could watch from the starboard port when they swung around the far face of the Moon. He picked out the landmarks made familiar to him by a thousand photographs with nostalgic pleasure, as if he were returning to his own country. McIntyre brought her slowly down as they came back around to the Earthward face, and prepared to land in Mare Imbrium between Aristillus and Archimedes, about ten miles from Luna City.

It was not a bad landing, all things considered. He had to land without coaching from the ground, and he had no second pilot to punch the stadimeter for him. In his anxiety to make it gentle he missed his destination by some thirty miles, but he did his cold-sober best. At that, it was rather bumpy.

As they scooted along to a stop, throwing up powdery pumice on each side, Charlie came up to the control station.

"How's our passenger?" Mac demanded.

"I'll see, but I wouldn't make any bets. That landing stunk, Mac."

"Damn it, I did my best."

"I know you did, skipper. Forget it."

But the passenger was alive and conscious, though bleeding from the nose, and with a pink foam on his lips. He was feebly trying to get himself out of his cocoon. They helped him, working together.

"Where are the vacuum suits?" was his first remark.

"Steady, Mr. Harriman. You can't go out there yet. We've got to give you some first aid."

"Get me that suit! First aid can wait."

Silently they did as he ordered. His left leg was practically useless, and they had to help him through the lock, one on each side. But with his inconsiderable mass having a lunar weight of only twenty pounds, he was no burden. They found a place some fifty yards from the ship where they could prop him up and let him look, a chunk of scoria supporting his head.

McIntyre put his helmet against the old man's and spoke. "We'll leave you here to enjoy the view while we get ready for the trek into town. It's a forty-miler, pretty near, and we'll have to break out spare air bottles and rations and stuff. We'll be back soon."

Harriman nodded without answering, and squeezed their gauntlets with a grip that was surprisingly strong.

He sat very quiet, rubbing his hands against the soil of the Moon and sensing the curiously light pressure of his body against the ground. At long last there was peace in his heart. His hurts had ceased to pain him. He was where he had longed to be—he had followed his need. Overhead hung the Earth in third quarter, a green-blue giant moon. The Sun's upper limb crowned the crags of Archimedes to his left. And underneath—the Moon; the soil of the Moon itself. He was on the Moon!

He lay back still while a bath of content flowed over him like a tide at flood, and soaked into his very marrow.

His attention strayed momentarily, and he thought once again that his name was called. Silly, he thought; I'm getting old—my mind wanders.

Back in the cabin Charlie and Mac were rigging shoulder yokes on a stretcher. "There. That will do," Mac commented. "We'd better stir Pop out; we ought to be going."

"I'll get him," Charlie replied. "I'll just pick him up and carry him. He don't weigh nothing."

Charlie was gone longer than McIntyre had expected him to be. He returned alone. Mac waited for him to close the lock and swing back his helmet. "Trouble?"

"Never mind the stretcher, skipper. We won't be needin' it. Yeah, I mean it," he continued. "I did what was necessary."

McIntyre bent down without a word and commenced to strap on the wide skis necessary to negotiate the powdery ash. Charlie followed his example. Then they swung spare air bottles over their shoulders and passed out through the lock. They didn't bother to close the outer door of the lock behind them.

Charlie looked toward the relaxed figure propped up on the bed of Lunar pumice, face fixed toward the Earth. "Well," he grunted, "he hit the Moon—"

BLACK DESTROYER / by A. E. Van Vogt

Speculation on inter-planetary travel leads inevitably to speculation on the types of life pioneers from Earth will encounter.
There are so many things to take into account: atmospheric
conditions, vegetation, climate, etc. Even planets grow old and
the civilizations that people them crumble and die, leaving
behind them dregs. Such a dreg was Coeurl, who had lost everything, even dim memories of greatness, in a primitive, ravening
hunger that could never be satiated.

ON AND ON COEURL PROWLED! The black, moonless,
almost starless night yielded reluctantly before a grim reddish dawn that crept up from his left. A vague, dull light
it was, that gave no sense of approaching warmth, no comfort, nothing but a cold, diffuse lightness, slowly revealing a
nightmare landscape.

Black, jagged rock and black, unliving plain took form
around him, as a pale-red sun peered at last above the
grotesque horizon. It was then Coeurl recognized suddenly
that he was on familiar ground.

He stopped short. Tenseness flamed along his nerves. His
muscles pressed with sudden, unrelenting strength against
his bones. His great forelegs—twice as long as his hindlegs—
twitched with a shuddering movement that arched every
razor-sharp claw. The thick tentacles that sprouted from
his shoulders ceased their weaving undulation, and grew taut
with anxious alertness.

Utterly appalled, he twisted his great cat head from side
to side, while the little hairlike tendrils that formed each
ear vibrated frantically, testing every vagrant breeze, every
throb in the ether.

But there was no response, no swift tingling along his
intricate nervous system, not the faintest suggestion any-

19

where of the presence of the all-necessary id. Hopelessly, Coeurl crouched, an enormous catlike figure silhouetted against the dim reddish skyline, like a distorted etching of a black tiger resting on a black rock in a shadow world.

He had known this day would come. Through all the centuries of restless search, this day had loomed ever nearer, blacker, more frightening—this inevitable hour when he must return to the point where he began his systematic hunt in a world almost depleted of id-creatures.

The truth struck in waves like an endless, rhythmic ache at the seat of his ego. When he had started, there had been a few id-creatures in every hundred square miles, to be mercilessly rooted out. Only too well Coeurl knew in this ultimate hour that he had missed none. There were no id-creatures left to eat. In all the hundreds of thousands of square miles that he had made his own way by right of ruthless conquest—until no neighboring coeurl dared to question his sovereignty—there was no id to feed the otherwise immortal engine that was his body.

Square foot by square foot he had gone over it. And now —he recognized the knoll of rock just ahead, and the black rock bridge that formed a queer, curling tunnel to his right. It was in that tunnel he had lain for days, waiting for the simple-minded, snakelike id-creature to come forth from its hole in the rock to bask in the sun—his first kill after he had realized the absolute necessity of organized extermination.

He licked his lips in brief gloating memory of the moment his slavering jaws tore the victim into precious toothsome bits. But the dark fear of an idless universe swept the sweet remembrance from his consciousness, leaving only certainty of death.

He snarled audibly, a defiant, devilish sound that quavered on the air, echoed and re-echoed among the rocks, and shuddered back along his nerves—an instinctive and hellish expression of his will to live.

And then—abruptly—it came.

He saw it emerge out of the distance on a long downward slant, a tiny glowing spot that grew enormously into a metal ball. The great shining globe hissed by above Coeurl, slowing visibly in quick deceleration. It sped over the black line of hills to the right, hovered almost motionless for a second, then sank down out of sight.

Coeurl exploded from his startled immobility. With tiger speed, he flowed down among the rocks. His round, black eyes burned with the horrible desire that was an agony within him. His ear tendrils vibrated a message of id in such tremendous quantities that his body felt sick with the pangs of his abnormal hunger.

The little red sun was a crimson ball in the purple-black heavens when he crept up from behind a mass of rock and gazed from its shadows at the crumbling, gigantic ruins of the city that sprawled below him. The silvery globe, in spite of its great size, looked strangely inconspicuous against that vast, fairylike reach of ruins. Yet about it was a leashed aliveness, a dynamic quiescence that, after a moment, made it stand out, dominating the foreground. A massive, rock-crushing thing of metal, it rested on a cradle made by its own weight in the harsh, resisting plain which began abruptly at the outskirts of the dead metropolis.

Coeurl gazed at the strange, two-legged creatures who stood in little groups near the brilliantly lighted opening that yawned at the base of the ship. His throat thickened with the immediacy of his need; and his brain grew dark with the first wild impulse to burst forth in furious charge and smash these flimsy, helpless-looking creatures whose bodies emitted the id-vibrations.

Mists of memory stopped that mad rush when it was still only electricity surging through his muscles. Memory that brought fear in an acid stream of weakness, pouring along his nerves, poisoning the reservoirs of his strength. He had time to see that the creatures wore things over their real bodies, shimmering transparent material that glittered in strange, burning flashes in the rays of the sun.

Other memories came suddenly. Of dim days when the city that spread below was the living, breathing heart of an age of glory that dissolved in a single century before flaming guns whose wielders knew only that for the survivors there would be an ever-narrowing supply of id.

It was the remembrance of those guns that held him there, cringing in a wave of terror that blurred his reason. He saw himself smashed by balls of metal and burned by searing flame.

Came cunning—understanding of the presence of these creatures. This, Coeurl reasoned for the first time, was a scientific expedition from another star. In the olden days, the coeurls had thought of space travel, but disaster came too swiftly for it ever to be more than a thought.

Scientists meant investigation, not destruction. Scientists in their way were fools. Bold with knowledge, he emerged into the open. He saw the creatures become aware of him. They turned and stared. One, the smallest of the group, detached a shining metal rod from a sheath, and held it casually in one hand. Coeurl loped on, shaken to his core by the action; but it was too late to turn back.

Commander Hal Morton heard little Gregory Kent, the chemist, laugh with the embarrassed half gurgle with which he invariably announced inner uncertainty. He saw Kent fingering the spindly metalite weapon.

Kent said: "I'll take no chances with anything as big as that."

Commander Morton allowed his own deep chuckle to echo along the communicators. "That," he grunted finally, "is one of the reasons why you're on this expedition, Kent—because you never leave anything to chance."

His chuckle trailed off into silence. Instinctively, as he watched the monster approach them across that black rock plain, he moved forward until he stood a little in advance of the others, his huge form bulking the transparent metalite suit. The comments of the men pattered through the radio communicator into his ears:

"I'd hate to meet that baby on a dark night in an alley."

"Don't be silly. This is obviously an intelligent creature. Probably a member of the ruling race."

"It looks like nothing else than a big cat, if you forget those tentacles sticking out from its shoulders, and make allowances for those monster forelegs."

"Its physical development," said a voice, which Morton recognized as that of Siedel, the psychologist, "presupposes an animal-like adaptation to surroundings, not an intellectual one. On the other hand, its coming to us like this is not the act of an animal but of a creature possessing a mental awareness of our possible identity. You will notice that its movements are stiff, denoting caution, which suggests fear and consciousness of our weapons. I'd like to get a good look at the ends of its tentacles. If they taper into handlike appendages that can really grip objects, then the conclusion would be inescapable that it is a descendant of the in-habitants of this city. It would be a great help if we could establish communication with it, even though appearances indicate that it has degenerated into a historyless primitive."

Coeurl stopped when he was still ten feet from the fore-most creature. The sense of id was so overwhelming that his brain drifted to the ultimate verge of chaos. He felt as if his limbs were bathed in molten liquid; his very vision was not quite clear, as the sheer sensuality of his desire thundered through his being.

The men—all except the little one with the shining metal rod in his fingers—came closer. Coeurl saw that they were frankly and curiously examining him. Their lips were mov-ing, and their voices beat in a monotonous, meaningless rhythm on his ear tendrils. At the same time he had the sense of waves of a much higher frequency—his own com-munication level—only it was a machine-like clicking that jarred his brain. With a distinct effort to appear friendly, he broadcast his name from his ear tendrils, at the same time pointing at himself with one curving tentacle.

Gourlay, chief of communications, drawled: "I got a sort of static in my radio when he wiggled those hairs, Morton. Do you think—"

"Looks very much like it," the leader answered the un-finished question. "That means a job for you, Gourlay. If it speaks by means of radio waves, it might not be alto-gether impossible that you can create some sort of television picture of its vibrations, or teach him the Morse code."

"Ah," said Siedel. "I was right. The tentacles each de-velop into seven strong fingers. Provided the nervous sys-tem is complicated enough, those fingers could, with train-ing, operate any machine."

Morton said: "I think we'd better go in and have some lunch. Afterward, we've got to get busy. The material men can set up their machines and start gathering data on the planet's possibilities, and so on. The others can do a little careful exploring. I'd like some notes on architecture and on the scientific development of this race, and particularly what happened to wreck the civilization. On earth civilization after civilization crumbled, but always a new one sprang up in its dust. Why didn't that happen here? Any questions?"

"Yes. What about pussy? Look, he wants to come in with us."

Commander Morton frowned, an action that emphasized the deep-space pallor of his face. "I wish there was some way we could take it with us, without forcibly capturing it. Kent, what do you think?"

"I think we should first decide whether it's an it or a him, and call it one or the other. I'm in favor of him. As for taking him in with us—" The little chemist shook his head decisively. "Impossible. This atmosphere is twenty-eight per cent chlorine. Our oxygen would be pure dynamite to his lungs."

The commander chuckled. "He doesn't believe that, apparently." He watched the catlike monster follow the first two men through the great door. The men kept an anxious distance from him, then glanced at Morton questioningly. Morton waved his hand. "O. K. Open the second lock and let him get a whiff of the oxygen. That'll cure him."

A moment later, he cursed his amazement. "By Heaven, he doesn't even notice the difference! That means he hasn't any lungs, or else the chlorine is not what his lungs use. Let him in! You bet he can go in! Smith, here's a treasure house for a biologist—harmless enough if we're careful. We can always handle him. But what a metabolism!"

Smith, a tall, thin, bony chap with a long, mournful face, said in an oddly forceful voice: "In all our travels, we've found only two higher forms of life. Those dependent on chlorine, and those who need oxygen—the two elements that support combustion. I'm prepared to stake my reputation that no complicated organism could ever adapt itself to both gases in a natural way. At first though I should say here is an extremely advanced form of life. This race long ago discovered truths of biology that we are just beginning to suspect. Morton, we mustn't let this creature get away if we can help it."

"If his anxiety to get inside is any criterion," Commander Morton laughed, "then our difficulty will be to get rid of him."

He moved into the lock with Coeurl and the two men. The automatic machinery hummed; and in a few minutes they were standing at the bottom of a series of elevators that led up to the living quarters.

"Does that go up?" One of the men flicked a thumb in the direction of the monster.

"Better send him up alone, if he'll go in."

Coeurl offered no objection, until he heard the door slam behind him; and the closed cage shot upward. He whirled with a savage snarl, his reason swirling into chaos. With one leap, he pounced at the door. The metal bent under his plunge, and the desperate pain maddened him. Now, he was all trapped animal. He smashed at the metal with his paws, bending it like so much tin.´ He tore great bars loose with his thick tentacles. The machinery screeched; there were horrible jerks as the limitless power pulled the cage along in spite of projecting pieces of metal that scraped the outside walls. And then the cage stopped, and he snatched off the rest of the door and hurtled into the corridor.

He waited there until Morton and the men came up with drawn weapons. "We're fools," Morton said. "We should have shown him how it works. He thought we'd double-crossed him."

He motioned to the monster, and saw the savage glow fade from the coal-black eyes as he opened and closed the door with elaborate gestures to show the operation.

Coeurl ended the lesson by trotting into the large room to his right. He lay down on the rugged floor, and fought down the electric tautness of his nerves and muscles. A very fury of rage against himself for his fright consumed him. It seemed to his burning brain that he had lost the advantage of appearing a mild and harmless creature. His strength must have startled and dismayed them.

It meant greater danger in the task which he now knew he must accomplish: To kill everything in the ship, and take the machine back to their world in search of unlimited id.

With unwinking eyes, Coeurl lay and watched the two men clearing away the loose rubble from the metal doorway of the huge old building. His whole body ached with the hunger of his cells for id. The craving tore through his palpitant muscles, and throbbed like a living thing in his brain. His every nerve quivered to be off after the men who had wandered into the city. One of them, he knew, had gone—alone.

The dragging minutes fled; and still he restrained himself, still he lay there watching, aware that the men knew he

watched. They floated a metal machine from the ship to
the rock mass that blocked the great half-open door, under
the direction of a third man. No flicker of their fingers
escaped his fierce stare, and slowly, as the simplicity of the
machinery became apparent to him, contempt grew upon him.

He knew what to expect finally, when the flame flared in
incandescent violence and ate ravenously at the hard rock
beneath. But in spite of his preknowledge, he deliberately
jumped and snarled as if in fear, as that white heat burst
forth. His ear tendrils caught the laughter of the men,
their curious pleasure at his simulated dismay.

The door was released, and Morton came over and went
inside with the third man. The latter shook his head.

"It's a shambles. You can catch the drift of the stuff.
Obviously, they used atomic energy, but . . . but it's in
wheel form. That's a peculiar development. In our science,
atomic energy brought in the nonwheel machine. It's possible that here they've progressed *further to* a new type of
wheel mechanics. I hope their libraries are better preserved
than this, or we'll never know. What could have happened
to a civilization to make it vanish like this?"

A third voice broke through the communicators: "This is
Siedel. I heard your question, Pennons. Psychologically and
sociologically speaking, the only reason why a territory becomes uninhabited is lack of food."

"But they're so advanced scientifically, why didn't they
develop space flying and go elsewhere for their food?"

"Ask Gunlie Lester," interjected Morton. "I heard him
expounding some theory even before we landed."

The astronomer answered the first call. "I've still got to
verify all my facts, but this desolate world is the only
planet revolving around that miserable red sun. There's nothing else. No moon, not even a planetoid. And the nearest
star system is *nine hundred light-years away*.

"So tremendous would have been the problem of the
ruling race of this world, that in one jump they would not
only have had to solve interplanetary but interstellar space
traveling. When you consider how slow our own development was—first the moon, then Venus—each success leading
to the next, and after centuries to the nearest stars; and last
of all to the anti-accelerators that permitted galactic travel
—considering all this, I maintain it would be impossible for
any race to create such machines without practical experi-

ence. And, with the nearest star so far away, they had no
incentive for the space adventuring that makes for experience."

Coeurl was trotting briskly over to another group. But
now, in the driving appetite that consumed him, and in the
frenzy of his high scorn, he paid no attention to what they
were doing. Memories of past knowledge, jarred into activity
by what he had seen, flowed into his consciousness in an
ever developing and more vivid stream.

From group to group he sped, a nervous dynamo—jumpy,
sick with his awful hunger. A little car rolled up, stopping
in front of him, and a formidable camera whirred as it
took a picture of him. Over on a mound of rock, a gigantic
telescope was rearing up toward the sky. Nearby, a disinte-
grating machine drilled its searing fire into an ever-deepening
hole, down and down, straight down.

Coeurl's mind became a blur of things he watched with
half attention. And ever more imminent grew the moment
when he knew he could no longer carry on the torture of
acting. His brain strained with an irresistible impatience; his
body burned with the fury of his eagerness to be off after
the man who had gone alone into the city.

He could stand it no longer. A green foam misted his
mouth, maddening him. He saw that, for the bare moment,
nobody was looking.

Like a shot from a gun, he was off. He floated along
in great, gliding leaps, a shadow among the shadows of the
rocks. In a minute, the harsh terrain hid the spaceship and
the two-legged beings.

Coeurl forgot the ship, forgot everything but his purpose,
as if his brain had been wiped clear by a magic, memory-
erasing brush. He circled widely, then raced into the city,
along deserted streets, taking short cuts with the ease of
familiarity, through gaping holes in time-weakened walls,
through long corridors of moldering buildings. He slowed
to a crouching lope as his ear tendrils caught the id vibrations.

Suddenly, he stopped and peered from a scatter of fallen
rock. The man was standing at what must once have been a
window, sending the glaring rays of his flashlight into the
gloomy interior. The flashlight clicked off. The man, a heavy-
set, powerful fellow, walked off with quick, alert steps.

Coeurl didn't like that alertness. It presaged trouble; it meant lightning reaction to danger.

Coeurl waited till the human being had vanished around a corner, then he padded into the open. He was running now, tremendously faster than a man could walk, because his plan was clear in his brain. Like a wraith, he slipped down the next street, past a long block of buildings. He turned the first corner at top speed; and then, with dragging belly, crept into the half-darkness between the building and a huge chunk of débris. The street ahead was barred by a solid line of loose rubble that made it like a valley, ending in a narrow, bottle-like neck. The neck had its outlet just below Coeurl.

His ear tendrils caught the low-frequency waves of whistling. The sound throbbed through his being; and suddenly terror caught with icy fingers at his brain. The man would have a gun. Suppose he leveled one burst of atomic energy —*one burst*—before his own muscles could whip out in murder fury.

A little shower of rocks streamed past. And then the man was beneath him. Coeurl reached out and struck a single crushing blow at the shimmering transparent headpiece of the spacesuit. There was a tearing sound of metal and a gushing of blood. The man doubled up as if part of him had been telescoped. For a moment, his bones and legs and muscles combined miraculously to keep him standing. Then he crumpled with a metallic clank of his space armor.

Fear completely evaporated, Coeurl leaped out of hiding. With ravenous speed, he smashed the metal and the body within it to bits. Great chunks of metal, torn piecemeal from the suit, sprayed the ground. Bones cracked. Flesh crunched.

It was simple to tune in on the vibrations of the id, and to create the violent chemical disorganization that freed it from the crushed bone. The id was, Coeurl discovered, mostly in the bone.

He felt revived, almost reborn. Here was more food than he had had in the whole past year.

Three minutes, and it was over, and Coeurl was off like a thing fleeing dire danger. Cautiously, he approached the glistening globe from the opposite side to that by which he had left. The men were all busy at their tasks. Gliding noiselessly, Coeurl slipped unnoticed up to a group of men.

Morton stared down at the horror of tattered flesh, metal and blood on the rock at his feet, and felt a tightening in his throat that prevented speech. He heard Kent say:

"He *would* go alone, damn him!" The little chemist's voice held a sob imprisoned; and Morton remembered that Kent and Jarvey had chummed together for years in the way only two men can.

"The worst part of it is," shuddered one of the men, "it looks like a senseless murder. His body is spread out like little lumps of flattened jelly, but it seems to be all there. I'd almost wager that if we weighed everything here, there'd still be one hundred and seventy-five pounds by earth gravity. That'd be about one hundred and seventy pounds here."

Smith broke in, his mournful face lined with gloom: "The killer attacked Jarvey, and then discovered his flesh was alien—uneatable. Just like our big cat. Wouldn't eat anything we set before him—" His words died out in sudden, queer silence. Then he said slowly: "Say, what about that creature? He's big enough and strong enough to have done this with his own little paws."

Morton frowned. "It's a thought. After all, he's the only living thing we've seen. We can't just execute him on suspicion, of course—"

"Besides," said one of the men, "he was never out of my sight."

Before Morton could speak, Siedel, the psychologist, snapped, "Positive about that?"

The man hesitated. "Maybe he was for a few minutes. He was wandering around so much, looking at everything."

"Exactly," said Siedel with satisfaction. He turned to Morton. "You see, commander, I, too, had the impression that he was always around; and yet, thinking back over it, I find gaps. There were moments—probably long minutes— when he was completely out of sight."

Morton's face was dark with thought, as Kent broke in fiercely: "I say, take no chances. Kill the brute on suspicion before he does any more damage."

Morton said slowly: "Korita, you've been wandering around with Cranessy and Van Horne. Do you think pussy is a descendant of the ruling class of this planet?"

The tall Japanese archeologist stared at the sky as if collecting his mind. "Commander Morton," he said finally, respectfully, "there is a mystery here. Take a look, all of you, at that majestic skyline. Notice the almost Gothic outline of the architecture. In spite of the megalopolis which they created, these people were close to the soil. The buildings are not simply ornamented. They are ornamental in themselves. Here is the equivalent of the Doric column, the Egyptian pyramid, the Gothic cathedral, growing out of the ground, earnest, big with destiny. If this lonely, desolate world can be regarded as mother earth, then the land had a warm, spiritual place in the hearts of the race.

"The effect is emphasized by the winding streets. Their machines prove they were mathematicians, but they were artists first; and so they did not create the geometrically designed cities of the ultra-sophisticated world metropolis. There is a genuine artistic abandon, a deep joyous emotion written in the curving and unmathematical arrangements of houses, buildings and avenues; a sense of intensity, of divine belief in an inner certainty. This is not a decadent, hoary-with-age civilization, but a young and vigorous culture, confident, strong with purpose.

"There it ended. Abruptly, as if at this point culture had its Battle of Tours, and began to collapse like the ancient Mohammedan civilization. Or as if in one leap it spanned the centuries and entered the period of contending states. In the Chinese civilization that period occupied 480-230 B. C., at the end of which the State of Tsin saw the beginning of the Chinese Empire. This phase Egypt experienced between 1780-1580 B. C., of which the last century was the 'Hyksos'—unmentionable—time. The classical experienced it from Chæronea—338—and, at the pitch of horror, from the Gracchi—133—to Actium—31 B. C. The West European Americans were devastated by it in the nineteenth and twentieth centuries, and modern historians agree that, nominally, we entered the same phase fifty years ago; though, of course, we have solved the problem.

"You may ask, commander, what has all this to do with your question? My answer is: there is no record of a culture entering abruptly into the period of contending states. It is always a slow development; and the first step is a merciless questioning of all that was once held sacred. Inner certainities cease to exist, are dissolved before the ruthless probings of scientific and analytic minds. The skeptic becomes the highest type of being.

"I say that this culture ended abruptly in its most flourishing age. The sociological effects of such a catastrophe would be a sudden vanishing of morals, a reversion to almost bestial criminality, unleavened by any sense of ideal, a callous indifference to death. If this . . . this pussy is a descendant of such a race, then he will be a cunning creature, a thief in the night, a cold-blooded murderer, who would cut his own brother's throat for gain."

"That's enough!" It was Kent's clipped voice. "Commander, I'm willing to act the role of executioner."

Smith interrupted sharply: "Listen, Morton, you're not going to kill that cat yet, even if he is guilty. He's a biological treasure house."

Kent and Smith were glaring angrily at each other. Morton frowned at them thoughtfully, then said: "Korita, I'm inclined to accept your theory as a working basis. But one question: Pussy comes from a period earlier than our own? That is, we are entering the highly civilized era of our culture, while he became suddenly historyless in the most vigorous period of his. *But* it is possible that his culture is a later one on this planet than ours is in the galactic-wide system we have civilized?"

"Exactly. His may be the middle of the tenth civilization of his world; while ours is the end of the eighth sprung from Earth, each of the ten, of course, having been built on the ruins of the one before it."

"In that case, pussy would not know anything about the skepticism that made it possible for us to find him out so positively as a criminal and murderer?"

"No; it would be literally magic to him."

Morton was smiling grimly. "Then I think you'll get your wish, Smith. We'll let pussy live; and if there are any fatalities, now that we know him, it will be due to rank carelessness. There's just the chance, of course, that we're wrong. Like Siedel, I also have the impression that he was always around. But now—we can't leave poor Jarvey here like this. We'll put him in a coffin and bury him."

"No, we won't!" Kent barked. He flushed. "I beg your pardon, commander. I didn't mean it that way. I maintain pussy wanted something from that body. It looks to be all there, but something must be missing. I'm going to find out what, and pin this murder on him so that you'll have to believe it beyond the shadow of a doubt."

It was late night when Morton looked up from a book and saw Kent emerge through the door that led from the laboratories below.

Kent carried a large, flat bowl in his hands; his tired eyes flashed across at Morton, and he said in a weary, yet harsh, voice: "Now watch!"

He started toward Coeurl, who lay sprawled on the great rug, pretending to be asleep.

Morton stopped him. "Wait a minute, Kent. Any other time, I wouldn't question your actions, but you look ill; you're overwrought. What have you got there?"

Kent turned, and Morton saw that his first impression had been but a flashing glimpse of the truth. There were dark pouches under the little chemist's gray eyes—eyes that gazed feverishly from sunken cheeks in an ascetic face.

"I've found the missing element," Kent said. "It's phosphorus. There wasn't so much as a square millimeter of phosphorus left in Jarvey's bones. Every bit of it had been drained out—by what superchemistry I don't know. There are ways of getting phosphorus out of the human body. For instance, a quick way was what happened to the workman who helped build this ship. Remember, he fell into fifteen tons of molten metalite—at least, so his relatives claimed—but the company wouldn't pay compensation until the metalite, on analysis, was found to contain a high percentage of phosphorus—"

"What about the bowl of food?" somebody interrupted. Men were putting away magazines and books, looking up with interest.

"It's got organic phosphorus in it. He'll get the scent, or whatever it is that he uses instead of scent—"

"I think he gets the vibrations of things," Gourlay interjected lazily. "Sometimes, when he wiggles those tendrils, I get a distinct static on the radio. And then, again, there's no reaction, just as if he's moved higher or lower on the wave scale. He seems to control the vibrations at will."

Kent waited with obvious impatience until Gourlay's last word, then abruptly went on: "All right, then, when he gets the vibration of the phosphorus and reacts to it like an animal, then—well, we can decide what we've proved by his reaction. May I go ahead, Morton?"

"There are three things wrong with your plan," Morton said. "In the first place, you seem to assume that he is only animal; you seem to have forgotten he may not be hungry after Jarvey; you seem to think he will not be suspicious. But set the bowl down. His reaction may tell us something."

Coeurl stared with unblinking black eyes as the man set the bowl before him. His ear tendrils instantly caught the id-vibrations from the contents of the bowl—and he gave it not even a second glance.

He recognized this two-legged being as the one who had held the weapon that morning. Danger! With a snarl, he floated to his feet. He caught the bowl with the finger-like appendages at the end of one looping tentacle, and emptied its contents into the face of Kent, who shrank back with a yell.

Explosively, Coeurl flung the bowl aside and snapped a hawser-thick tentacle around the cursing man's waist. He didn't bother with the gun that hung from Kent's belt. It was only a vibration gun, he sensed—atomic powered, but not an atomic disintegrator. He tossed the kicking Kent onto the nearest couch—and realized with a hiss of dismay that he should have disarmed the man.

Not that the gun was dangerous—but, as the man furiously wiped the gruel from his face with one hand, he reached with the other for his weapon. Coeurl crouched back as the gun was raised slowly and a white beam of flame was discharged at his massive head.

His ear tendrils hummed as they canceled the efforts of the vibration gun. His round, black eyes narrowed as he caught the movement of men reaching for their metalite guns. Morton's voice lashed across the silence.

"Stop!"

Kent clicked off his weapon; and Coeurl crouched down, quivering with a fury at this man who had forced him to reveal something of his power.

"Kent," said Morton coldly, "you're not the type to lose your head. You deliberately tried to kill pussy, knowing that the majority of us are in favor of keeping him alive. You know what our rule is: If anyone objects to my decisions, he must say so *at the time*. If the majority object, my decisions are overruled. In this case, no one but you objected, and, therefore, your action in taking the law into your own hands is most reprehensible, and automatically debars you from voting for a year."

Kent stared grimly at the circle of faces. "Korita was right when he said ours was a highly civilized age. It's decadent." Passion flamed harshly in his voice. "My God, isn't there a man here who can see the horror of the situation? Jarvey dead only a few hours, and this creature, whom we all know to be guilty, lying there unchained, planning his next murder; and the victim is right here in this room. What kind of men are we—fools, cynics, ghouls—or is it that our civilization is so steeped in reason that we can contemplate a murderer sympathetically?"

He fixed brooding eyes on Coeurl. "You were right, Morton, that's no animal. That's a devil from the deepest hell of this forgotten planet, whirling its solitary way around a dying sun."

"Don't go melodramatic on us," Morton said. "Your analysis is all wrong, so far as I am concerned. We're not ghouls or cynics; we're simply scientists, and pussy here is going to be studied. Now that we suspect him, we doubt his ability to trap any of us. One against a hundred hasn't a chance." He glanced around. "Do I speak for all of us?"

"Not for me, commander!" It was Smith who spoke, and, as Morton stared in amazement, he continued: "In the excitement and momentary confusion, no one seems to have noticed that when Kent fired his vibration gun, the beam hit this creature squarely on his cat head—and didn't hurt him."

Morton's amazed glance went from Smith to Coeurl, and back to Smith again. "Are you certain it hit him? As you say, it all happened so swiftly—when pussy wasn't hurt I simply assumed that Kent had missed him."

"He hit him in the face," Smith said positively. "A vibration gun, of course, can't even kill a man right away—but it can injure him. There's no sign of injury on pussy, though, not even a singed hair."

"Perhaps his skin is a good insulation against heat of any kind."

"Perhaps. But in view of our uncertainty, I think we should lock him up in the cage."

While Morton frowned darkly in thought, Kent spoke up. "Now you're talking sense, Smith."

Morton asked: "Then you would be satisfied, Kent, if we put him in the cage?"

Kent considered, finally: "Yes. If four inches of micro-steel can't hold him, we'd better give him the ship."

Coeurl followed the men as they went out into the corridor. He trotted docilely along as Morton unmistakably motioned him through a door he had not hitherto seen. He found himself in a square, solid metal room. The door clanged metallically behind him; he felt the flow of power as the electric lock clicked home.

His lips parted in a grimace of hate, as he realized the trap, but he gave no other outward reaction. It occurred to him that he had progressed a long way from the sunk-into-primitiveness creature who, a few hours before, had gone incoherent with fear in an elevator cage. Now, a thousand memories of his powers were reawakened in his brain; ten thousand cunnings were, after ages of disuse, once again part of his very being.

He sat quite still for a moment on the short, heavy haunches into which his body tapered, his ear tendrils examining his surroundings. Finally, he lay down, his eyes glowing with contemptuous fire. The fools! The poor fools!

It was about an hour later when he heard the man—Smith—fumbling overhead. Vibrations poured upon him, and for just an instant he was startled. He leaped to his feet in pure terror—and then realized that the vibrations *were* vibrations, not atomic explosions. Somebody was taking pictures of the inside of his body.

He crouched down again, but his ear tendrils vibrated, and he thought contemptuously: the silly fool would be surprised when he tried to develop those pictures.

After a while the man went away, and for a long time there were noises of men doing things far away. That, too, dried away slowly.

Coeurl lay waiting, as he felt the silence creep over the ship. In the long ago, before the dawn of immortality, the coeurls, too, had slept at night; and the memory of it had been revived the day before when he saw some of the men dozing. At last, the vibration of two pairs of feet, pacing, pacing endlessly, was the only human-made frequency that throbbed on his ear tendrils.

Tensely, he listened to the two watchmen. The first one walked slowly past the cage door. Then about thirty feet behind him came the second. Coeurl sensed the alertness of these men; knew that he could never surprise either while they walked separately. It meant—he must be doubly careful!

Fifteen minutes, and they came again. The moment they were past, he switched his senses from their vibrations to a vastly higher range. The pulsating violence of the atomic engines stammered its soft story to his brain. The electric dynamos hummed their muffled song of pure power. He felt the whisper of that flow through the wires in the walls of his cage, and through the electric lock of his door. He forced his quivering body into straining immobility, his senses seeking, searching, to tune in on that sibilant tempest of energy. Suddenly, his ear tendrils vibrated in harmony— he caught the surging change into shrillness of that rippling force wave.

There was a sharp click of metal on metal. With a gentle touch of one tentacle, Coeurl pushed open the door, and glided out into the dully gleaming corridor. For just a moment he felt contempt, a glow of superiority, as he thought of the stupid creatures who dared to match their wit against a coeurl. And in that moment, he suddenly thought of other coeurls. A queer, exultant sense of race pounded through his being; the driving hate of centuries of ruthless competition yielded reluctantly before pride of kinship with the future rulers of all space.

Suddenly, he felt weighed down by his limitations, his need for other coeurls, his aloneness—one against a hundred, with the stake all eternity; the starry universe itself beckoned his rapacious, vaulting ambition. If he failed, there would never be a second chance—no time to revive long-rotted machinery, and attempt to solve the secret of space travel.

He padded along on tensed paws—through the salon— into the next corridor—and came to the first bedroom door. It stood half open. One swift flow of synchronized muscles, one swiftly lashing tentacle that caught the unresisting throat of the sleeping man, crushing it; and the lifeless head rolled crazily, the body twitched once.

Seven bedrooms; seven dead men. It was the seventh taste of murder that brought a sudden return of lust, a pure, unbounded desire to kill, return of a millennium-old habit of destroying everything containing the precious id.

As the twelfth man slipped convulsively into death, Coeurl emerged abruptly from the sensuous joy of the kill to the sound of footsteps.

They were not near—that was what brought wave after wave of fright swirling into the chaos that suddenly became his brain.

The watchmen were coming slowly along the corridor toward the door of the cage where he had been imprisoned. In a moment, the first man would see the open door—and sound the alarm.

Coeurl caught at the vanishing remnants of his reason. With frantic speed, careless now of accidental sounds, he raced—along the corridor with its bedroom doors—through the salon. He emerged into the next corridor, cringing in awful anticipation of the atomic flame he expected would stab into his face.

The two men were together, standing side by side. For one single instant, Coeurl could scarcely believe his tremendous good luck. Like a fool the second had come running when he saw the other stop before the open door. They looked up, paralyzed, before the nightmare of claws and tentacles, the ferocious cat head and hate-filled eyes.

The first man went for his gun, but the second, physically frozen before the doom he saw, uttered a shriek, a shrill cry of horror that floated along the corridors—and ended in a curious gurgle, as Coeurl flung the two corpses with one irresistible motion the full length of the corridor. He didn't want the dead bodies found near the cage. That was his one hope.

Shaking in every nerve and muscle, conscious of the terrible error he had made, unable to think coherently, he plunged into the cage. The door clicked softly shut behind him. Power flowed once more through the electric lock.

He crouched tensely, simulating sleep, as he heard the rush of many feet, caught the vibration of excited voices. He knew when somebody actuated the cage audioscope and looked in. A few moments now, and the other bodies would be discovered.

"Siedel gone!" Morton said numbly. "What are we going to do without Siedel? And Breckenridge! And Goulter and—Horrible!"

He covered his face with his hands, but only for an instant. He looked up grimly, his heavy chin outthrust as he stared into the stern faces that surrounded him. "If anybody's got so much as a germ of an idea, bring it out."

"Space madness!"

"I've thought of that. But there hasn't been a case of a man going mad for fifty years. Dr. Eggert will test everybody, of course, and right now he's looking at the bodies with that possibility in mind."

As he finished, he saw the doctor coming through the door. Men crowded aside to make way for him.

"I heard you, commander," Dr. Eggert said, "and I think I can say right now that the space-madness theory is out. The throats of these men have been squeezed to a jelly. No human being could have exerted such enormous strength without using a machine."

Morton saw that the doctor's eyes kept looking down the corridor, and he shook his head and groaned:

"It's no use suspecting pussy, doctor. He's in his cage, pacing up and down. Obviously heard the racket and— Man alive! You can't suspect him. That cage was built to hold literally *anything*—four inches of micro-steel—and there's not a scratch on the door. Kent, even you won't say, 'Kill him on suspicion,' because there can't be any suspicion, unless there's a new science here, beyond anything we can imagine—"

"On the contrary," said Smith flatly, "we have all the evidence we need. I used the telefluor on him—you know the arrangement we have on top of the cage—and tried to take some pictures. They just blurred. Pussy jumped when the telefluor was turned on, as if he felt the vibrations.

"You all know what Gourlay said before? This beast can apparently receive and send vibrations of any lengths. The way he dominated the power of Kent's gun is final proof of his special ability to interfere with energy."

"What in the name of all the hells have we got here?" One of the men groaned. "Why, if he can control that power, and sent it out in any vibrations, there's nothing to stop him killing all of us."

"Which proves," snapped Morton, "that he isn't invincible, or he would have done it long ago."

Very deliberately, he walked over to the mechanism that controlled the prison cage.

"You're not going to open the door!" Kent gasped, reaching for his gun.

"No, but if I pull this switch, electricity will flow through the floor, and electrocute whatever's inside. We've never had to use this before, so you had probably forgotten about it."

He jerked the switch hard over. Blue fire flashed from the metal, and a bank of fuses above his head exploded with a single bang.

Morton frowned. "That's funny. Those fuses shouldn't have blown! Well, we can't even look in, now. That wrecked the audios, too."

Smith said: "If he could interfere with the electric lock, enough to open the door, then he probably probed every possible danger and was ready to interfere when you threw that switch."

"At least, it proves he's vulnerable to our energies!" Morton smiled grimly. "Because he rendered them harmless. The important thing is, we've got him behind four inches of the toughest of metal. At the worst we can open the door and ray him to death. But first, I think we'll try to use the telefluor power cable—"

A commotion from inside the cage interrupted his words. A heavy body crashed against a wall, followed by a dull thump.

"He knows what we were trying to do!" Smith grunted to Morton. "And I'll bet it's a very sick pussy in there. What a fool he was to go back into that cage and does he realize it!"

The tension was relaxing; men were smiling nervously, and there was even a ripple of humorless laughter at the picture Smith drew of the monster's discomfiture.

"What I'd like to know," said Pennons, the engineer, "is, why did the telefluor meter dial jump and waver at full power when pussy made that noise? It's right under my nose here, and the dial jumped like a house afire!"

There was silence both without and within the cage, then Morton said: "It may mean he's coming out. Back, everybody, and keep your guns ready. Pussy was a fool to think he could conquer a hundred men, but he's by far the most formidable creature in the galactic system. He may come out of that door, rather than die like a rat in a trap. And he's just tough enough to take some of us with him—if we're not careful."

The men backed slowly in a solid body; and somebody said: "That's funny. I thought I heard the elevator."

"Elevator!" Morton echoed. "Are you sure, man?"

"Just for a moment I was!" The man, a member of the crew, hesitated. "We were all shuffling our feet—"

"Take somebody with you, and go look. Bring whoever dared to run off back here—"

There was a jar, a horrible jerk, as the whole gigantic body of the ship careened under them. Morton was flung to the floor with a violence that stunned him. He fought back to consciousness, aware of the other men lying all around him. He shouted: "Who the devil started those engines!"

The agonizing acceleration continued; his feet dragged with awful exertion, as he fumbled with the nearest audioscope, and punched the engine-room number. The picture that flooded onto the screen brought a deep bellow to his lips:

"It's pussy! He's in the engine room—and we're heading straight out into space."

The screen went black even as he spoke, and he could see no more.

It was Morton who first staggered across the salon floor to the supply room where the spacesuits were kept. After fumbling almost blindly into his own suit, he cut the effects of the body-torturing acceleration, and brought suits to the semiconscious men on the floor. In a few moments, other men were assisting him; and then it was only a matter of minutes before everybody was clad in metalite, with anti-acceleration motors running at half power.

It was Morton then who, after first looking into the cage, opened the door and stood, silent as the others crowded about him, to stare at the gaping hole in the rear wall. The hole was a frightful thing of jagged edges and horribly bent metal, and it opened upon another corridor.

"I'll swear," whispered Pennons, "that it's impossible. The ten-ton hammer in the machine shops couldn't more than dent four inches of micro with one blow—and we only heard one. It would take at least a minute for an atomic disintegrator to do the job. Morton, this is super-being."

Morton saw that Smith was examining the break in the wall. The biologist looked up. "If only Breckenridge weren't dead! We need a metallurgist to explain this. Look!"

He touched the broken edge of the metal. A piece crumbled in his finger and slithered away in a fine shower of dust to the floor. Morton noticed for the first time that there was a little pile of metallic debris and dust.

"You've hit it." Morton nodded. "No miracle of strength here. The monster merely used his special powers to interfere with the electronic tensions holding the metal together. That would account, too, for the drain on the telefluor power cable that Pennons noticed. The thing used the power with his body as a transforming medium, smashed through the wall, ran down the corridor to the elevator shaft, and so down to the engine room."

"In the meantime, commander," Kent said quietly, "we are faced with a super-being in control of the ship, completely dominating the engine room and its almost unlimited power, and in possession of the best part of the machine shops."

Morton felt the silence, while the men pondered the chemist's words. Their anxiety was a tangible thing that lay heavily upon their faces; in every expression was the growing realization that here was the ultimate situation in their lives; their very existence was at stake and perhaps much more. Morton voiced the thought in everybody's mind:

"Suppose he wins. He's utterly ruthless, and he probably sees galactic power within his grasp."

"Kent is wrong," barked the chief engineer. "The thing doesn't dominate the engine room. We've still got the control room, and that gives us *first* control of all the machines. You fellows may not know the mechanical set-up we have; but, though he can eventually disconnect us, we can cut off all the switches in the engine room *now*. Commander, why didn't you just shut off the power instead of putting us into spacesuits? At the very least you could have adjusted the ship to the acceleration."

"For two reasons," Morton answered. "Individually, we're safer within the force fields of our spacesuits. And we can't afford to give up our advantages in panicky moves."

"Advantages! What other advantages have we got?"

"We know things about him," Morton replied. "And right now, we're going to make a test. Pennons, detail five men to each of the four approaches to the engine room. Take atomic disintegrators to blast through the big doors. They're all shut, I noticed. He's locked himself in.

"Selenski, you go up to the control room and shut off

everything except the drive engines. Gear them to the master switch, and shut them off all at once. One thing, though—leave the acceleration on full blast. No anti-acceleration must be applied to the ship. Understand?"

"Aye, sir!" The pilot saluted.

"And report to me through the communicators if any of the machines start to run again." He faced the man. "I'm going to lead the main approach. Kent, you take No. 2; Smith, No. 3, and Pennons, No. 4. We're going to find out right now if we're dealing with unlimited science, or a creature limited like the rest of us. I'll bet on the second possibility."

Morton had an empty sense of walking endlessly, as he moved, a giant of a man in his transparent space armor, along the glistening metal tube that was the main corridor of the engine-room floor. Reason told him the creature had already shown feet of clay, yet the feeling that here was an invincible being persisted.

He spoke into the communicator: "It's no use trying to sneak up on him. He can probably hear a pin drop. So just wheel up your units. He hasn't been in that engine room long enough to do anything.

"As I've said, this is largely a test attack. In the first place, we could never forgive ourselves if we didn't try to conquer him now, before he's had time to prepare against us. But, aside from the possibility that we can destroy him immediately, I have a theory.

"The idea goes something like this: Those doors are built to withstand accidental atomic explosions, and it will take fifteen minutes for the atomic disintegrators to smash them. True, the drive will be on, but that's straight atomic explosion. My theory is, he can't touch stuff like that; and in a few minutes you'll see what I mean—I hope."

His voice was suddenly crisp: "Ready, Selenski?"

"Aye, ready."

"Then cut the master switch."

The corridor—the whole ship, Morton knew—was abruptly plunged into darkness. Morton clicked on the dazzling light of his spacesuit; the other men did the same, their faces pale and drawn.

"Blast!" Morton barked into his communicator.

The mobile units throbbed; and then pure atomic flame

ravened out and poured upon the hard metal of the door. The first molten droplet rolled reluctantly, not down, but up the door. The second was more normal. It followed a shaky downward course. The third rolled sideways—for this was pure force, not subject to gravitation. Other drops followed until a dozen streams trickled sedately yet unevenly in every direction—streams of hellish, sparkling fire, bright as fairy gems, alive with the coruscating fury of atoms suddenly tortured, and running blindly, crazy with pain.

The minutes ate at time like a slow acid. At last Morton asked huskily:

"Selenski?"

"Nothing yet, commander."

Morton half whispered: "But he must be doing something. He can't be just waiting in there like a cornered rat. Selenski?"

"Nothing, commander."

Seven minutes, eight minutes, then twelve.

"Commander!" It was Selenski's voice, taut. "He's got the electric dynamo running."

Morton drew a deep breath, and heard one of his men say:

"That's funny. We can't get any deeper. Boss, take a look at this."

Morton looked. The little scintillating streams had frozen rigid. The ferocity of the disintegrators vented in vain against metal grown suddenly invulnerable.

Morton sighed. "Our test is over. Leave two men guarding every corridor. The others come up to the control room."

He seated himself a few minutes later before the massive control keyboard. "So far as I'm concerned the test was a success. We know that of all the machines in the engine room, the most important to the monster was the electric dynamo. He must have worked in a frenzy of terror while we were at the doors."

"Of course, it's easy to see what he did," Pennons said. "Once he had the power he increased the electronic tensions of the door to their ultimate."

"The main thing is this," Smith chimed in. "He works with vibrations only so far as his special powers are concerned, and the energy must come from outside himself. Atomic energy in its pure form, not being vibration, he can't handle any differently than we can."

Kent said glumly: "The main point in my opinion is that he stopped us cold. What's the good of knowing that his control over vibrations did it? If we can't break through those doors with our atomic disintegrators, we're finished."

Morton shook his head. "Not finished—but we'll have to do some planning. First, though, I'll start these engines. It'll be harder for him to get control of them when they're running."

He pulled the master switch back into place with a jerk. There was a hum, as scores of machines leaped into violent life in the engine room a hundred feet below. The noises sank to a steady vibration of throbbing power.

Three hours later, Morton paced up and down before the men gathered in the salon. His dark hair was uncombed; the space pallor of his strong face emphasized rather than detracted from the outthrust aggressiveness of his jaw. When he spoke, his deep voice was crisp to the point of sharpness:

"To make sure that our plans are fully co-ordinated, I'm going to ask each expert in turn to outline his part in the overpowering of this creature. Pennons first!"

Pennons stood up briskly. He was not a big man, Morton thought, yet he looked big, perhaps because of his air of authority. This man knew engines, and the history of engines. Morton had heard him trace a machine through its evolution from a simple toy to the highly complicated modern instrument. He had studied machine development on a hundred planets; and there was literally nothing fundamental that he didn't know about mechanics. It was almost weird to hear Pennons, who could have spoken for a thousand hours and still only have touched upon his subject, say with absurd brevity:

"We've set up a relay in the control room to start and stop every engine rhythmically. The trip lever will work a hundred times a second, and the effect will be to create vibrations of every description. There is just a possibility that one or more of the machines will burst, on the principle of soldiers crossing a bridge in step—you've heard that old story, no doubt—but in my opinion there is no real danger of a break of that tough metal. The main purpose is simply to interfere with the interference of the creature, and smash through the doors."

"Gourlay next!" barked Morton.

Gourlay climbed lazily to his feet. He looked sleepy, as

if he was somewhat bored by the whole proceedings, yet Morton knew he loved people to think him lazy, a good-for-nothing slouch, who spent his days in slumber and his nights catching forty winks. His title was chief communication engineer, but his knowledge extended to every vibration field; and he was probably, with the possible exception of Kent, the fastest thinker on the ship. His voice drawled out, and—Morton noted—the very deliberate assurance of it had a soothing effect on the men—anxious faces relaxed, bodies leaned back more restfully:

"Once inside," Gourlay said, "we've rigged up vibration screens of pure force that should stop nearly everything he's got on the ball. They work on the principle of reflection, so that everything he sends will be reflected back to him. In addition, we've got plenty of spare electric energy that we'll just feed him from mobile copper cups. There must be a limit to his capacity for handling power with those insulated nerves of his."

"Selenski!" called Morton.

The chief pilot was already standing, as if he had anticipated Morton's call. And that, Morton reflected, was the man. His nerves had that rocklike steadiness which is the first requirement of the master controller of a great ship's movements; yet that very steadiness seemed to rest on dynamite ready to explode at its owner's volition. He was not a man of great learning, but he "reacted" to stimuli so fast that he always seemed to be anticipating.

"The impression I've received of the plan is that it must be cumulative. Just when the creature thinks that he can't stand any more, another thing happens to add to his trouble and confusion. When the uproar's at its height, I'm supposed to cut in the anti-accelerators. The commander thinks with Gunlie Lester that these creatures will know nothing about anti-acceleration. It's a development, pure and simple, of the science of interstellar flight, and couldn't have been developed in any other way. We think when the creature feels the first effects of the anti-acceleration—you all remember the caved-in feeling you had the first month—it won't know what to think or do."

"Korita next."

"I can only offer you encouragement," said the archeologist, "on the basis of my theory that the monster has all the characteristics of a criminal of the early ages of any civilization, complicated by an apparent reversion to primitiveness. The suggestion has been made by Smith that his knowledge of science is puzzling, and could only mean that we are dealing with an actual inhabitant, not a descendant of the inhabitants of the dead city we visited. This would ascribe a virtual immortality to our enemy, a possibility which is borne out by his ability to breathe both oxygen and chlorine—or neither—but even that makes no difference. He comes from a certain age in his civilization; and he has sunk so low that his ideas are mostly memories of that age.

"In spite of all the powers of his body, he lost his head in the elevator the first morning, until he remembered. He placed himself in such a position that he was forced to reveal his special powers against vibrations. He bungled the mass murders a few hours ago. In fact, his whole record is one of the low cunning of the primitive, egotistical mind which has little or no conception of the vast organization with which it is confronted.

"He is like the ancient German soldier who felt superior to the elderly Roman scholar, yet the latter was part of a mighty civilization of which the Germans of that day stood in awe.

"You may suggest that the sack of Rome by the Germans in later years defeats my argument; however, modern historians agree that the 'sack' was an historical accident, and not history in the true sense f the word. The movement of the 'Sea-peoples' which set i   ainst the Egyptian civilization from 1400 B. C. succeeded   ly as regards the Cretan island-realm—their mighty expe itions against the Libyan and Phoenician coasts, with the accompaniment of Viking fleets, failed as those of the Huns failed against the Chinese Empire. Rome would have been abandoned in any event. Ancient, glorious Samarra was desolate by the tenth century; Pataliputra, Asoka's great capital, was an immense and completely uninhabited waste of houses when the Chinese traveler Hsinan-tang visited it about A. D. 635.

"We have, then, a primitive, and that primitive is now far out in space, completely outside of his natural habitat. I say, let's go in and win."

One of the men grumbled, as Korita finished: "You can talk about the sack of Rome being an accident, and about this fellow being a primitive, but the facts are facts. It looks to me as if Rome is about to fall again; and it won't be no primitive that did it, either. This guy's got plenty of what it takes."

Morton smiled grimly at the man, a member of the crew. "We'll see about that—right now!"

In the blazing brilliance of the gigantic machine shop, Coeurl slaved. The forty-foot, cigar-shaped spaceship was nearly finished. With a grunt of effort, he completed the laborious installation of the drive engines, and paused to survey his craft.

Its interior, visible through the one aperture in the outer wall, was pitifully small. There was literally room for nothing but the engines—and a narrow space for himself.

He plunged frantically back to work as he heard the approach of the men, and the sudden change in the tempest-like thunder of the engines—a rhythmical off-and-on hum, shriller in tone, sharper, more nerve-racking than the deep-throated, steady throb that had preceded it. Suddenly, there were the atomic disintegrators again at the massive outer doors.

He fought them off, but never wavered from his task. Every mighty muscle of his powerful body strained as he carried great loads of tools, machines and instruments, and dumped them into the bottom of his makeshift ship. There was no time to fit anything into place, no time for anything —no time—no time.

The thought pounded at his reason. He felt strangely weary for the first time in his long and vigorous existence. With a last, tortured heave, he jerked the gigantic sheet of metal into the gaping aperture of the ship—and stood there for a terrible minute, balancing it precariously.

He knew the doors were going down. Half a dozen disintegrators concentrating on one point were irresistibly, though slowly, eating away the remaining inches. With a gasp, he released his mind from the doors, and concentrated every ounce of his mind on the yard-thick outer wall, toward which the blunt nose of his ship was pointing.

His body cringed from the surging power that flowed from the electric dynamo through his ear tendrils into that resisting wall. The whole inside of him felt on fire, and he knew that he was dangerously close to carrying his ultimate load.

And still he stood there, shuddering with the awful pain, holding the unfastened metal plate with hard-clenched tentacles. His massive head pointed as in dread fascination at that bitterly hard wall.

He heard one of the engine-room doors crash inward. Men shouted; disintegrators rolled forward, their raging power unchecked. Coeurl heard the floor of the engine room hiss in protest, as those beams of atomic energy tore everything in their path to bits. The machines rolled closer; cautious footsteps sounded behind them. In a minute they would be at the flimsy doors separating the engine room from the machine shop.

Suddenly, Coeurl was satisfied. With a snarl of hate, a vindictive glow of feral eyes, he ducked into his little craft, and pulled the metal plate down into place as if it was a hatchway.

His ear tendrils hummed, as he softened the edges of the surrounding metal. In an instant, the plate was more than welded—it was part of his ship, a seamless, rivetless part of a whole that was solid opaque metal except for two transparent areas, one in the front, one in the rear.

His tentacle embraced the power drive with almost sensuous tenderness. There was a forward surge of his fragile machine, straight at the great outer wall of the machine shops. The nose of the forty-foot craft touched—and the wall dissolved in a glittering shower of dust.

Coeurl felt the barest retarding movement; and then he kicked the nose of the machine out into the cold of space, twisted it about, and headed back in the direction from which the big ship had been coming all these hours.

Men in space armor stood in the jagged hole that yawned in the lower reaches of the gigantic globe. The men and the great ship grew smaller. Then the men were gone; and there was only the ship with its blaze of a thousand blurring portholes. The ball shrank incredibly, too small now for individual portholes to be visible.

Almost straight ahead, Coeurl saw a tiny, dim, reddish ball—his own sun, he realized. He headed toward it at full speed. There were caves where he could hide and with other coeurls build secretly a spaceship in which they could reach other planets safely—now that he knew how.

His body ached from the agony of acceleration, yet he dared not let up for a single instant. He glanced back, half in terror. The globe was still there, a tiny dot of light in the immense blackness of space. Suddenly it twinkled and was gone.

For a brief moment, he had the empty, frightened impression that just before it disappeared, it moved. But he could see nothing. He could not escape the belief that they had shut off all their lights, and were sneaking up on him in the darkness. Worried and uncertain, he looked through the forward transparent plate.

A tremor of dismay shot through him. The dim red sun toward which he was heading was not growing larger. *It was becoming smaller* by the instant, and it grew visibly tinier during the next five minutes, became a pale-red dot in the sky—and vanished like the ship.

Fear came then, a blinding surge of it, that swept through his being and left him chilled with the sense of the unknown. For minutes, he stared frantically into the space ahead, searching for some landmark. But only the remote stars glimmered there, unwinking points against a velvet background of unfathomable distance.

Wait! One of the points was growing larger. With every muscle and nerve tensed, Coeurl watched the point becoming a dot, a round ball of light—red light. Bigger, bigger, it grew. Suddenly, the red light shimmered and turned white —and there, before him, was the great globe of the spaceship, lights glaring from every porthole, the very ship which a few minutes before he had watched vanish behind him.

Something happened to Coeurl in that moment. His brain was spinning like a flywheel, faster, faster, more incoherently. Suddenly, the wheel flew apart into a million aching fragments. His eyes almost started from their sockets as, like a maddened animal, he raged in his small quarters.

His tentacles clutched at precious instruments and flung them insensately; his paws smashed in fury at the very walls of his ship. Finally, in a brief flash of sanity, he knew that he couldn't face the inevitable fire of atomic disintegrators.

It was a simple thing to create the violent disorganization that freed every drop of id from his vital organs.

They found him lying dead in a little pool of phosphorus.

"Poor pussy," said Morton. "I wonder what he thought when he saw us appear ahead of him, after his own sun disappeared. Knowing nothing of anti-accelerators, he

couldn't know that we could stop short in space, whereas it
would take him more than three hours to decelerate; and
in the meantime he'd be drawing farther and farther away
from where he wanted to go. He couldn't know that by stopping, we flashed past him at millions of miles a second. Of
course, he didn't have a chance once he left our ship. The
whole world must have seemed topsy-turvy."

"Never mind the sympathy," he heard Kent say behind
him. "We've got a job—to kill every cat in that miserable
world."

Korita murmured softly: "That should be simple. They
are but primitives; and we have merely to sit down, and they
will come to us, cunningly expecting to delude us."

Smith snapped: "You fellows make me sick! Pussy was
the toughest nut we ever had to crack. He had everything he
needed to defeat us—"

Morton smiled as Korita interrupted blandly: "Exactly,
my dear Smith, except that he reacted according to the
biological impulses of his type. His defeat was already fore-
shadowed when we unerringly analyzed him as a criminal
from a certain era of his civilization.

"It was history, honorable Mr. Smith, our knowledge of
history that defeated him," said the Japanese archeologist,
reverting to the ancient politeness of his race.

TIME LOCKER / by Lewis Padgett

Mr. Padgett does more playing with time, time plus the fourth dimension—and concocts a locker that needed no lock. Wherein things shrank out of sight and out of time . . . until it was timely and convenient for them to reappear. A good place to hide stolen property, but even in the fourth dimension, crime does not pay!

GALLOWAY PLAYED by ear, which would have been all right had he been a musician—but he was a scientist. A drunken and erratic one, but good. He'd wanted to be an experimental technician, and would have been excellent at it, for he had a streak of genius at times. Unfortunately, there had been no funds for such specialized education, and now Galloway, by profession an integrator machine supervisor, maintained his laboratory purely as a hobby. It was the damndest-looking lab in six states. Galloway had spent ten months building what he called a liquor organ, which occupied most of the space. He could recline on a comfortably padded couch and, by manipulating buttons, siphon drinks from marvelous quantity, quality, and variety down his scarified throat. Since he had made the liquor organ during a protracted period of drunkenness, he never remembered the basic principles of its construction. In a way, that was a pity.

There was a little of everything in the lab, much of it incongruous. Rheostats had little skirts on them, like ballet dancers, and vacuously grinning faces of clay. A generator was conspicuously labeled, "Monstro," and a much smaller one rejoiced in the name of "Bubbles." Inside a glass retort was a china rabbit, and Galloway alone knew how it had got there. Just inside the door was a hideous iron dog, originally intended for Victorian lawns or perhaps for Hell, and its hollowed ears served as sockets for test tubes.

"But how do you do it?" Vanning asked.

Galloway, his lank form reclining under the liquor organ, siphoned a shot of double Martini into his mouth. "Huh?"

"You heard me. I could get you a swell job if you'd use that screwball brain of yours. Or even learn to put up a front."

"Tried it," Galloway mumbled. "No use. I can't work when I concentrate, except at mechanical stuff. I think my subconscious must have a high I.Q."

Vanning, a chunky little man with a scarred, swarthy face, kicked his heels against Monstro. Sometimes Galloway annoyed him. The man never realized his own potentialities, or how much they might mean to Horace Vanning, Commerce Analyst. The "commerce," of course, was extra-legal, but the complicated trade relationships of 1970 left many loopholes a clever man could slip through. The fact of the matter was, Vanning acted in an advisory capacity to crooks. It paid well. A sound knowledge of jurisprudence was rare in these days; the statutes were in such a tangle that it took years of research before one could even enter a law school. But Vanning had a staff of trained experts, a colossal library of transcripts, decisions, and legal data, and, for a suitable fee, he could have told Dr. Crippen how to get off scot-free.

The shadier side of his business was handled in strict privacy, without assistants. The matter of the neuro-gun, for example—

Galloway had made that remarkable weapon, quite without realizing its importance. He had hashed it together one evening, piecing out the job with court plaster when his welder went on the fritz. And he'd given it to Vanning, on request. Vanning didn't keep it long. But already he had earned thousands of credits by lending the gun to potential murderers. As a result, the police department had a violent headache.

A man in the know would come to Vanning and say, "I heard you can beat a murder rap. Suppose I wanted to—"

"Hold on! I can't condone anything like that."

"Huh? But—"

"Theoretically, I suppose a perfect murder might be possible. Suppose a new sort of gun had been invented, and suppose—just for the sake of an example—it was in a locker at the Newark Stratoship Field."

"Huh?"

"I'm just theorizing. Locker Number 79, combination thirty-blue-eight. These little details always help one to visualize a theory, don't they?"

"You mean—"

"Of course if our murderer picked up this imaginary gun and used it, he'd be smart enough to have a postal box ready, addressed to . . . say . . . Locker 40, Brooklyn Port. He could slip the weapon into the box, seal it, and get rid of the evidence at the nearest mail conveyor. But that's all theorizing. Sorry I can't help you. The fee for an interview is three thousand credits. The receptionist will take your check."

Later, conviction would be impossible. Ruling 875-M, Illinois Precinct, case of State vs. Dupson, set the precedent. Cause of death must be determined. Element of accident must be considered. As Chief Justice Duckett had ruled during the trial of Sanderson vs. Sanderson, which involved the death of the accused's mother-in-law—

Surely the prosecuting attorney, with his staff of toxicological experts, must realize that—

And in short, your honor, I must respectfully request that the case be dismissed for lack of evidence and proof of *casus mortis*—

Galloway never even found out that his neuro-gun was a dangerous weapon. But Vanning haunted the sloppy laboratory, avidly watching the results of his friend's scientific doodling. More than once he had acquired handy little devices in just this fashion. The trouble was, Galloway wouldn't *work!*

He took another sip of Martini, shook his head, and unfolded his lanky limbs. Blinking, he ambled over to a cluttered workbench and began toying with lengths of wire.

"Making something?"

"Dunno. Just fiddling. That's the way it goes. I put things together, and sometimes they work. Trouble is, I never know exactly what they're going to do. *Tsk!*" Galloway dropped the wires and returned to his couch. "Hell with it."

He was, Vanning reflected, an odd duck. Galloway was essentially amoral, thoroughly out of place in this too-complicated world. He seemed to watch, with a certain wry amusement, from a vantage point of his own, rather disinterested for the most part. And he made things—

But always and only for his own amusement. Vanning sighed and glanced toward the laboratory, his orderly soul shocked by the melee. Automatically he picked up a rumpled smock from the floor, and looked for a hook. Of course there was none. Galloway, running short of conductive metal, had long since ripped them out and used them in some gadget or other.

The so-called scientist was creating a zombie, his eyes half closed. Vanning went over to a metal locker in one corner and opened the door. There were no hooks, but he folded the smock neatly and laid it on the floor of the locker. Then he went back to his perch on Monstro.

"Have a drink?" Galloway asked.

Vanning shook his head. "Thanks, no. I've got a case coming up tomorrow."

"There's always thiamin. Filthy stuff. I work better when I've got pneumatic cushions around my brain."

"Well, I don't."

"It is purely a matter of skill," Galloway hummed, "to which each may attain if he will. . . . What are you gaping at?"

"That—locker," Vanning said, frowning in a baffled way. "What the—" He got up. The metal door hadn't been securely latched and had swung open. Of the smock Vanning had placed within the metal compartment there was no trace.

"It's the paint," Galloway explained sleepily. "Or the treatment. I bombarded it with gamma rays. But it isn't good for anything."

Vanning went over and swung a fluorescent into a more convenient position. The locker wasn't empty, as he had at first imagined. The smock was no longer there, but instead there was a tiny blob of—something, pale-green and roughly spherical.

"It melts things?" Vanning asked, staring.

"Uh-huh. Pull it out. You'll see."

Vanning felt hesitant about putting his hand inside the locker. Instead, he found a long pair of test-tube clamps and teased the blob out. It was—

Vanning hastily looked away. His eyes hurt. The green blob was changing in color, shape and size. A crawling, nongeometrical blur of motion rippled over it. Suddenly the clamps were remarkably heavy.

No wonder. They were gripping the original smock.

"It does that, you know," Galloway said absently. "Must be a reason, too. I put things in the locker and they get small. Take 'em out, and they get big again. I suppose I could sell it to a stage magician." His voice sounded doubtful.

Vanning sat down, fingering the smock and staring at the metal locker. It was oblong, approximately 3 x 3 x 5, lined with what seemed to be grayish paint, sprayed on. Outside, it was shiny black.

"How'd you do it?"

"Huh? I dunno. Just fiddling around." Galloway sipped his zombie. "Maybe it's a matter of dimensional extension. My treatment may have altered the spatio-temporal relationships inside the locker. I wonder what that means?" he murmured in a vague aside. "Words frighten me sometimes."

Vanning was thinking about tesseracts. "You mean it's bigger inside than it is outside?"

"A paradox, a paradox, a most delightful paradox. You tell *me*. I suppose the inside of the locker isn't in this space-time continuum at all. Here, shove that bench in it. You'll see." Galloway made no move to rise; he waved toward the article of furniture in question.

"You're right. That bench is bigger than the locker."

"So it is. Shove it in a bit at a time. That corner first. Go ahead."

Vanning wrestled with the bench. Despite his shortness, he was stockily muscular.

"Lay the locker on its back. It'll be easier."

"I . . . *uh!* . . . O. K. Now what?"

"Edge the bench down into it."

Vanning squinted at his companion, shrugged, and tried to obey. Of course the bench wouldn't go into the locker. One corner did, that was all. Then naturally, the bench stopped, balancing precariously at an angle.

"Well?"

"Wait."

The bench moved. It settled slowly downward. As Vanning's jaw dropped, the bench seemed to crawl into the locker, with the gentle motion of a not-too-heavy object

sinking through water. It wasn't sucked down. It melted down.
The portion still outside the locker was unchanged. But that,
too, settled, and was gone.

Vanning craned forward. A blur of movement hurt his
eyes. Inside the locker was—something. It shifted its con-
tours, shrank, and became a spiky sort of scalene pyramid,
deep-purple in hue.

It seemed to be less than four inches across at its widest
point.

"I don't believe it," Vanning said.

Galloway grinned. "As the Duke of Wellington remarked
to the subaltern, it was a damned small bottle, sir."

"Now, wait a minute. How the devil could I put an eight-
foot bench inside of a five-foot locker?"

"Because of Newton," Galloway said. "Gravity. Go fill a
test tube with water and I'll show you."

"Wait a minute . . . O. K. Now what?"

"Got it brim-full? Good. You'll find some sugar cubes
in that drawer labeled 'Fuses.' Lay a cube on top of the
test tube, one corner down so it touches the water."

Vanning racked the tube and obeyed. "Well?"

"What do you see?"

"Nothing. The sugar's getting wet. And melting."

"So there you are," Galloway said expansively. Vanning
gave him a brooding look and turned back to the tube.
The cube of sugar was slowly dissolving and melting down.
Presently it was gone.

"Air and water are different physical conditions. In air a
sugar cube can exist as a sugar cube. In water it exists in
solution. The corner of it extending into water is subject
to aqueous conditions. So it alters physically, though not
chemically. Gravity does the rest."

"Make it clearer."

"The analogy's clear enough, dope. The water represents
the particular condition existing inside that locker. The sugar
cube represents the workbench. Now! The sugar soaked up
the water and gradually dissolved it, so gravity could pull
the cube down into the tube as it melted. See?"

"I think so. The bench soaked up the . . . the *x* condition
inside the locker, eh? A condition that shrank the bench—"

"*In partis,* not *in toto.* A little at a time. You can shove
a human body into a small container of sulphuric acid,
bit by bit."

"Oh," Vanning said, regarding the cabinet askance. "Can you get the bench out again?"

"Do it yourself. Just reach in and pull it out."

"Reach in? I don't want my hand to melt!"

"It won't. The action isn't instantaneous. You saw that yourself. It takes a few minutes for the change to take place. You can reach into the locker without any ill effects, if you don't leave your hand exposed to the conditions for more than a minute or so. I'll show you." Galloway languidly arose, looked around, and picked up an empty demijohn. He dropped this into the locker.

The change wasn't immediate. It occurred slowly, the demijohn altering its shape and size till it was a distorted cube the apparent size of a cube of sugar. Galloway reached down and brought it up again, placing the cube on the floor. It grew. It was a demijohn again.

"Now the bench. Look out."

Galloway rescued the little pyramid. Presently it became the original workbench.

"You see? I'll bet a storage company would like this. You could probably pack all the furniture in Brooklyn in here, but there'd be trouble in getting what you wanted out again. The physical change, you know—"

"Keep a chart," Vanning suggested absently. "Draw a picture of how the thing looks inside the locker, and note down what it was."

"The legal brain," Galloway said. "I want a drink." He returned to his couch and clutched the siphon in a grip of death.

"I'll give you six credits for the thing," Vanning offered.

"Sold. It takes up too much room anyway. Wish I could put it inside itself." The scientist chuckled immoderately. "That's very funny."

"Is it?" Vanning said. "Well, here you are." He took credit coupons from his wallet. "Where'll I put the dough?"

"Stuff it into Monstro. He's my bank. . . . Thanks."

"Yeah. Say, elucidate this sugar business a bit, will you? It isn't just gravity that affects the cube so it slips into a test tube. Doesn't the water soak up into the sugar—"

"You're right at that. Osmosis. No, I'm wrong. Osmosis has something to do with eggs. Or is that ovulation? Conduction, convection—absorption! Wish I'd studied physics; then I'd know the right words. Just a zoot stoop, that's me. I shall take the daughter of the Vine to spouse," Galloway finished incoherently and sucked at the siphon.

"Absorption," Vanning scowled. "Only not water, being soaked up by the sugar. The . . . the *conditions* existing inside the locker, being soaked up by your workbench—in that particular case.

"Like a sponge or a blotter."

"The bench?"

"Me," Galloway said succinctly, and relapsed into a happy silence, broken by occasional gurgles as he poured liquor down his scarified gullet. Vanning sighed and turned to the locker. He carefully closed and latched the door before lifting the metal cabinet in his muscular arms.

"Going? G'night. Fare thee well, fare thee well—"

"Night."

"*Fare*—thee—well!" Galloway ended, in a melancholy outburst of tunefulness, as he turned over preparatory to going to sleep.

Vanning sighed again and let himself out into the coolness of the night. Stars blazed in the sky, except toward the south, where the aurora of Lower Manhattan dimmed them. The glowing white towers of skyscrapers rose in a jagged pattern. A sky-ad announced the virtues of Vambulin—"It Peps You Up."

His speeder was at the curb. Vanning edged the locker into the trunk compartment and drove toward the Hudson Floataway, the quickest route downtown. He was thinking about Poe—

The Purloined Letter, which had been hidden in plain sight, but re-folded and re-addressed, so that its superficial appearance was changed. Holy Hutton! What a perfect safe the locker would make! No thief could crack it, for the obvious reason that it wouldn't be locked. No thief would *want t*o clean it out. Vanning could fill the locker with credit coupons and instantly they'd become unrecognizable. It was the ideal cache.

How the devil did it work?

There was little use in asking Galloway. He played by ear. A primrose by the river's rim a simple primrose was to him—not *Primula vulgaris*. Syllogisms were unknown to him. He reached the conclusion without the aid of either major or minor premises.

Vanning pondered. Two objects cannot occupy the same space at the same time. Ergo, there was a different sort of space in the locker—

But Vanning was jumping at conclusions. There was another answer—the right one. He hadn't guessed it yet.

Instead, he tooled the speeder downtown to the office building where he maintained a floor, and brought the locker upstairs in the freight lift. He didn't put it in his private office; that would have been too obvious. He placed the metal cabinet in one of the storerooms, sliding a file cabinet in front of it for partial concealment. It wouldn't do to have the clerks using this particular locker.

Vanning stepped back and considered. Perhaps—

A bell rang softly. Preoccupied, Vanning didn't hear it at first. When he did, he went back to his own office and pressed the acknowledgment button on the Winchell. The gray, harsh, bearded face of Counsel Hatton appeared, filling the screen.

"Hello," Vanning said.

Hatton nodded. "I've been trying to reach you at your home. Thought I'd try the office—"

"I didn't expect you to call now. The trial's tomorrow. It's a bit late for discussion, isn't it?"

"Dugan & Sons wanted me to speak to you. I advised against it."

"Oh?"

Hatton's thick gray brows drew together. "I'm prosecuting, you know. There's plenty of evidence against MacIlson."

"So you say. But peculation's a difficult charge to prove."

"Did you get an injunction against scop?"

"Naturally," Vanning said. "You're not using truth serum on my client!"

"That'll prejudice the jury."

"Not on medical grounds. Scop affects MacIlson harmfully. I've got a covering prognosis."

"Harmfully is right!" Hatton's voice was sharp. "Your client embezzled those bonds, and I can prove it."

"Twenty-five thousand in credits, it comes to, eh? That's a lot for Dugan & Sons to lose. What about that hypothetical case I posed? Suppose twenty thousand were recovered—"

"Is this a private beam? No recordings?"

"Naturally. Here's the cut-off." Vanning held up a metal-tipped cord. "This is strictly *sub rosa*."

"Good," Counsel Hatton said. "Then I can call you a lousy shyster."

"Tch!"

"Your gag's too old. It's moth-eaten. MacIlson swiped five grand in bonds, negotiable into credits. The auditors start checking up. MacIlson comes to you. You tell him to take twenty grand more, and offer to return that twenty if Dugan & Sons refuse to prosecute. MacIlson splits with you on the five thousand, and on the plat standard, that ain't hay."

"I don't admit to anything like that."

"Naturally you don't, not even on a closed beam. But it's tacit. However, the gag's moth-eaten, and my clients won't play ball with you. They're going to prosecute."

"You called me up just to tell me that?"

"No, I want to settle the jury question. Will you agree to let 'em use scop on the panel?"

"O. K.," Vanning said. He wasn't depending on a fixed jury tomorrow. His battle would be based on legal technicalities. With scop-tested talesmen, the odds would be even. And such an arrangement would save days or weeks of argument and challenge.

"Good," Hatton grunted. "You're going to get your pants licked off."

Vanning replied with a mild obscenity and broke the connection. Reminded of the pending court fight, he forced the matter of the fourth-dimensional locker out of his mind and left the office. Later—

Later would be time enough to investigate the possibilities of the remarkable cabinet more thoroughly. Just now, he didn't want his brain cluttered with nonessentials. He went to his apartment, had the servant mix him a short highball, and dropped into bed.

And, the next day, Vanning won his case. He based it on complicated technicalities and obscure legal precedents. The crux of the matter was that the bonds had not been converted into government credits. Abstruse economic charts proved that point for Vanning. Conversion of even five thousand credits would have caused a fluctuation in the graph line, and no such break existed. Vanning's experts went into monstrous detail.

In order to prove guilt, it would have been necessary to show, either actually or by inference, that the bonds had been in existence since last December 20th, the date of their most recent check-and-recording. The case of Donovan vs. Jones stood as a precedent.

Hatton jumped to his feet. "Jones later confessed to his defalcation, your honor!"

"Which does not affect the original decision," Vanning said smoothly. "Retroaction is not admissible here. The verdict was not proven."

"Counsel for the defense will continue."

Counsel for the defense continued, building up a beautifully intricate edifice of casuistic logic.

Hatton writhed. "Your honor! I—"

"If my learned opponent can produce one bond—just one of the bonds in question—I will concede the case."

The presiding judge looked sardonic. "Indeed! If such a piece of evidence could be produced, the defendant would be jailed as fast as I could pronounce sentence. You know that very well, Mr. Vanning. Proceed."

"Very well. My contention, then, is that the bonds never existed. They were the result of a clerical error in notation."

"A clerical error in a Pederson Calculator?"

"Such errors have occurred, as I shall prove. If I may call my next witness—"

Unchallenged, the witness, a math technician, explained how a Pederson Calculator can go haywire. He cited cases.

Hatton caught him up on one point. "I protest this proof. Rhodesia, as everyone knows, is the location of a certain important experimental industry. Witness has refrained from stating the nature of the work performed in this particular Rhodesian factory. Is it not a fact that the Henderson United Company deals largely in radioactive ores?"

"Witness will answer."

"I can't. My records don't include that information."

"A significant omission," Hatton snapped. "Radioactivity damages the intricate mechanism of a Pederson Calculator. There is no radium nor radium by-product in the offices of Dugan & Sons."

Vanning stood up. "May I ask if those offices have been fumigated lately?"

"They have. It is legally required."

"A type of chlorine gas was used."

"Yes."

"I wish to call my next witness."

The next witness, a physicist in the Ultra Radium Institute, explained that gamma radiations affect chlorine strongly, causing ionization. Living organisms could assimilate by-products of radium and transmit them in turn. Certain clients of Dugan & Sons had been in contact with radioactivity—

"This is ridiculous, your honor! Pure theorization—"

Vanning looked hurt. "I cite the case of Dangerfield vs. Austro Products, California, 1963. Ruling states that the uncertainty factor is prime admissible evidence. My point is simply that the Pederson Calculator which records the bonds could have been in error. If this be true, there were no bonds, and my client is guiltless."

"Counsel will continue," said the judge, wishing he were Jeffries so he could send the whole damned bunch to the scaffold. Jurisprudence should be founded on justice, and not be a three-dimensional chess game. But, of course, it was the natural development of the complicated political and economic factors of modern civilization. It was already evident that Vanning would win his case.

And he did. The jury was directed to find for the defendant. On a last, desperate hope, Hatton raised a point of order and demanded scop, but his petition was denied. Vanning winked at his opponent and closed his brief case.

That was that.

Vanning returned to his office. At four-thirty that afternoon trouble started to break. The secretary announced a Mr. MacIlson, and was pushed aside by a thin, dark, middle-aged man lugging a gigantic suedette suitcase.

"Vanning! I've got to see you—"

The attorney's eye hooded. He rose from behind his desk, dismissing the secretary with a jerk of his head. As the door closed, Vanning said brusquely, "What are you doing here? I told you to stay away from me. What's in that bag?"

"The bonds," MacIlson explained, his voice unsteady. "Something's gone wrong—"

"You crazy fool! Bringing the bonds here—" With a leap Vanning was at the door, locking it. "Don't you realize that if Hatton gets his hands on that paper, you'll be yanked back to jail? And I'll be disbarred. Get 'em out of here."

"Listen a minute, will you? I took the bonds to Finance Unity, as you told me, but . . . but there was an officer there, waiting for me. I saw him just in time. If he'd caught me—"

Vanning took a deep breath. "You were supposed to leave the bonds in that subway locker for two months."

MacIlson pulled a news sheet from his pocket. "But the government's declared a freeze on ore stocks and bonds. It'll go into effect in a week. I couldn't wait—the money would have been tied up indefinitely."

"Let's see that paper." Vanning examined it and cursed softly. "Where'd you get this?"

"Bought it from a boy outside the jail. I wanted to check the current ore quotations."

"Uh-huh. I see. Did it occur to you that this sheet might be faked?"

MacIlson's jaw dropped. "Fake?"

"Exactly. Hatton figured I might spring you, and had this paper ready. You bit. You led the police right to the evidence, and a swell spot you've put me in."

"B-but—"

Vanning grimaced. "Why do you suppose you saw that cop at Finance Unity? They could have nabbed you any time. But they wanted to scare you into heading for my office, so they could catch both of us on the same hook. Prison for you, disbarment for me. Oh, hell!"

MacIlson licked his lips. "Can't I get out a back door?"

"Through the cordon that's undoubtedly waiting? Orbs! Don't be more of a sap than you can help."

"Can't you—hide the stuff?"

"Where? They'll ransack this office with X rays. No, I'll just—" Vanning stopped. "Oh. Hide it, you said. *Hide it*—"

He whirled to the dictograph. "Miss Horton? I'm in conference. Don't disturb me for anything. If anybody hands you a search warrant, insist on verifying it through headquarters. Got me? O. K."

Hope had returned to MacIlson's face. "Is it all right?"

"Oh, shut up!" Vanning snapped. "Wait here for me. Be back directly." He headed for a side door and vanished. In a surprising short time he returned, awkwardly lugging a metal cabinet.

"Help me . . . *uh!* . . . here. In this corner. Now get out."

"But—"

"Flash," Vanning ordered. "Everything's under control. Don't talk. You'll be arrested, but they can't hold you without evidence. Come back as soon as you're sprung." He urged MacIlson to the door, unlocked it, and thrust the man through. After that, he returned to the cabinet, swung open the door, and peered in. Empty. Sure.

The suedette suitcase—

Vanning worked it into the locker, breathing hard. It took a little time, since the valise was larger than the metal cabinet. But at last he relaxed, watching the brown case shrink and alter its outline till it was tiny and distorted, the shape of an elongated egg, the color of a copper cent piece.

"Whew!" Vanning said.

Then he leaned closer, staring. Inside the locker, something was moving. A grotesque little creature less than four inches tall and visible. It was a shocking object, all cubes and angles, a bright green in tint, and it was obviously alive. Someone knocked on the door.

The tiny—thing—was busy with the copper-colored egg. Like an ant, it was lifting the egg and trying to pull it away. Vanning gasped and reached into the locker. The fourth-dimensional creature dodged. It wasn't quick enough. Vanning's hand descended, and he felt wriggling movement against his palm. He squeezed.

The movement stopped. He let go of the dead thing and pulled his hand back swiftly.

The door shook under the impact of fists.

Vanning closed the locker and called, "Just a minute."

"Break it down," somebody ordered.

But that wasn't necessary. Vanning put a painful smile on his face and turned the key. Counsel Hatton came in, accompanied by b   licemen. "We've got MacIlson," he said.

"Oh? Why?"

For answer Hatton jerked his hand. The officers began to search the room. Vanning shrugged.

"You've jumped the gun," he said. "Breaking and entering—"

"We've got a warrant."

"Charge?"

"The bonds, of course." Hatton's voice was weary. "I don't know where you've hid that suitcase, but we'll find it."

"What suitcase?" Vanning wanted to know.

"The one MacIlson had when he came in. The one he didn't have when he went out."

"The game," Vanning said sadly, "is up. You win."

"Eh?"

"If I tell you what I did with the suitcase, will you put in a good word for me?"

"Why . . . yeah. Where—"

"I ate it," Vanning said, and retired to the couch, where he settled himself for a nap. Hatton gave him a long, hating look. The officers tore in—

They passed by the locker, after a casual glance. The X rays revealed nothing, in walls, floor, ceiling, or articles of furniture. The other offices were searched, too. Vanning applauded the painstaking job.

In the end, Hatton gave up. There was nothing else he could do.

"I'll clap suit on you tomorrow," Vanning promised. "Same time I get a habeas corpus on MacIlson."

"Step to hell," Hatton growled.

" 'By now."

Vanning waited till his unwanted guests had departed. Then, chuckling quietly, he went to the locker and opened it.

The copper-colored egg that represented the suedette suitcase had vanished. Vanning groped inside the locker, finding nothing.

The significance of this didn't strike Vanning at first. He swung the cabinet around so that it faced the window. He looked again, with identical results.

The locker was empty.

Twenty-five thousand credits in negotiable ore bonds had disappeared.

Vanning started to sweat. He picked up the metal box and shook it. That didn't help. He carried it across the room and set it up in another corner, returning to search the floor with painstaking accuracy. *Holy—*

Hatton?

No. Vanning hadn't let the locker out of his sight from the time the police had entered till they left. An officer had swung open the cabinet's door, looked inside, and closed it again. After that the door had remained shut, till just now.

The bonds were gone.

So was the abnormal little creature Vanning had crushed. All of which meant—what?

Vanning approached the locker and closed it, clicking the

latch into position. Then he reopened it, not really expecting that the copper-colored egg would reappear.

He was right. It didn't.

Vanning staggered to the Winchell and called Galloway.

"Whatzit? Huh? Oh. What do you want?" The scientist's
gaunt face appeared on the screen, rather the worse for wear.
"I got a hangover. Can't use thiamin, either. I'm allergic to it.
How'd your case come out?"

"Listen," Vanning said urgently, "I put something inside
that damn locker of yours and now it's gone."

"The locker? That's funny."

"No! The thing I put in it. A . . . a suitcase."

Galloway shook his head thoughtfully. "You never know,
do you? I remember once I made a—"

"The hell with that. I want that suitcase back!"

"An heirloom?" Galloway suggested.

"No, there's money in it."

"Wasn't that a little foolish of you? There hasn't been a
bank failure since 1949. Never suspected you were a miser,
Vanning. Like to have the stuff around, so you can run
it through your birdlike fingers, eh?"

"You're drunk."

"I'm *trying*," Galloway corrected. "But I've built up an
awful resistance over a period of years. It takes time. Your
call's already set me back two and a half drinks. I must put
an extension on the siphon, so I can Winchell and guzzle
at the same time."

Vanning almost chattered incoherently into the mike. "My
suitcase! What happened to it? I want it back."

"Well, I haven't got it."

"Can't you find out where it is?"

"Dunno. Tell me the details. I'll see what I can figure out."

Vanning complied, revising his story as caution prompted.

"O. K.," Galloway said at last, rather unwillingly. "I hate
working out theories, but just as a favor. . . . My diagnosis
will cost you fifty credits."

"What? Now listen—"

"Fifty credits," Galloway repeated unflinchingly. "Or no
prognosis."

"How do I know you can get it back for me?"

"Chances are I can't. Still, maybe . . . I'll have to go over
to Mechanistra and use some of their machines. They

charge a good bit, too. But I'll need forty-brainpower calculators—"

"O. K., O. K.!" Vanning growled. "Hop to it. I want that suitcase back."

"What interests me is that little bug you squashed. In fact, that's the only reason I'm tackling your problem. Life in the fourth dimension—" Galloway trailed off, murmuring. His face faded from the screen. After a while Vanning broke the connection.

He re-examined the locker, finding nothing new. Yet the suedette suitcase had vanished from it, into thin air. Oh, hell!

Brooding over his sorrows, Vanning shrugged into a top coat and dined vinously at the Mahattan Roof. He felt very sorry for himself.

The next day he felt even sorrier. A call to Galloway had given the blank signal, so Vanning had to mark time. About noon MacIlson dropped in. His nerves were shot.

"You took your time in springing me," he started immediately. "Well, what now? Have you got a drink anywhere around?"

"You don't need a drink," Vanning grunted. "You've got a skinful already, by the look of you. Run down to Florida and wait till this blows over."

"I'm sick of waiting. I'm going to South America. I want some credits."

"Wait'll I arrange to cash the bonds."

"I'll take the bonds. A fair half, as we agreed."

Vanning's eyes narrowed. "And walk out into the hands of the police. Sure."

MacIlson looked uncomfortable. "I'll admit I made a boner. But this time—no, I'll play smart now."

"You'll wait, you mean."

"There's a friend of mine on the roof parking lot, in a helicopter. I'll go up and slip him the bonds, and then I'll just walk out. The police won't find anything on me."

"I said no," Vanning repeated. "It's too dangerous."

"It's dangerous as things are. If they locate the bonds—"

"They won't."

"Where'd you hide 'em?"

"That's my business."

MacIlson glowered nervously. "Maybe. But they're in this

building. You couldn't have finagled 'em out yesterday before the cops came. No use playing your luck too far. Did
they use X rays?"

"Yeah." -

"Well, I heard Counsel Hatton's got a batch of experts
going over the blueprints on this building. He'll find your
safe. I'm getting out of here before he does."

Vanning patted the air. "You're hysterical. I've taken care
of you, haven't I? Even though you almost screwed the whole
thing up."

"Sure," MacIlson said, pulling at his lip. "But I"— He
chewed a fingernail. "Oh, damn! I'm sitting on the edge of
a volcano with termites under me. I can't stay here and wait
till they find the bonds. They can't extradite me from South
America—where I'm going, anyway."

"You're going to wait," Vanning said firmly. "That's your
best chance."

There was suddenly a gun in MacIlson's hand. "You're going to give me half the bonds. Right now. I don't trust you a
little bit. You figure you can stall me along—hell, get those
bonds!"

"No," Vanning said.

"I'm not kidding."

"I know you aren't. I can't get the bonds."

"Eh? Why not?"

"Ever heard of a time lock?" Vanning asked, his eye
watchful. "You're right; I put the suitcase in a concealed
safe. But I can't open that safe till a certain number of hours
have passed."

"Mm-m." MacIlson pondered. "When—"

"Tomorrow."

"All right. You'll have the bonds for me then?"

"If you want them. But you'd better change your mind.
It'd be safer."

For answer MacIlson grinned over his shoulder as he
went out. Vanning sat motionless for a long time. He was,
frankly, scared.

The trouble was, MacIlson was a manic-depressive type.
He'd kill. Right now, he was cracking under the strain, and
imagining himself a desperate fugitive. Well—precautions
would be advisable.

Vanning called Galloway again, but got no answer. He left

a message on the recorder and thoughtfully looked into the locker again. It was empty, depressingly so.

That evening Galloway let Vanning into his laboratory. The scientist looked both tired and drunk. He waved comprehensively toward a table, covered with scraps of paper.

"What a headache you gave me! If I'd known the principles behind that gadget, I'd have been afraid to tackle it. Sit down. Have a drink. Got the fifty credits?"

Silently Vanning handed over the coupons. Galloway shoved them into Monstro. "Fine. Now—" He settled himself on the couch. "Now we start. The fifty credit question."

"Can I get the suitcase back?"

"No," Galloway said flatly. "At least, I don't see how it can be worked. It's in another spatio-temporal sector."

"Just what does that mean?"

"It means the locker works something like a telescope, only the thing isn't merely visual. The locker's a window, I figure. You can reach through it as well as look through it. It's an opening into Now plux x."

Vanning scowled. "So far you haven't said anything."

"So far all I've got is theory, and that's all I'm likely to get. Look. I was wrong originally. The things that went into the locker didn't appear in another space, because there would have been a spatial constant. I mean, they wouldn't have got smaller. Size is size. Moving a one-inch cube from here to Mars wouldn't make it any larger or smaller."

"What about a different density in the surrounding medium? Wouldn't that crush an object?"

"Sure, and it'd stay squashed. It wouldn't return to its former size and shape when it was taken out of the locker again. X plus y never equals xy. But x times y—"

"So?"

"That's a pun," Galloway broke off to explain. "The things we put in the locker went into time. Their time-rate remained constant, but not the spatial relationships. Two things can't occupy the same place at the same time. Ergo, your suitcase went into a different time. Now plus x. And what x represents I don't know, though I suspect a few million years."

Vanning looked dazed. "The suitcase is a million years in the future?"

"Dunno how far, but—I'd say plenty. I haven't enough

factors to finish the equation. I reasoned by induction, mostly, and the results are screwy as hell. Einstein would have
loved it. My theorem shows that the universe is expanding
and contracting at the same time."

"What's that got to do—"

"Motion is relative," Galloway continued inexorably.
"That's a basic principle. Well, the universe is expanding,
spreading out like a gas, but its component parts are
shrinking at the same time. The *parts* don't actually grow,
you know—not the suns and atoms. They just run away
from the central point. Galloping off in all directions . . .
where was I? Oh. Actually, the universe, taken as a unit, is
shrinking."

"So, it's shrinking. Where's my suitcase?"

"I told you. In the future. Inductive reasoning showed
that. It's beautifully simple and logical. And it's quite impossible of proof, too. A hundred, a thousand, a million
years ago the Earth—the universe—was larger than it is now.
And it continues to contract. Sometime in the future the
Earth will be just half as large as it is now. Only we won't
notice it because the universe will be proportionately smaller."

Galloway went on dreamily. "We put a workbench into
the locker, so it emerged sometime in the future. The
locker's an open window into a different time, as I told
you. Well, the bench was affected by the conditions of that
period. It ' rank, after we gave it a few seconds to soak
up the en| >py or something. Do I mean entropy? Allah
knows. Oh, vell."

"It turned into a pyramid."

"Maybe there's a geometric distortion, too. Or it might
be a visual illusion. Perhaps we can't get the exact focus.
I doubt if things will really look different in the future—
except that they'll be smaller—but we're using a window
into the fourth dimension. We're taking a pleat in time.
It must be like looking through a prism. The alteration in
size is real, but the shape and color are altered to our eyes
by the fourth-dimensional prism."

"The whole point, then, is that my suitcase is in the future.
Eh? But why did it disappear from the locker?"

"What about that little creature you squashed? Maybe he
had pals. They wouldn't be visible till they came into the very
narrow focus of the whatchmaycallit, but—figure it out.

Sometime in the future, in a hundred or a thousand or a million years, a suitcase suddenly appears out of thin air. One of our descendants investigates. You kill him. His pals come along and carry the suitcase away, out of range of the locker. In space it may be anywhere, and the time factor's an unknown quantity. Now plus x. It's a time locker. Well?"

"Hell!" Vanning exploded. "So that's all you can tell me? I'm supposed to chalk it up to profit and loss?"

"Uh-huh. Unless you want to crawl into the locker yourself after your suitcase. Lord knows where you'd come out, though. The proportions of the air probably would have changed in a few thousand years. There might be other alterations, too."

"I'm not that crazy."

So there he was. The bonds were gone, beyond hope of redemption. Vanning could resign himself to that loss, once he knew the securities wouldn't fall into the hands of the police. But MacIlson was another matter, especially after a bullet spattered against the glassolex window of Vanning's office.

An interview with McIlson had proved unsatisfactory. The defaulter was convinced that Vanning was trying to bilk him. He was removed forcibly, yelling threats. He'd go to the police—he'd confess—

Let him. There was no proof. The hell with him. But, for safety's sake, Vanning clapped an injunction on his quondam client.

It didn't land. MacIlson clipped the official on the jaw and fled. Now, Vanning suspected, he lurked in dark corners, armed, and anxious to commit homicide. Obviously a manic-depressive type.

Vanning took a certain malicious pleasure in demanding a couple of plain-clothes men to act as his guards. Legally, he was within his rights, since his life had been threatened. Until MacIlson was under sufficient restriction, Vanning would be protected. And he made sure that his guards were two of the best shots on the Manhattan force. He also found out that they had been told to keep their eyes peeled for the missing bonds and the suedette suitcase. Vanning Winchelled Counsel Hatton and grinned at the screen.

"Any luck yet?"

"What do you mean?"

"My watchdogs. Your spies. They won't find the bonds, Hatton. Better call 'em off. Why make the poor devils do two jobs at once?"

"One job would be enough. Finding the evidence. If Mac-Ilson drilled you, I wouldn't be too unhappy."

"Well, I'll see you in court," Vanning said. "You're prosecuting Watson, aren't you?"

"Yes. Are you waiving scop?"

"On the jurors? Sure. I've got this case in the bag."

"That's what you think," Hatton said, and broke the beam.

Chuckling, Vanning donned his topcoat, collected the guards, and headed for court. There was no sign of Mac-Ilson—

Vanning won the case, as he had expected. He returned to his offices, collected a few unimportant messages from the switchboard girl, and walked toward his private suite. As he opened the door, he saw the suedette suitcase on the carpet in one corner.

He stopped, hand frozen on the latch. Behind him he could hear the heavy footsteps of the guards. Over his shoulder Vanning said, "Wait a minute," and dodged into the office, slamming and locking the door behind him. He caught the tail end of a surprised question.

The suitcase. There it was, unequivocally. And, quite as unequivocally, the two plain-clothes men, after a very brief conference, were hammering on the door, trying to break it down.

Vanning turned green. He took a hesitant step forward, and then saw the locker, in the corner to which he had moved it. The time locker—

That was it. If he shoved the suitcase inside the locker, it would become unrecognizable. Even if it vanished again, that wouldn't matter. What mattered was the vital importance of getting rid—immediately!—of incriminating evidence.

The door rocked on its hinges. Vanning scuttled toward the suitcase and picked it up. From the corner of his eye he saw movement.

In the air above him, a hand had appeared. It was the hand of a giant, with an immaculate cuff fading into emptiness. Its huge fingers were reaching down—

Vanning screamed and sprang away. He was too slow. The hand descended, and Vanning wriggled impotently against the palm.

The hand contracted into a fist. When it opened, what was left of Vanning dropped squashily to the carpet, which it stained.

The hand withdrew into nothingness. The door fell in and the plain-clothes men stumbled over it as they entered.

It didn't take long for Hatton and his cohorts to arrive. Still, there was little for them to do except clean up the mess. The suedette bag, containing twenty-five thousand credits in negotiable bonds, was carried off to a safer place. Vanning's body was scraped up and removed to the morgue. Photographers flashed pictures, fingerprint experts insufflated their white power, X ray men worked busily. It was all done with swift efficiency, so that within an hour the office was empty and the door sealed.

Thus there were no spectators to witness the advent of a gigantic hand that appeared from nothingness, groped around as though searching for something, and presently vanished once more—

The only person who could have thrown light on the matter was Galloway, and his remarks were directed to Monstro, in the solitude of his laboratory. All he said was:

"So that's why that workbench materialized for a few minutes here yesterday. Hm-m-m. Now plus x—and x equals about a week. Still, why not? It's all relative. But—I never thought the universe was shrinking *that* fast!"

He relaxed on the couch and siphoned a double Martini. "Yeah, that's it," he murmured after a while. "Whew! I guess Vanning must have been the only guy who ever reached into the middle of next week and—killed himself! I think I'll get tight."

And he did.

MECHANICAL MICE / by Maurice A. Hugi

We are on the threshold of the robot age. Automatic pilots are true robots. They are machines that perform set duties faithfully and well without the personal supervision of their masters, man. Increase the functions and capabilities of such machines; elaborate, develop, modify their design and—you have robots. But what happens if (and when) a robot develops the power to think? Who wins the ensuing struggle, man or machine? Pessimistic author Hugi thinks the machine will be the victor and tells a spine-tingling tale of the triumphant Robot Mother and her murderous brood.

IT'S ASKING for trouble to fool around with the unknown. Burman did it! Now there are quite a lot of people who hate like the very devil anything that clicks, ticks, emits whirring sounds, or generally behaves like an asthmatic alarm clock. They've got mechanophobia. Dan Burman gave it to them.

Who hasn't heard of the Burman Bullfrog Battery? The same chap! He puzzled it out from first to last and topped it with his now world-famous slogan: "Power in Your Pocket." It was no mean feat to concoct a thing the size of a cigarette packet that would pour out a hundred times as much energy as its most efficient competitor. Burman differed from everyone else in thinking it a mean feat.

Burman looked me over very carefully, then said, "When that technical journal sent you around to see me twelve years ago, you listened sympathetically. You didn't treat me as if I were an idle dreamer or a congenital idiot. You gave me a decent write-up, and started all the publicity that eventually made me much money."

"Not because I loved you," I assured him, "but because I was honestly convinced that your battery was good."

"Maybe." He studied me in a way that conveyed he was anxious to get something off his chest. "We've been pretty pally since that time. We've filled in some idle hours together, and I feel that you're the one of my few friends to whom I can make a seemingly silly confession."

"Go ahead," I encouraged. We had been pretty pally, as he'd said. It was merely that we liked each other, found each other congenial. He was a clever chap, Burman, but there was nothing of the pedantic professor about him. Fortyish, normal, neat, he might have been a fashionable dentist to judge by appearances.

"Bill," he said, very seriously, "I didn't invent that damn battery."

"No?"

"No!" he confirmed. "I pinched the idea. What makes it madder is that I wasn't quite sure of what I was stealing and, crazier still, I don't know from whence I stole it."

"Which is as plain as a pikestaff," I commented.

"That's nothing. After twelve years of careful, exacting work I've built something else. It must be the most complicated thing in creation." He banged a fist on his knee, and his voice rose complainingly. "And now that I've done it, I don't know what I've done."

"Surely when an inventor experiments he knows what he's doing?"

"Not me!" Burman was amusingly lugubrious. "I've invented only one thing in my life, and that was more by accident than by good judgment." He perked up. "But that one thing was the key to a million notions. It gave me the battery. It has nearly given me things of greater importance. On several occasions it has nearly, but not quite, placed within my inadequate hands and half-understanding mind plans that would alter this world far beyond your conception." Leaning forward to lend emphasis to his speech, he said, "Now it has given me a mystery that has cost me twelve years of work and a nice sum of money. I finished it last night. I don't know what the devil it is."

"Perhaps if I had a look at it—"

"Just what I'd like you to do." He switched rapidly to mounting enthusiasm. "It's a beautiful job of work, even

though I say so myself. Bet you that you can't say what is
is, or what it's supposed to do."

"Assuming it can do something," I put in.

"Yes," he agreed. "But I'm positive it has a function of
some sort." Getting up, he opened a door. "Come along."

It was a stunner. The thing was a metal box with a glossy,
rhodium-plated surface. In general size and shape it bore a
faint resemblance to an upended coffin, and had the same,
brooding, ominous air of a casket waiting for its owner to
give up the ghost.

There were a couple of small glass windows in its front
through which could be seen a multitude of wheels as
beautifully finished as those in a first-class watch. Elsewhere,
several tiny lenses stared with sphinx-like indifference. There
were three small trapdoors in one side, two in the other, and
a large one in the front. From the top, two knobbed rods of
metal stuck up like goat's horns, adding a satanic touch to
the thing's vague air of yearning for midnight burial.

"It's an automatic layer-outer," I suggested, regarding the
contraption with frank dislike. I pointed to one of the trapdoors. "You shove the shroud in there, and the corpse comes
out the other side reverently composed and ready wrapped."

"So you don't like its air, either," Burman commented. He
lugged open a drawer in a nearby tier, hauled out a mass of
drawings. "These are its innards. It has an electric circuit,
valves, condensers, and something that I can't quite understand, but which I suspect to be a tiny, extremely efficient
electric furnace. It has parts I recognize as cog-cutters and
pinion-shapers. It embodies several small-scale multiple
stampers, apparently for dealing with sheet metal. There are
vague suggestions of an assembly line ending in that large
compartment shielded by the door in front. Have a look at
the drawings yourself. You can see it's an extremely complicated device for manufacturing something only little less
complicated."

The drawings showed him to be right. But they didn't
show everything. An efficient machine designer could cor-
rectly have deduced the gadget's function if given complete
details. Burman admitted this, saying that some parts he had
made "on the spur of the moment," while others he had been
"impelled to draw." Short of pulling the machine to pieces,

there was enough data to whet the curiosity, but not enough
to satisfy it.

"Start the damn thing and see what it does."

"I've tried," said Burman. "It won't start. There's no starting handle, nothing to suggest how it can be started. I tried
everything I could think of, without result. The electric circuit ends in those antennae at the top, and I even sent current through those, but nothing happened."

"Maybe it's a self-starter," I ventured. Staring at it, a
thought struck me. "Timed," I added.

"Eh?"

"Set for an especial time. When the dread hour strikes, it'll
go of its own accord, like a bomb."

"Don't be so melodramatic," said Burman, uneasily.

Bending down, he peered into one of the tiny lenses.

"Bz-z-z!" murmured the contraption in a faint undertone
that was almost inaudible.

Burman jumped a foot. Then he backed away, eyed the
thing warily, turned his glance at me.

"Did you hear that?"

"Sure!" Getting the drawings, I mauled them around. That
little lens took some finding, but it was there all right. It has
a selenium cell behind it. "An eye," I said. "It saw you, and
reacted. So it isn't dead even if it does just stand there seeing
no evil, hearing no evil, speaking no evil." I put a white
handkerchief against the lens.

"Bz-z-z!" repeated th coffin, emphatically.

Taking the handkerc ef, Burman put it against the other
lenses. Nothing happer ed. Not a sound was heard, not a
funeral note. Just nothing.

"It beats me," he confessed.

I'd got pretty fed up by this time. If the crazy article had
performed, I'd have written it up and maybe I'd have started
another financial snowball rolling for Burman's benefit. But
you can't do anything with a box that buzzes whenever it
feels temperamental. Firm treatment was required, I decided.

"You've been all nice and mysterious about how you got
hold of this brain wave," I said. "Why can't you go to the
same source for information about what it's supposed to be?"

"I'll tell you—or, rather, I'll show you."

From his safe, Burman dragged out a box, and from the

box he produced a gadget. This one was far simpler than the useless mass of works over by the wall. It looked just like one of those old-fashioned crystal sets, except that the crystal was very big, very shiny, and was set in a horizontal vacuum tube. There was the same single dial, the same cat's whisker. Attached to the lot by a length of flex was what might have been a pair of headphones, except in place of the phones were a pair of polished, smoothly rounded copper circles shaped to fit outside the ears and close against the skull.

"My one and only invention," said Burman, not without a justifiable touch of pride.

"What is it?"

"A time-traveling device."

"Ha, ha!" My laugh was very sour. I'd read about such things. In fact, I'd written about them. They were buncombe. Nobody could travel through time, either backward or forward. "Let me see you grow hazy and vanish into the future."

"I'll show you something very soon." Burman said it with assurance I didn't like. He said it with the positive air of a man who knows darned well that he can do something that everybody else knows darned well can't be done. He pointed to the crystal set. "It wasn't discovered at the first attempt. Thousands must have tried and failed. I was the lucky one. I must have picked a peculiarly individualistic crystal; I still don't know how it does what it does; I've never been able to repeat its performance even with a crystal apparently identical."

"And it enables you to travel in time?"

"Only forward. It won't take me backward, not even as much as one day. But it can carry me forward an immense distance, perhaps to the very crack of doom, perhaps everlastingly through infinity."

I had him now! I'd got him firmly entangled in his own absurdities. My loud chuckle was something I couldn't control.

"You can travel forward, but not backward, not even one day back. Then how the devil can you return to the present once you've gone into the future?"

"Because I never leave the present," he replied, evenly. "I don't partake of the future. I merely survey it from the vantage point of the present. All the same, it is time-traveling in the correct sense of the term." He seated himself. "Look here, Bill, what are you?"

"Who, me?"

"Yes, what are you." He went on to provide the answer. "Your name is Bill. You're a body and a mind. Which of them is Bill?"

"Both," I said, positively.

"True—but they're different parts of you. They're not the same even though they go around like Siamese twins." His voice grew serious. "Your body moves always in the present, the dividing line between the past and the future. But your mind is more free. It can think, and is in the present. It can remember, and at once is in the past. It can imagine, and at once is in the future, in its own choice of all the possible futures. *Your mind can travel through time!*"

He'd outwitted me. I could find points to pick upon and argue about, but I knew that fundamentally he was right. I'd not looked at it from this angle before, but he was correct in saying that anyone could travel through time within the limits of his own memory and imagination. At that very moment I could go back twelve years and see him in my mind's eye as a younger man, paler, thinner, more excitable, not so cool and self-possessed. The picture was as perfect as my memory was excellent. For that brief spell I was twelve years back in all but the flesh.

"I call this thing a psychophone," Burman went on. "When you imagine what the future will be like, you make a characteristic choice of all the logical possibilities, you pick your favorite from a multitude of likely futures. The psychophone, somehow—the Lord alone knows how—tunes into future *reality*. It makes you depict within your mind the future as it will be shaped in actuality, eliminating all the alternatives that will not occur."

"An imagination-stimulator, a dream-machine," I scoffed, not feeling as sure of myself as I sounded. "How do you know it's giving you the McCoy?"

"Consistency," he answered, gravely. "It repeats the same features and the same trends far too often for the phenomena to be explained as mere coincidence. Besides," he waved a presuasive hand, "I got the battery from the future. It works, doesn't it?"

"It does," I agreed, reluctantly. I pointed to his psychophone. "I, too, may travel in time. How about letting me have a try? Maybe I'll solve your mystery for you."

"You can try if you wish," he replied, quite willingly. He

pulled a chair into position. "Sit here, and I'll let you peer into the future."

Clipping the headband over my cranium, and fitting the copper rings against my skull where it sprouted ears, Burman connected his psychophone to the mains, switched it on; or rather he did some twiddling that I assumed was a mode of switching on.

"All you have to do," he said, "is to close your eyes, compose yourself, then try and permit your imagination to wander into the future."

He meddled with the cat's whisker. A couple of times he said, "Ah!" And each time he said it I got a peculiar dithery feeling around my unfortunate ears. After a few seconds of this, he drew it out to, "A-a-ah!" I played unfair, and peeped beneath lowered lids. The crystal was glowing like rats' eyes in a forgotten cellar. A furtive crimson.

Closing my own optics, I let my mind wander. Something was flowing between those copper electrodes, a queer, indescribable something that felt with stealthy fingers at some secret portion of my brain. I got the asinine notion that they were the dexterous digits of a yet-to-be-born magician who was going to shout, "Presto!" and pull my abused lump of think-meat out of a thirtieth century hat—assuming they'd wear hats in the thirtieth century.

What was it like, or, rather, what would it be like in the thirtieth century? Would there be retrogression? Would humanity again be composed of scowling, fur-kilted creatures lurking in caves? Or had progress continued—perhaps even to the development of men like gods?

Then it happened! I swear it! I pictured, quite voluntarily, a savage, and then a huge-domed individual with glittering eyes—the latter being my version of the ugliness we hope to attain. Right in the middle of their erratic dreaming, those weird fingers warped my brain, dissolved my phantoms, and replaced them with a dictated picture which I witnessed with all the helplessness and clarity of a nightmare.

I saw a fat man spouting. He was quite an ordinary man as far as looks went. In fact, he was so normal that he looked henpecked. But he was attired in a Roman toga, and he wore a small, black box where his laurel wreath ought to have been. His audience was similarly dressed, and all were balancing their boxes like a convention of fish porters.

What Fatty was orating sounded gabble to me, but he said his piece as if he meant it.

The crowd was in the open air, with great, curved rows of seats visible in the background. Presumably an outside auditorium of some sort. Judging by the distance of the back rows, it must have been a devil of a size. Far behind its sweeping ridge a great edifice jutted into the sky, a cubical erection with walls of glossy squares, like an immense glass-house.

"F'wot?" bellowed Fatty, with obvious heat. "Wuk, wuk, wuk, mor, noon'n'ni'! Bok onned, ord this, ord that." He stuck an indignant finger against the mysterious object on his cranium. "Bok onned, wuk, wuk, wuk. F'wot?" he glared around. "F'nix!" The crowd murmured approval somewhat timidly. But it was enough for Fatty. Making up his mind, he flourished a plump fist and shouted, "Th'ell wit'm!" Then he tore his box from his pate.

Nobody said anything, nobody moved. Dumb and wide-eyed, the crowd just stood and stared as if paralyzed by the sight of a human being sans box. Something with a long, slender streamlined body and broad wings soared gracefully upward in the distance, swooped over the auditorium, but still the crowd neither moved nor uttered a sound.

A smile of triumph upon his broad face, Fatty bawled, "Lem see'm make wuk now! Lem see'm—"

He got no further. With a rush of mistiness from its tail, but in perfect silence, the soaring thing hovered and sent down a spear of faint, silvery light. The light touched Fatty. He rotted where he stood, like a victim of ultra-rapid leprosy. He rotted, collapsed, crumbled within his sagging clothes, became dust as once he had been dust. It was horrible.

The watchers did not flee in utter panic; not one expression of fear, hatred or disgust came from their tightly closed lips. In perfect silence they stood there, staring, just staring, like a horde of wooden soldiers. The thing in the sky circled to survey its handiwork, then dived low over the mob, a stubby antenna in its prow sparking furiously. As one man, the crowd turned left. As one man it commenced to march, left, right, left, right.

Tearing off the headband, I told Burman what I'd seen, or what his contraption had persuaded me to think that I'd seen. "What the deuce did it mean?"

"Automatons," he murmured. "Glasshouses and reaction ships." He thumbed through a big diary filled with notations in his own hands. "Ah, yes, looks like you were very early in the thirtieth century. Unrest was persistent for twenty years prior to the Antibox Rebellion."

"What rebellion?"

"The Antibox—the revolt of the automatons against the thirty-first century Technocrats. Jackson-Dkj-99717, a successful and cunning schemer with a warped box, secretly warped hundreds of other boxes, and eventually led the rebels to victory in 3047. His great-grandson, a greedy, thick-headed individual, caused the rebellion of the Boxless Freemen against his own clique of Jacksocrats."

I gaped at this recital, then said, "The way you tell it makes it sound like history."

"Of course it's history," he asserted. "History that is yet to be." He was pensive for a while. "Studying the future will seem a weird process to you, but it appears quite a normal procedure to me. I've done it for years, and maybe familiarity has bred contempt. Trouble is though, that selectivity is poor. You can pick on some especial period twenty times in succession, but you'll never find yourself in the same month, or even the same year. In fact, you're fortunate if you strike twice in the same decade. Result is that my data is very erratic."

"I can imagine that," I told him. "A good guesser can guess the correct time to within a minute or two, but never within ten or even fifty seconds."

"Quite!" he responded. "So the hell of it has been that mine was the privilege of watching the panorama of the future, but in a manner so sketchy that I could not grasp its prizes. Once I was lucky enough to watch a twenty-fifth century power pack assembled from first to last. I got every detail before I lost the scene which I've never managed to hit upon again. But I made that power pack—and you know the result."

"So that's how you concocted your famous battery!"

"It is! But mine, good as it may be, isn't as good as the one I saw. Some slight factor is missing." His voice was suddenly tight when he added, "I missed something because I had to miss it!"

"Why?" I asked, completely puzzled.

"Because history, past or future, permits no glaring paradox. Because, having snatched this battery from the twenty-fifth century, I am recorded in that age as the twentieth-century inventor of the thing. They've made a mild improvement to it in those five centuries, but that improvement was automatically withheld from me. Future history is as fixed and unalterable by those of the present time as is the history of the past."

"Then," I demanded, "explain to me that complicated contraption which does nothing but say *bz-z-z*."

"Damn it!" he said, with open ire, "that's just what's making me crazy! It can't be a paradox, it just can't." Then, more carefully, "So it must be a seeming paradox."

"O.K. You tell me how to market a seeming paradox, and the commercial uses thereof, and I'll give it a first-class write-up."

Ignoring my sarcasm, he went on, "I tried to probe the future as far as human minds can probe. I saw nothing, nothing but the vastness of a sterile floor upon which sat a queer machine, gleaming there in silent, solitary majesty. Somehow, it seemed aware of my scrutiny across the gulf of countless ages. It held my attention with a power almost hypnotic. For more than a day, for a full thirty hours, I kept that vision without losing it—the longest time I have ever kept a future scene."

"Well?"

"I drew it. I made complete drawings of it, performing the task with all the easy confidence of a trained machine draughtsman. Its insides could not be seen, but somehow they came to me, somehow I knew them. I lost the scene at four o'clock in the morning, finding myself with masses of very complicated drawings, a thumping head, heavy-lidded eyes, and a half-scared feeling in my heart." He was silent for a short time. "A year later I plucked up courage and started to build the thing I had drawn. It cost me a hell of a lot of time and a hell of a lot of money. But I did it—it's finished."

"And all it does is buzz," I remarked, with genuine sympathy.

"Yes," he sighed, doubtfully.

There was nothing more to be said. Burman gazed moodily at the wall, his mind far, far away. I fiddled aimlessly with the copper earpieces of the psychophone. My imagination, I reckoned, was as good as anyone's, but for the life of me I could neither imagine nor suggest a profitable market for a metal coffin filled with watchmaker's junk. No, not even if it did make odd noises.

A faint, smooth *whir* came from the coffin. It was a new sound that swung us round to face it pop-eyed. *Whir-r-r!* it went again. I saw finely machined wheels spin behind the window in its front.

"Good heavens!" said Burman.

Bz-z-z! Whir-r! Click! The whole affair suddenly slid side-wise on its hidden castors.

The devil you know isn't half so frightening as the devil you don't. I don't mean that this sudden demonstration of life and motion got us scared, but it certainly made us leery, and our hearts put in an extra dozen bumps a minute. This coffin-thing was, or might be, a devil we didn't know. So we stood there, side by side, gazing at it fascinatedly, feeling apprehensive of we knew not what.

Motion ceased after the thing had slid two feet. It stood there, silent, imperturbable, its front lenses eyeing us with glassy lack of expression. Then it slid another two feet. Another stop. More meaningless contemplation. After that, a swifter and farther slide that brought it right up to the laboratory table. At that point it ceased moving, began to emit varied but synchronized ticks like those of a couple of sympathetic grandfather clocks.

Burman said, quietly, "Something's going to happen!"

If the machine could have spoken it would have taken the words right out of his mouth. He'd hardly uttered the sentence when a trapdoor in the machine's side fell open, a jointed, metallic arm snaked cautiously through the opening and reached for a marine chronometer standing on the table.

With a surprised oath, Burman dashed forward to rescue the chronometer. He was too late. The arm grabbed it, whisked it into the machine, the trapdoor shut with a hard snap, like the vicious clash of a sprung bear trap. Simultaneously, another trapdoor in the front flipped open, another jointed arm shot out and in again, spearing with ultra-rapid motion too fast to follow. That trapdoor also snapped shut, leaving Burman gaping down at his torn clothing from which his expensive watch and equally expensive gold chain had been ripped away.

"Good heavens!" said Burman, backing from the machine.

We stood looking at it a while. It didn't move again, just posed there ticking steadily as if ruminating upon its welcome meal. Its lenses looked at us with all the tranquil lack of interest of a well-fed cow. I got the idiotic notion that it was happily digesting a mess of cogs, pinions and wheels.

Because its subtle air of menace seemed to have faded away, or maybe because we sensed its entire preoccupation with the task in hand, we made an effort to rescue Burman's valuable timepiece. Burman tugged mightily at the trapdoor through which his watch had gone, but failed to move it. I tugged with him, without result. The thing was sealed as solidly as if welded in. A large screwdriver failed to pry it open. A crowbar, or a good jimmy would have done the job, but at that point Burman decided that he didn't want to damage the machine which had cost him more than the watch.

Tick-tick-tick! went the coffin, stolidly. We were back where we'd started, playing with our fingers, and no wiser than before. There was nothing to be done, and I felt that the accursed contraption knew it. So it stood there, gaping through its lenses, and jeered *tick-tick-tick*. From its belly, or where its belly would have been if it'd had one, a slow warmth radiated. According to Burman's drawings, that was the location of the tiny electric furnace.

The thing was functioning; there could be no doubt about that! If Burman felt the same way as I did, he must have been pretty mad. There we stood, like a couple of prize boobs, not knowing what the machine was supposed to do, and all the time it was doing under our very eyes whatever it was designed to do.

From where was it drawing its power? Were those antennae sticking like horns from its head busily sucking current from the atmosphere? Or was it, perhaps, absorbing radio power? Or did it have internal energy of its own? All the evidence suggested that it was making something, giving birth to something, but giving birth to what?

Tick-tick-tick! was the only reply.

Our questions were still unanswered, our curiosity was still unsatisfied, and the machine was still ticking industriously at the hour of midnight. We surrendered the problem until next morning. Burman locked and double-locked his laboratory before we left.

Police officer Burke's job was a very simple one. All he had to do was walk round and round the block, keeping a wary eye on the stores in general and the big jewel depot in particular, phoning headquarters once per hour from the post at the corner.

Night work suited Burke's taciturn disposition. He could wander along, communing with himself, with nothing to bother him or divert him from his inward ruminations. In that particular section nothing ever happened at night, nothing.

Stopping outside the gem-bedecked window, he gazed through the glass and the heavy grille behind it to where a low-power bulb shed light over the massive safe. There was a rajah's ransom in there. The guard, the grille, the automatic alarms and sundry ingenious traps preserved it from the adventurous fingers of anyone who wanted to ransom a rajah. Nobody had made the brash attempt in twenty years. Nobody had even made a try for the contents of the grille-protected window.

He glanced upward at a faintly luminescent path of cloud behind which lay the hidden moon. Turning, he strolled on. A cat snaked past him, treading cautiously, silently, and hugging the angle of the wall. His sharp eyes detected its slinking shape even in the nighttime gloom, but he ignored it and progressed to the corner.

Back of him, the cat came below the window through which he had just stared. It stopped, one forefoot half-raised, its ears locked forward. Then it flattened belly-low against the concrete, its burning orbs wide, alert, intent. Its tail waved slowly from side to side.

Something small and bright came skittering toward it, moving with mouselike speed and agility in the angle of the wall. The cat tensed as the object came nearer. Suddenly, the thing was within range, and the cat pounced with lithe eagerness. Hungry paws dug at a surface that was not soft and furry, but hard, bright and slippery. The thing darted around like a clockwork toy as the cat vainly tried to hold it. Finally, with an angry snarl, the cat swiped it viciously, knocking it a couple of yards where it rolled onto its back and emitted softly protesting clicks and tiny, urgent impulses that its feline attacker could not sense.

Gaining the gutter with a single leap, the cat crouched again. Something else was coming. The cat muscled, its eyes glowed. Another object slightly similar to the curious thing it had just captured, but a little bit bigger, a fraction noisier, and much different in shape. It resembled a small, gold-plated cylinder with a tonical front from which projected a slender blade, and it slid along swiftly on invisible wheels.

Again the cat leaped. Down on the corner, Burke heard its brief shriek and following gurgle. The sound didn't bother Burke—he'd heard cats and rats and other vermin make all sorts of queer noises in the night. Phlegmatically, he continued on his beat.

Three quarters of an hour later, Police Officer Burke had worked his way around to the fatal spot. Putting his flash on the body, he rolled the supine animal over with his foot. Its throat was cut. Its throat had been cut with an utter savagery that had half-severed its head from its body. Burke scowled down at it. He was no lover of cats himself, but he found difficulty in imagining anyone hating like that!

"Somebody," he muttered, "wants flaying alive."

His big foot shoved the dead cat back into the gutter where street cleaners could cart it away in the morning. He turned his attention to the window, saw the light still glowing upon the untouched safe. His mind was still on the cat while his eyes looked in and said that something was wrong. Then he dragged his attention back to business, realized what was wrong, and sweated at every pore. It wasn't the safe, it was the window.

In front of the window the serried trays of valuable rings still gleamed undisturbed. To the right, the silverware still shone untouched. But on the left had been a small display of delicate and extremely expensive watches. They were no longer there, not one of them. He remembered that right in front had rested a neat, beautiful calendar-chronometer priced at a year's salary. That, too, was gone.

The beam of his flash trembled as he tried the gate, found it fast, secure. The door behind it was firmly locked. The transom was closed, its heavy wire guard still securely fixed. He went over the window, eventually found a small, neat hole, about two inches in diameter, down in the corner on the side nearest the missing display.

Burke's curse was explosive as he turned and ran to the corner. His hand shook with indignation while it grabbed the telephone from its box. Getting headquarters, he recited his story. He thought he'd a good idea of what had happened, fancied he'd read once of a similar stunt being pulled else-where.

"Looks like they cut a disk with a rotary diamond, lifted it out with a suction cup, then fished through the hole with a telescopic rod." He listened a moment, then said, "Yes, yes. That's just what gets me—the rings are worth ten times as much."

His still-startled eyes looked down the street while he paid attention to the voice at the other end of the line. The eyes wandered slowly, descended, found the gutter, remained fixed on the dim shape lying therein. Another dead cat! Still clinging to his phone, Burke moved out as far as the cord would allow, extended a boot, rolled the cat away from the curb. The flash settled on it. Just like the other—ear to ear!

"And listen," he shouted into the phone, "some maniac's wandering around slaughtering cats."

Replacing the phone, he hurried back to the maltreated window, stood guard in front of it until the police car rolled up. Four piled out.

The first said, "Cats! I'll say somebody's got it in for cats! We passed two a couple of blocks away. They were bang in the middle of the street, flat in the headlights, and had been damn near guillotined. Their bodies were still warm."

The second grunted, approached the window, stared at the small, neat hole and said. "The mob that did this would be too cute to leave a print."

"They weren't too cute to leave the rings," growled Burke.

"Maybe you've got something there," conceded the other. "If they've left the one, they might have left the other. We'll test for prints, anyway."

A taxi swung into the dark street, pulled up behind the police car. An elegantly dressed, fussy, and very agitated individual got out, rushed up to the waiting group. Keys jangled in his pale, moist hand.

"Maley, the manager—you phoned me," he explained, breathlessly. "Gentlemen, this is terrible, terrible! The win-dow show is worth thousands, thousands! What a loss, what a loss!"

"How about letting us in?" asked one of the policemen, calmly.

"Of course, of course."

Jerkily, he opened the gate, unlocked the door, using about six keys for the job. They walked inside. Maley switched on the lights, stuck his head between the plate glass shelves, surveyed the depleted window.

"My watches, my watches," he groaned.

"It's awful, it's awful!" said one of the policemen, speaking with beautiful solemnity. He favored his companions with a sly wink.

Maley leaned farther over, the better to inspect an empty corner. "All gone, all gone," he moaned, "all my show of the finest makes in—*Yeeouw!*" His yelp made then jump. Maley bucked as he tried to force himself through the obstructing shelves toward the grille and the window beyond it. "My watch! My own watch!"

The others tiptoed, stared over his shoulders, saw the gold buckle of a black velvet fob go through the hole in the window. Burke was the first outside, his ready flash searching the concrete. Then he spotted the watch. It was moving rapidly along, hugging the angle of the wall, but it stopped dead as his beam settled upon it. He fancied he saw something else, equally bright and metallic, scoot swiftly into the darkness beyond the circle of his beam.

Picking up the watch, Burke stood and listened. The noises of the others coming out prevented him from hearing clearly, but he could have sworn he'd heard a tiny whirring noise, and a swift, juicy ticking that was not coming from the instrument in his hand. Must have been only his worried fancy. Frowning deeply, he returned to his companions.

"There was nobody," he asserted. "It must have dropped out of your pocket and rolled."

Damn it, he thought, could a watch roll that far? What the devil was happening this night? Far up the street, something screeched, then it bubbled. Burke shuddered—he could make a shrewd guess at that! He looked at the others, but apparently they hadn't heard the noise.

The papers gave it space in the morning. The total was sixty watches and eight cats, also some oddments from the small stock of a local scientific instrument maker. I read about it on my way down to Burman's place. The details were fairly lavish, but not complete. I got them completely at a later time when we discovered the true significance of what had occurred.

Burman was waiting for me when I arrived. He appeared both annoyed and bothered. Over in the corner, the coffin

was ticking away steadily, its noise much louder than it had
been the previous day. The thing sounded a veritable hive of
industry.

"Well?" I asked.

"It's moved around a lot during the night," said Burman.
"It's smashed a couple of thermometers and taken the mer-
cury out of them. I found some drawers and cupboards shut,
some open, but I've an uneasy feeling that it's made a
thorough search through the lot. A packet of nickel foil has
vanished, a coil of copper wire has gone with it." He
pointed an angry finger at the bottom of the door through
which I'd just entered. "And I blame it for gnawing ratholes
in that. They weren't there yesterday."

Sure enough, there were a couple of holes in the bottom
of that door. But no rat made those—they were neat and
smooth and round, almost as if a carpenter had cut them
with a keyhole saw.

"Where's the sense in it making those?" I questioned. "It
can't crawl through apertures that size."

"Where's the sense in the whole affair?" Burman coun-
tered. He glowered at the busy machine which stared back at
him with its expressionless lenses and churned steadily on.
Tick-tick-tick! persisted the confounded thing. Then, *whir-
thump-click!*

I opened my mouth intending to voice a nice, sarcastic
comment at the machine's expense when there came a very
tiny, very subtle and extremely high-pitched whine. Something small, metallic, glittering shot through one of the rat
holes, fled across the floor toward the churning monstrosity.
A trapdoor opened and swallowed it with such swiftness
that it had disappeared before I realized what I'd seen. The
thing had been a cylindrical, polished object resembling the
shuttle of a sewing machine, but about four times the size.
And it had been dragging something also small and metallic.

Burman stared at me; I stared at Burman. Then he foraged
around the laboratory, found a three-foot length of half-inch
steel pipe. Dragging a chair to the door, he seated himself,
gripped the pipe like a bludgeon, and watched the rat holes.
Imperturbably, the machine watched him and continued to
tick-tick-tick.

Ten minutes later, there came a sudden click and another
tiny whine. Nothing darted inward through the holes, but
the curious object we'd already seen—or another one exactly

like it—dropped out of the trap, scooted to the door by which we were waiting. It caught Burman by surprise. He made a mad swipe with the steel as the thing skittered elusively past his feet and through a hole. It had gone even as the weapon walloped the floor.

"Damn!" said Burman, heartily. He held the pipe loosely in his grip while he glared at the industrious coffin. "I'd smash it to bits except that I'd like to catch one of these small gadgets first."

"Look out!" I yelled.

He was too late. He ripped his attention away from the coffin toward the holes, swinging up the heavy length of pipe, a startled look on his face. But his reaction was far too slow. Three of the little mysteries were through the holes and halfway across the floor before his weapon was ready to swing. The coffin swallowed them with the crash of a trapdoor.

The invading trio had rushed through in single file, and I'd got a better picture of them this time. The first two were golden shuttles, much like the one we'd already seen. The third was bigger, speedier, and gave me the notion that it could dodge around more dexterously. It had a long, sharp projection in front, a wicked, ominous thing like a surgeon's scalpel. Sheer speed deprived me of a good look at it, but I fancied that the tip of the scalpel had been tinged with red. My spine exuded perspiration.

Came an irritated scratching upon the outside of the door and a white-tipped paw poked tentatively through one of the holes. The cat backed to a safe distance when Burman opened the door, but looked lingeringly toward the laboratory. Its presence needed no explaining—the alert animal must have caught a glimpse of those infernal little whizzers. The same thought struck both of us; cats are quick on the pounce, very quick. Given a chance, maybe this one could make a catch for us.

We enticed it in with fair words and soothing noises. Its eagerness overcame its normal caution toward strangers, and it entered. We closed the door behind it; Burman got his length of pipe, sat by the door, tried to keep one eye on the holes and the other on the cat. He couldn't do both, but he tried. The cat sniffed and prowled around, mewed defeatedly. Its behavior suggested that it was seeking by sight rather than scent. There wasn't any scent.

With feline persistence, the animal searched the whole laboratory. It passed the buzzing coffin several times, but ignored it completely. In the end, the cat gave it up, sat on the corner of the laboratory table and started to wash its face.

Tick-tick-tick! went the big machine. Then *whir-thump!* A trap popped open, a shuttle fell out and raced for the door. A second one followed it. The first was too fast even for the cat, too fast for the surprised Burman as well. Bang! The length of steel tube came down viciously as the leading shuttle bulleted triumphantly through a hole.

But the cat got the second one. With a mighty leap, paws extended claws out, it caught its victim one foot from the door. It tried to handle the slippery thing, failed, lost it for an instant. The shuttle whisked around in a crazy loop. The cat got it again, lost it again, emitted an angry snarl, batted it against the skirting board. The shuttle lay there, upside down, four midget wheels in its underside spinning madly with a high, almost inaudible whine.

Eyes alight with excitement, Burman put down his weapon, went to pick up the shuttle. At the same time, the cat slunk toward it ready to play with it. The shuttle lay there, helplessly functioning upon its back, before either could reach it the big machine across the room went *clunk!* opened a trap and ejected another gadget.

With astounding swiftness, the cat turned and pounced upon the newcomer, Then followed pandemonium. Its prey swerved agilely with a fitful gleam of gold; the cat swerved with it, cursed and spat. Black-and-white fur whirled around in a fighting haze in which gold occasionally glowed; the cat's hissings and spittings overlay a persistent whine that swelled and sank in the manner of accelerating or decelerating gears.

A peculiar gasp came from the cat, and blood spotted the floor. The animal clawed wildly, emitted another gasp followed by a gurgle. It shivered and flopped, a stream of crimson pouring from the great gash in its gullet.

We'd hardly had time to appreciate the full significance of the ghastly scene when the victor made for Burman. He was standing by the skirting board, the still-buzzing shuttle in his hand. His eyes were sticking out with utter horror, but he retained enough presence of mind to make a frantic jump a second before the bulleting menace reached his feet.

He landed behind the thing, but it reversed in its own length and came for him again. I saw the mirrorlike sheen of its scapel as it banked at terrific speed, and the sheen was drowned in sticky crimson two inches along the blade. Burman jumped over it again, reached the lab table, got up on that.

"Lord!" he breathed.

By this time I'd got the piece of pipe which he'd discarded. I hefted it, feeling its comfortable weight, then did my best to bat the buzzing lump of wickedness through the window and over the roofs. It was too agile for me. It whirled, accelerated, dodged the very tip of the descending steel, and flashed twice around the table upon which Burman had taken refuge. It ignored me completely. Somehow, I felt that it was responding entirely to some mysterious call from the shuttle Burman had captured.

I swiped desperately, missed it again, though I swear I missed by no more than a millimeter. Something whipped through the holes in the door, fled past me into the big machine. Dimly, I heard traps opening and closing, and beyond all other sounds that steady, persistent *tick-tick-tick*. Another furious blow that accomplished no more than to dent the floor and jar my arm to the shoulder.

Unexpectedly, unbelievably, the golden curse ceased its insane gyrations on the floor and around the table. With a hard click, and a whir much louder than before, it raced easily up one leg of the table and reached the top.

Burman left his sanctuary in one jump. He was still clinging to the shuttle. I'd never seen his face so white.

"The machine!" he said, hoarsely. "Bash it to hell!"

Thunk! went the machine. A trap gaped, released another demon with a scalpel. *Tzz-z-z!* a third shot in through the holes in the door. Four shuttles skimmed through behind it, made for the machine, reached it safely. A fifth came through more slowly. It was dragging an automobile valve spring. I kicked the thing against the wall even as I struck a vain blow at one with a scalpel.

With another jump, Burman cleared an attacker. A second sheared off the toe of his right shoe as he landed. Again he reached the table from which his first foe had departed. All three things with scalpels made for the table with a reckless vim that was frightening.

"Drop that damned shuttle," I yelled.

He didn't drop it. As the fighting trio whirred up the legs, he flung the shuttle with all his might at the coffin that had given it birth. It struck, dented the casing, fell the floor. Burman was off the table again. The thrown shuttle lay battered and noiseless, its small motive wheels stilled.

The armed contraptions scooting around the table seemed to change their purpose coincidently with the captured shuttle's smashing. Together, they dived off the table, sped through the holes in the door. A fourth came out of the machine, escorting two shuttles, and those too vanished beyond the door. A second or two later, a new thing, different from the rest, came in through one of the holes. It was long, round-bodied, snub-nosed, about half the length of a policeman's nightstick, had six wheels beneath, and a double row of peculiar serrations in front. It almost sauntered across the room while we watched it fascinatedly. I saw the serrations jerk and shift when it climbed the lower trap into the machine. They were midget caterpillar tracks!

Burman had had enough. He made up his mind. Finding the steel pipe, he gripped it firmly, approached the coffin. Its lenses seemed to leer at him as he stood before it. Twelve years of intensive work to be destroyed at a blow. Endless days and nights of effort to be undone at one stroke. But Burman was past caring. With a ferocious swing he demolished the glass, with a fierce thrust he shattered the assembly of wheels and cogs behind.

The coffin shuddered and slid beneath his increasingly angry blows. Trapdoors dropped open, spilled out lifeless samples of the thing's metallic brood. Grindings and raspings came from the accursed object while Burman battered it to pieces. Then it was silent, stilled, a shapeless, useless mass of twisted and broken parts.

I picked up the dented shape of the object that had sauntered in. It was heavy, astonishingly heavy, and even after partial destruction its workmanship looked wonderful. It had a tiny, almost unnoticeable eye in front, but the miniature lens was cracked. Had it returned for repairs and overhaul?

"That," said Burman, breathing audibly, "is that!"

I opened the door to see if the noise had attracted attention. It hadn't. There was a lifeless shuttle outside the door, a second a yard behind it. The first had a short length of brass chain attached to a tiny hook projecting from its rear. The nose cap of the second had opened fanwise, like an iris diaphragm, and a pair of jointed metal arms were folded inside, hugging a medium-sized diamond. It looked as if they'd been about to enter when Burman destroyed the big machine.

Picking them up, I brought them in. Their complete inactivity, though they were undamaged, suggested that they had been controlled by the big machine and had drawn their motive power from it. If so, then we'd solved our problem simply, and by destroying the one had destroyed the lot.

Burman got his breath back and began to talk.

He said, "The Robot Mother! That's what I made—a duplicate of the Robot Mother. I didn't realize it, but I was patiently building the most dangerous thing in creation, a thing that is a terrible menace because it shares with mankind the ability to propagate. Thank Heaven we stopped it in time!"

"So," I remarked, remembering that he claimed to have got it from the extreme future, "that's the eventual master, or mistress, of Earth. A dismal prospect for humanity, eh?"

"Not necessarily. I don't know just how far I got, but I've an idea it was so tremendously distant in the future that Earth had become sterile from humanity's viewpoint. Maybe we'd emigrated to somewhere else in the cosmos, leaving our semi-intelligent slave machines to fight for existence or die. They fought—and survived."

"And then wangle things to try and alter the past in their favor," I suggested.

"No, I don't think so." Burman had become much calmer by now. "I don't think it was a dastardly attempt so much as an interesting experiment. The whole affair was damned in advance because success would have meant an impossible paradox. There are no robots in the next century, nor any knowledge of them. Therefore the intruders in this time must have been wiped out and forgotten."

"Which means," I pointed out, "that you must not only have destroyed the machine, but also all your drawings, all your notes, as well as the psychopone, leaving nothing but a few strange events and a story for me to tell."

"Exactly—I shall destroy everything. I've been thinking over the whole affair, and it's not until now I've understood

that the psychopone can never be of the slightest use to me.
It permits me to discover or invent only those things that
history has decreed I shall invent, and which, therefore, I
shall find with or without the contraption. I can't play tricks
with history, past or future."

"Humph!" I couldn't find any flaw in his reasoning. "Did
you notice," I went on, "the touch of bee-psychology in our
antagonists? You build the hive, and from it emerged workers,
warriors, and"—I indicated the dead saunterer—"one drone."

"Yes," he said, lugubriously. "And I'm thinking of the
honey—eighty watches! Not to mention any other items the
late papers may report, plus any claims for slaughtered cats.
Good thing I'm wealthy."

"Nobody knows you've anything to do with those incidents. You can pay secretly if you wish."

"I shall," he declared.

"Well," I went on, cheerfully, "all's well that ends well.
Thank goodness we've got rid of what we brought upon ourselves."

With a sigh of relief, I strolled toward the door. A high
whine of midget motors drew my startled attention downward. While Burman and I stared aghast, a golden shuttle
slid easily through one of the rat holes, sensed the death
of the Robot Mother and scooted back through the other
hole before I could stop it.

If Burman had been shaken before, he was doubly so now.
He came over to the door, stared incredulously at the little
exit just used by the shuttle, then at the couple of other
undamaged but lifeless shuttles lying about the room.

"Bill," he mouthed, "your bee analogy was perfect. Don't
you understand? There's another swarm! A queen got loose!"

There was another swarm all right. For the next forty-eight
hours it played merry hell. Burman spent the whole time
down at headquarters trying to convince them that his evidence wasn't just a fantastic story, but what helped him
to persuade the police of his veracity was the equally fantastic reports that came rolling in.

To start with, old Gildersome heard a crash in his shop at
midnight, thought of his valuable stock of cameras and
miniature movie projectors, pulled on his pants and rushed
downstairs. A razor-sharp instrument stabbed him through the

right instep when halfway down, and he fell the rest of the way. He lay there, badly bruised and partly stunned, while things clicked, ticked and whirred in the darkness and the gloom. One by one, all the contents of his box of expensive lenses went through a hole in the door. A quantity of projector cogs and wheels went with them.

Ten people complained of being robbed in the night of watches and alarm clocks. Two were hysterical. One swore that the bandit was "a six-inch cockroach" which purred like a toy dynamo. Getting out of bed, he'd put his foot upon it and felt its old hardness wriggle away from beneath him. Filled with revulsion, he'd whipped his foot back into bed "just as another cockroach scuttled toward him." Burman did not tell that agitated complainant how near he had come to losing his foot.

Thirty more reports rolled in next day. A score of houses had been entered and four shops robbed by things that had the agility and furtiveness of rats—except that they emitted tiny ticks and buzzing noises. One was seen racing along the road by a homing railway worker. He tried to pick it up, lost his forefinger and thumb, stood nursing the stump until an ambulance rushed him away.

Rare metals and fine parts were the prey of these ticking marauders. I couldn't see how Burman or anyone else could wipe them out once and for all, but he did it. He did it by baiting them like rats. I went around with him, helping him on the job, while he consulted a map.

"Every report," said Burman, "leads to this street. An alarm clock that suddenly sounded was abandoned near here. Two automobiles were robbed of small parts near here. Shuttles have been seen going to and from this area. Five cats were dealt with practically on this spot. Every other incident has taken place within easy reach."

"Which means," I guessed, "that the queen is somewhere near this point?"

"Yes." He stared up and down the quiet empty street over which the crescent moon shed a sickly light. It was two o'clock in the morning. "We'll settle this matter pretty soon!"

He attached the end of a reel of firm cotton to a small piece of silver chain, nailed the reel to the wall, dropped the chain on the concrete. I did the same with the movement of a broken watch. We distributed several small cogs, a few clock wheels, several camera fittings, some small, tangled bunches of copper wire, and other attractive oddments.

Three hours later, we returned accompanied by the police. They had mallets and hammers with them. All of us were wearing steel leg-and-foot shields knocked up at short notice by a handy sheet-metal worker.

The bait had been taken! Several cotton strands had broken after being unreeled a short distance, but others were intact. All of them either led to or pointed to a steel grating leading to a cellar below an abandoned warehouse. Looking down, we could see a few telltale strands running through the window frame beneath.

Burman said, "Now!" and we went in with a rush. Rusty locks snapped, rotten doors collapsed, we poured through the warehouse and into the cellar.

There was a small, coffin-shaped thing against one wall, a thing that ticked steadily away while its lenses stared at us with ghastly lack of emotion. It was very similar to the Robot Mother, but only a quarter of the size. In the light of a police torch, it was a brooding, ominous thing of dreadful significance. Around it, an active clan swarmed over the floor buzzing and ticking in metallic fury.

Amid angry whirs and the crack of snapping scalpels on steel, we waded headlong through the lot. Burman reached the coffin first, crushing it with one mighty blow of his twelve-pound hammer, then bashing it to utter ruin with a rapid succession of blows. He finished exhausted. The daughter of the Robot Mother was no more, nor did her alien tribe move or stir.

Sitting down on a rickety wooden case, Burman mopped his brow and said, "Thank Heavens that's done!"

Tick-tick-tick!

He shot up, snatched his hammer, a wild look in his eyes.

"Only my watch," apologized one of the policemen. "It's a cheap one, and it makes a hell of a noise." He pulled it out to show the worried Burman.

"Tick! tick!" said the watch, with mechanical aplomb.

AS NEVER WAS / by P. Schuyler Miller

Consider, for a moment, the complexities and contradictions of time travel. It involves, for example, your living in a time before you were born; i.e., before you lived! Or, it may involve your traveling to the future and living in a time after you have died. Few illustrations of the completeness of the paradox that is time travel have been so well drawn as Mr. Miller's story of the knife. That knife of wonderful metal that—by ordinary logic—could never have been placed where—and when—it was found.

HAVE YOU ever dreamed of murder?

Have you ever set your elbows on the desk and let your head slump down on your hands, and closed your eyes, and dreamed of how it would feel to drive a knife up to the hilt in a scrawny, wrinkled throat, and twist it until the thin old blood begins to slime your fingers and drip from your wrist—until the piercing old eyes roll back and close, and the skinny old legs crumple and sag? Have you felt the blood pounding in your own temples, and savage satisfaction swarming up in you as you stare down on the hideous, sprawling thing you have destroyed?

And then have you opened your eyes and looked down at the mass of scribbled papers, and the meticulously drawn sectional charts, and the trait tables and correlation diagrams and all the other dead, dry details that make up your life's work? And picked up your pen and started making more scribbles on the papers and more checks on the charts and more little colored dots on the scattergrams, just as you've been doing three days out of every five since you were old enough to start the career for which you'd been tested and picked and trained?

Maybe I should go to a clinic and let the psychotherapists feed vitamins to my personality. Maybe I should go to a religious center and let the licensed clergy try to put this fear of Humanity into my reputed soul. Maybe I should go to a pleasure palace and let them mix me up a emotional hooker to jar the megrims out of my disposition, or go down and apply for a permit to wed and set about begetting another generation of archeologists who will grow up to be just as tired and bored and murderous as their illustrious father.

Night after night and day after day I dream of what might have happened that day in the laboratory if I had picked up the knife and slit the gullet of the man who had just injected the time-stream concept into the quietly maturing science of human archeology. If I could have seen ahead— If I could have guessed what would happen to all the romantic visions he had worked so hard to inspire in me—

Why should I dream? I was a child then; I had no way of looking ahead; the knife was just another knife. And I think if *he* had known—if he had been able to see ahead and watch the science to which he had devoted his every waking moment for a long lifetime degenerate into a variety of three-dimensional bookkeeping—he'd have cut his own heart out and offered it to me in apology.

He was a great old man. He was my grandfather.

You've seen the knife. Everyone has, I guess. I was the first, after him, ever to see it, and I was about ten years old. I was sitting in a chair in his laboratory, waiting for him to come back. It was a wooden chair, something his grandfather had used, and maybe other people before that. The laboratory was just a big room at the back of the house, with a concrete floor and plenty of light from a row of windows over the worktable. There were hundreds of potsherds strewn over the table where he'd been classifying and matching them for restoration. There were trays of stone implements, and cheap wooden boxes full of uncatalogued stuff with the dirt still on it. There was a row of battered-looking notebooks, bound in imitation leather, fraying at the corners and stained with ink and dirt. There was a pot that had been half restored, the sherds joined so neatly that you could barely see where they fitted together, and a little ivory goddess whose cracks and chips were being replaced with a plastic filler until you'd never have known she was five thousand years old.

That was what an archeologist's laboratory was like in those days. Of course, we've outgrown all that. His experiment, and the knife he brought back and tossed down on the table for me to look at, have ended all that. Archeology has found its place among the major sciences. It's no longer a kind of bastard stepchild of art and anthropology. We have money for the best equipment, the newest gadgets. We have laboratories designed by the best architects to fit the work we do in them. We can call on the technicians of a score of other sciences to do our dirty work, or can train ourselves to know as much as they do if we're reactionaries like me. We have our own specialists, just as learned and as limited as any hairsplitter in biochemistry or galactic physics. We have prestige—recognition—everything he never had in his day, when he was acknowledged master in his field, and we have him to thank for it all. But Walter Toynbee, if he were living now, would dry up and die in this kind of laboratory his grandson has. He'd push his charts and his correlations back and drop his head in his hands and dream. He'd plan out his own murder.

I'd been sitting there for nearly six hours. I'd been over the worktable from one end to the other, three times. I'd picked up every potsherd—turned them over—studied them with all the solemn intentness of ten years old—put them back exactly where I'd found them, as he had taught me. I'd found four sherds that would fit onto the pot he was restoring, and two that made an ear for a little clay figurine shaped like a fat, happy puppy. I'd taken down his books, one by one, and looked at the plates and figures as I had done many times before. I had even taken down one of his notebooks and slowly leafed through it, trying to spell out the straggling hand-writing and make sense of the precise sketches, until a loose slip of paper fell out from among the pages and I slipped it hurriedly back and put the book away.

All one corner of the laboratory was taken up by the time shuttle. It had cost more than the air surveys, all the expeditions, all the books and photographs and restorations of his whole career. The copper bus bars that came in through the wall behind it were like columns in some Mayan colonnade. The instrument panel was like something you'd imagine on—well, on a time machine. The machine itself was a block of dull gray lead with a massive steel door in one side of it, the time cell floating in the magnetic bearing between the pole pieces which set up the field.

Ours are neater now, but inside they're about the same. Old Walter Toynbee was an artist to the core, and Balmer, who built the machine for him from Malecewicz's notes, had a flair for functional design. It was the first shuttle big enough and powerful enough to push a man and his baggage more than twenty years into the future—or the past, for that matter. Malecewicz had gone back fifteen years. He never returned. His equations showed why that was, and the archeological world, which had been rubbing its hands in anticipation of striking up a speaking acquaintance with Hatshepsut and Queen Shub-Ad, went back to its trowels and whiskbrooms with sighs of resignation. All but my grandfather. All but Walter Toynbee.

Malecewicz had never taken time to really work out his theory of the time function and lapsed interval, or he might be alive now. Laymen will still ask you why we archeologists don't simply climb into a shuttle with a solido camera and slip back to Greece of Elam or maybe Atlantis, and film what went on instead of tediously slicing the dust of millennia over the graveyards of past civilizations. It can be done, but the man who does it must be utterly self-centered, wrapped up in knowledge for its own sake, utterly unconcerned with his duties to his fellow men. As any schoolchild learns, the time shuttler who goes into the past introduces an alien variable into the spacio-temporal matrix at the instant when he emerges. The time-stream forks, an alternative universe is born in which his visit is given its proper place, and when he returns it will be to a future level in the new world which he has created. His own universe is forever barred to him.

The future is by nature different. All that we are now and all that we have seen or become from moment to moment is integral in the structure and flow of our particular thread of time. The man who visits the future is not changing it: his visit is a foredestined part of that future. As the ancients might have said: "It is written." Though I should imagine that the writing is in the matrix of spacetime and not in the record book of God.

Walter Toynbee was a brilliant man who might have made a success of many sciences. He had money to guarantee him such comfort as he might want, and he chose the science which most attracted him—archeology. He was the last of the great amateurs. He had known Malecewciz well—financed some of his experimental work—and when the physicist failed to return he wheedled the trustees of the university into turning the man's notes over to him. He showed them almost at once where Malecewicz had gone and why he would never return, and he saw immediately that there was no such barrier between Man and his tomorrows. Inside of a week he and Balmer were moving cases of artifacts out of the back room to make room for the shuttle. Night after night they sat up into the wee hours, arguing over fantastic-looking diagrams. In two months the power lines were coming in across the fields, straight from the generators at Sheldon Forks, and Balmer's men were pouring the colossal concrete base on which the machine would sit.

It was past dinner time. I had been sitting there alone since a little after one o'clock, when he had stepped into the shuttle and asked me to wait until he returned. There it sat, just as it had sat for the last six hours, shimmering a little as though the air around it were hot and humming like a swarm of bees deep in an old beech. I got down a big book of plates of early Sumerian cylinder seals and began to turn the pages slowly. The sameness of them had grown boring when I realized that the humming had stopped.

I looked up at the lead cube. It was no longer shimmering. I closed the book and put it carefully back on the shelf, just as the great steel door of the shuttle swung silently open, and my grandfather stepped down out of the time cell.

He had been digging. His breeches and heavy jacket were covered with whitish dust. Dirt made grimy gutters under his eyes and filled in the creases and wrinkles of his face and neck. He had a stubble of dirty gray beard on his chin, which hadn't been there six hours before, and his shirt was dark with sweat. He was tired, but there was a gleam of satisfaction in his sharp black eyes and a kind of grin on his wrinkled face.

The battered canvas bag in which he kept his tools and records was slung over one shoulder. He slapped at his thighs and puffs of dust spurted from his trousers. He took off the shabby felt hat which he always wore, and his thin gray hair was damp and draggled. He came over to the table, fumbling with the buckle on the bag. I watched his knotted fingers wide-eyed, for I had seen them pull many wonders out of that dusty wallet. I can hear his triumphant chuckle as he drew out a knife—the knife—and tossed it ringing on the table among the sherds.

You've seen it, of course. It's been in the pictures many times, and there are solidographs of the thing in most museums. I saw it then for the first time—ever—in our time.

He hadn't washed it. There was dirt on the fine engraving of the dull-black hilt, and caked in the delicate filigree of the silver guard. But the blade was clean, and it was as you have seen it—cold, gleaming, metallic blue—razor-edged—and translucent.

Maybe you've had a chance to handle it, here in the museum. Where the blade thins down to that feather-edge you can read the small print through it. Where it's thicker, along the rib that reinforces the back of the blade, it's cloudy—milky looking. There has been engraving on the blade, too, but it has been ground or worn down until it is illegible. That is odd, because the blade is harder than anything we know except diamond. There is no such metal in the System or the Galaxy, so far as we know, except in this one well-worn and apparently very ancient knife blade.

It must be old. Not only is the engraving on the blade obliterated by wear; there is the telltale little serif near the hilt, where that utterly keen, hard edge has been worn back a little by use and honing. The black stuff of the hilt looks newer, and the carving is clearer, though still very old. Grandfather thought that it was made of some very heavy wood, possibly impregnated with a plastic of some sort, and that it had been made to replace an earlier hilt which had become worn out or broken. The metal of the guard and the plate and rivets which hold the hilt are ordinary silver, in one of the new stainless alloys which were just then coming into fairly general use.

Well—there it was. Walter Toynbee, who was probably the most competent archeologist the world has yet seen, had gone into the future in a Malecewicz shuttle. He had dug up a knife, and brought it back with him. And it was made of a material—a metal—of which our science knew absolutely nothing.

Three days later Walter Toynbee was dead. It may have been some virus picked up in that distant future which he had visited, to which our generation of mankind had developed no resistance. It may have been the strain of the

trip into time, or the excitement and exertion of what he
did there. He washed up, and we went home together to
supper. We had it together, in the kitchen, because the family
had finished and the dishes were done. Grandfather examined the knife while we were eating, but he wouldn't talk
about it then. He was tired: he wanted to sleep. He never
awoke.

In my father, old Walter's only son, the family talents
had taken another turn. He was a more practical man than
his father, and had done his noted parent many a good
turn by husbanding and stimulating the family fortunes
when they most needed it. Where Grandfather had been
interested in the minutiae and complexities of the ancient
cultures whose dust he cleared away, Father was one of
the then popular cyclic historians who tried to see civilization as a whole—as a kind of super-organism—and to find
recurring patterns in Man's gradual progression from the
jungle to Parnassus. I am not implying that old Walter had
no interest in synthesis and generalization—it is, as a matter of fact, a tradition that he had adopted the name
Toynbee out of admiration for an historian of that name
—a scholar of scholars—who lived and wrote in the early
years of the last century. There is a letter among his papers
which suggests that our original patronym may have been
Slavic. If so, it might also explain his long and warm
friendship with the unfortunate Malecewicz.

Be that as it may, Grandfather's death set in motion
events whose result is all too familiar to all who have
chosen to identify their lives with the pursuit of archeology.
By the time the public lamentations had begun to die away,
the press found a new sensation in the knife. The experts
mulled over it and reported with remarkable unanimity
that the engraving on the blade and hilt, while clearly of
the same provenance, resembled no known human script or
style of decoration. Finding their progress blocked, they
called on the metallurgists and chemists to identify the blue
metal of the blade, and on the botanists to specify the wood
—if it was wood—of which the hilt was made.

Need I continue? There was more quibbling for its own
sake in those days than there is now. Every expert was
jealous of his personal acumen and insistent upon being the
Only Right Man. It was considered fitting and proper that

experts should disagree. But it gradually dawned on everyone concerned that here was something where there could be no disagreement, and what was more, something which might very well open new vistas of human progress.

Physically and chemically the blue stuff was a metal, though it was no metal chemistry had ever described or imagined. When they had succeeded in sawing out a sliver of the blade for tests, and finally got it into solution, its chemical behavior placed it quite outside the periodic system of the elements. The physicists went to work on another sample with X rays and spectographs, and arrived at much the same result. The more they studied it, the less they knew, for sooner or later some experiment would succeed in knocking over any hypothesis which they might have built up on the basis of their previous investigations.

Out of it all eventually came the judgment which stands today: that the blue stuff might well be some familiar metal, but that its atomic and molecular structure—and consequently its physical and chemical properties—had been modified or tampered with in a manner unknown to our science, making it to all intents and purposes a new state of matter. The botanists returned the same report. The black material had the structure of wood, and it might be any of several common tropical woods or it might be something quite alien, but it, too, had been hardened—indurated—through internal transformations which left it something entirely new to our planet.

That ended the first stage of the battle. When the experts threw up their hands in despair, the attack shifted to another quarter. The knife came back to my father, and he promptly made it the nucleus of a Toynbee Museum of Human Acculturation at his and Malecewicz's university, where it is today. But it was common knowledge that old Walter had brought the thing from the future. That meant somewhere in the coming centuries of our race was a science which could create such unheard of things as the blue metal, and that the stuff was sufficiently common with them for knives to be made of it. Its electrical properties alone were such as to open a host of possible uses for it—Father had been offered a small fortune by a certain great electrical concern for the material in the knife alone—and science decided to visit that future civilization, learn its secrets, and profit suitably thereby.

So the experiments shifted to time traveling. Malecewicz's notes were unearthed again and published; Grandfather's shuttle was dismantled and reconstructed a dozen times; Balmer found himself in a position to charge almost any fee as a consultant to industrial laboratories, universities, and private speculators who were hot on the trail of tomorrow. Shuttles were built on every hand, and men—and women—disappeared into the future. One by one they straggled back, empty-handed and thoroughly disgruntled. The future had no such metal.

There was a brief period in which everyone who had failed to solve the problem of the knife tried to cast doubts on Walter Toynbee, but the thing existed, its nature was what it was, and presently the hubbub swung around full circle to the place it had started. Grandfather had been an archeologist. He had gone into the future, and excavated the knife from the detritus of what might conceivably have been a colony or a chance visitant from another world— even another galaxy—someone—or something—of which the rest of humanity at that moment in time was quite unaware. Archeology had found the thing. Science craved it. It was up to archeology to find it—or its source—again.

So we became, in the language of the popularizers, the Mother Science—spawning off all sorts of minuscule specialties, lording it over a score of devoutly adulatory slave sciences, enjoying our position and taking every advantage of it.

I grew up in that atmosphere. From the time I could talk and listen, Grandfather had filled me with the wonders of the past and the romance of their discovery. Now the whole world was awake to the glories of archeology as the science of sciences which would open a whole new world to struggling Mankind. Is it any wonder I chose to follow in my grandfather's footsteps?

Let me say now that men like my father and grandfather, who had needed no world-shaking anomaly to intrigue them with their chosen study, never lost their heads in the storm of recognition which swept over them. It might have been better if they had. Archeology was in the saddle; very well, it was going to ride—and ride hard. Projects which had been tabled for lack of funds were financed in a twinkling. Tools and instruments of investigation which had been regraded as extremists' pipe dreams were invented on demand. With new tools came new techniques, and with new techniques came a hierarchy of skilled technicians, statisticians in place of explorers, desk work in place of excavation, piddling with detail instead of drawing in broad strokes the panorama of advancing civilization which men like Schliemann, and Evans, and Breasted, and that first Toynbee—yes, and old Walter Toynbee after them all—had seen with clear and understanding eyes.

We have no one to blame but ourselves. I fully realize that. We dug our own hole; we furnished it lavishly; we built a wall around it to exclude the non-elite; we arranged to be fed and comforted while we dawdled with our trivia; and then we pulled the hole in on top of ourselves. We wore a rut so deep that we can never climb out of it. So I dream of cutting my grandfather's throat instead of realizing that if I were the man he was—if I had the courage to break away from the stultified pattern I have helped to make, and go primitive, dig in the dirt with a trowel, regain the thrill of new worlds—the barriers would disappear and I would be free again, as men were meant to be.

Of course, by the time I was old enough for the university the whole business was well under way. My father, with his cycles in mind, had instigated a project whereby Archeology—it rated the capital by now—would uncover and describe the entire growth, maturity, and decline of representative communities, our own included. A colleague —or maybe he was a competitor—at Harvard was all for starting all over again at the beginning and redigesting the entire corpus of archeological data accumulated by grubbers since the beginning of time, using the new statistical attacks and the college's vast new calculating machine. He got his money. Science had declared that Archeology was the magician which would presently pass out unbounded benefits to one and all, and one and all swarmed to get on Santa Claus' good side.

I served my apprenticeship doing the dirty work for the men who voyaged into the future and sent back reams and sheaves of notes out of which we desk-workers were supposed to pull blue metal rabbits. His was the era of specialism: when trained mechanics did the digging, when stenographers and solido-scanners took the notes, and when laboratory drudges squeezed out of them every possible drop of information which super-statistics could extract.

I remember the worst pest of them all—a man with as much personality as my grandfather, though of a different kind—who nearly imposed his infernal pattern on the science for a generation. He had been a mathematical physicist who turned to archeology in what he claimed was an attempt to fit human behavior "in its broader sense" into some set of universal field-equations he had distilled out of his stars and atoms, and which purported to express the Totality of All, or some such pat phrase, in a large nutshell.

Of course, any such over-view of civilization was music to my father's ears, and he gave the man the run of the Museum and a voice in all our activities. Hill—that was his name—at once announced the precept that it was quite unnecessary to *find* blue-metal knives in some future culture. By making a sufficiently exhaustive collection of data at any particular moment, and applying his field equations in their humano-cultural aspect—I am trying here to recall his jargon—it would be possible to predict accurately when and where such knives *must* be.

Hill had a shock of red hair, a barrel chest, and a loud voice. He spoke often and in the right places. Myriads of miserable students like myself had to mull over the tons of notes which expeditions under his direction sent back. We translated facts into symbols, put the symbols through his mill, and got out more symbols. Nine times, by count, he announced to the world that "now he had it"—and nine times by count a simple check up showed that the poor beleaguered natives of whatever era it was he had chosen as it had never heard of such a metal. Some of them had never heard of metal.

By the time I was twenty-three and had my own license to explore past and future indiscriminately, we had a pretty good overall view of the future of humanity. We had libraries of histories which had been written in millennia to come. We had gadgets and super-gadgets developed by future civilizations, some of which we could use and most of which we were able to misuse. The world we supposedly enjoy today was in the making, and you know what it is like.

I had done altogether too well at whipping the esteemed Dr. Hill's hodgepodge of miscellaneous data into some semblance of intelligibility. The powers that were—and are—announced that I might spend at the rest of my life, for the good of Humanity, fiddling with the same kind of stuff. But I was young, and I was a Toynbee. I stood up and demanded my rights, and they gave them to me. I could go out like the rest and hunt for the knife.

I am not a fool. Moreover, I had had the advantage of knowing my grandfather—better even than Father ever did. I knew how he would think and how he would react. He was the kind of man who went at things hard—all out —to the limit of his ability. It seemed clear enough to me that the first step in finding the knife was to determine what that limit was—although in thirteen years or so nobody had chosen that approach.

Balmer was still alive, and I made him dig out the plans and specifications he had drawn up when he made Grandfather's shuttle. I got hold of the notes the experts had made when they tore the machine apart after his death, and they checked. And then I had Balmer set me up just the same kind of old gray cube out of which Walter Toynbee had stumbled that day, with the blue knife in his dusty old ditty bag.

It was bigger, of course—I had to have room for the kind of equipment a field man considered necessary in my day. I'd never had any training or experience with the kind of work old Walter did with his own two hands, a camera, and a trowel. The profession had been mechanized, and it was silly not to use the best I could lay my hands on. The time field, though, was the same, and it should carry me just as far as it had carried its originator thirteen years before.

It did. Malecewicz, by stretching his original model, had been able to get fifteen years out of it. Grandfather's huge old vault of a machine lofted him nearly twenty times as far into the future of our race—and of our town. As I had suspected from the specifications of the machine, it dropped me somewhere near the middle of that interregnum which followed the Hemispheric wars, when half the cities of America had been reduced to rubble, disease and famine and put the population of the planet back into a hunting-fishing-food-gathering economy, and all that remained of

civilization was a memory which would some day be revived, restored, and started off again.

I am not saying that in thirteen years of trying nobody
had hit upon this particular period in the future. It is
true that having hit it they let common sense scare them
off. It was obvious that that level of culture could never
produce so sophisticated a scientific marvel as the knife.
There was no evidence in the ruins they found to show
that our own culture, up to and during the time of the
Wars, had done so. Ergo: onward and upward. Try another
thousand years. Try a million.

I had a slightly different point of view on the matter.
I knew Grandfather. He would go as far as his machine
could take him. I had duplicated that. He would look around
him for a promising site, get out his tools, and pitch in.
Well, I could do that, too.

There is enough uncertainty—backlash, if you want to
call it that—in the operation of any time shuttle so that
you can never be certain that you will hit any specific
moment or even any specific day or week in the future.
Put that down to mechanical imperfections, if you like—
I know some do—but I consider it a matter of the inexacti-
tude of the physical universe, and I doubt that there is
ever anything that we can do about it. You can approxi-
mate—hopping back and forth across the time you want until
you get reasonably close—but that is a makeshift solution,
borrowed from practical mathematics. I didn't try.

If you've read your history of the next five hundred
years, you'll know that the gas attacks toward the end of
the war had stripped the Atlantic coastal regions of vegetation and every other living thing. I got out of the shuttle
in a dusty landscape where the bare bones of the planet
stuck up in shattered stumps in a wind-swept desert of
gullied clay. I might be ahead of grandfather's time—in
which case I saw a paradox brewing—or I might be following him. As it turned out, it was the latter.

I knew from what others had learned that there was no
life in this coastal strip until much later. Gradually vegetation worked its way into the arid strip, insects and mammals
followed, men followed them—but this is no essay on the
future. There was no point in hunting for survivors; Grandfather certainly hadn't. For on all sides stretched the wreckage of our own city—or its counterpart of three centuries

from now—and I knew that he would have stood just as I was standing, looking it over with a appraising eye, wondering where to begin.

One mass of fallen masonry, half submerged in a drift of sand, towered higher than the rest. It would provide a vantage point from which to size up the situation. As I plodded toward it through the soft sand I found myself watching for his footprints, so certain was I that this must be the place and the time. It was nonsense, of course; my own tracks were filling in as the wind curled sand into them.

Then I saw it—and that day thirteen years before came rushing back to me. Of course there would be traces! Walter Toynbee would never in his life have abandoned a dig as promising as this—a dig where surface-scratching had yielded him a relic like the knife. But for his sickness and death he would have been planning a return expedition —a camp—a full-scale attack. Not half the equipment he had taken with him was in the shuttle when he returned. And there, at the eastern base of the mound, the tatters of a red bandanna whipping in the wind, a short-handled shovel was driven into a crack in the masonry.

I fingered the shreds of red cloth. It was his. He always had one stuffed in the pocket of his jeans. Duster—sun shield—lashing—he had a score of uses for them. Any field worker had in those days, before there was a tool for every purpose.

The crevice into which the shovel had been wedged widened as it went down. Sand had drifted into it, filling it to within a few feet of the top. By all the tenets of civilized archeology I should prepare my aërial plan of the entire complex of ruins, erect the light tower with its instrument board to establish a zero reference plane for the solidograph, and assemble the scanner. When a grid had been projected on the screen of the excavator, it would be time enough to think of beginning the actual investigation.

Do you believe in ghosts? As I stood there, with those shreds of faded red cloth in my hand, stroking the sand-polished handle of the shovel, I suddenly realized that so far as time itself went he might have been standing here only hours, or even minutes before me. It was as though he had turned his back for a moment, and I had stepped into his tracks there in the sand. I was a child again, tagging after him as he strode around the big laboratory with his giant's strides, pulling down a book here, running though a file of negatives there, gathering his tools around him before he set to work to unravel some perplexing situation in his digging. A thin cloud passed across the sun, and it was as though his shadow had fallen on me.

I pulled the shovel out of the crack in which he had wedged it. It was in good condition—perfectly usable. In my time we did not work with shovels or picks, but any fool could handle the thing. I dug it into the sand—scratched at the base of the crack. It would take only a few moments to deepen it enough so that I could crawl inside.

There was a kind of satisfaction to the work. I exercise in the public gymnasia—all young men of my age have to, to keep fit—but there was a difference. Using this primitive tool brought with it a feeling of accomplishment—of purpose—that I never found in mere exercise. I was strong, and it gratified me to see the hole deepen and the drift of sand grow behind me. Soon I had a tunnel into which I could crawl without bumping my head. I went back to the shuttle for a glow lamp and a pocket scanner, and plunged into the darkness.

After the first few feet I had no use for the lamp. My eyes grew accustomed to the dark, and I saw that shafts and streaks of light broke through gaps in the ruin overhead. Presently I found a hard floor under my feet, and then I came out into a room which was like a wedge—the ceiling fallen in one mass which hung diagonally between the wall over my head and the floor about twenty feet before me. Sunlight seeped in through a crevice to the left, striking on the wall and filling the whole place with a kind of diffuse glow. In that glow I saw footprints in the thick dust which covered the floor, and the table to which they led.

They were his footprints, of course. On that table he had found the knife. I stepped out of the doorway where I had been standing, an odd feeling of familiarity growing in me. I crossed the floor to the table. It had been covered with heavy glass, which lay in shreds on the dusty bronze. I could see the marks of his fingers in the dust where he had moved the broken glass aside. And I could see the outline of the knife, as sharp in the unstirred dust as it was when he picked it up in his gnarled old fingers thirteen years—or was it thirteen minutes?—before.

The crack of light was widening as the sun moved; the

place grew brighter. I brushed the dust away from the table top. It was heavy bronze; it told me nothing. And then, turning, I saw the opposite wall and the frieze in low relief which ran above the door—

I don't like the impossible. I don't like paradox. I sit here, toiling over my correlations—they have promised a machine by spring which will perform them for us more quickly and in far more detail than we have ever attempted—and when I grow tired I let my head slip down on my hands, and I dream of a day when I was a child. I dream of an old man and a knife—and murder.

I had had my chance. Others, more experienced and possibly more capable than I followed me. The entire ruin was excavated, with the most meticulous attention to technique, down to bedrock. And I . . . I was sent back to my correlations and my trait tables, to work up the data which other men would presently send me. Because strive as they will, they can find no other explanation than the one which—to me—seems obvious. The answer which is no answer—

You can go into the Toynbee Museum now, today, and see the knife in a guarded case, in the anteroom of the main exhibit hall. In the course of three hundred years that case will have been replaced by a bronze table and a cover of heavy glass. Bombs will fall, the building will crumble in ruins, and the knife will still be there. Dust will cover the ruins, and one day a gnarled old man in shabby clothes will shovel it away and creep inside. He will find the knife and carry it away. Later a younger man will come—and then others—many others, men and women both. And all the while, on the granite lintel above the door to the room where the knife is kept, will be the inscription:

WALTER TOYNBEE
1962—2035

My grandfather brought the knife back from the future. He died. It was placed in the museum named for him. It lay there for three hundred years, while the human race went mad trying to solve its secret—while all civilization was turned upside down in the search for something which never existed!

He found it in the museum where it had always been. He carried it back through time, and it was placed in that museum. It lay there until he came and found it, and carried it back through time—

It was a simple pattern—as simple as ever was. Must we think only in terms of a beginning and an end? Cannot a thing—even a person—exist in a closed cycle without beginning or end? Appearing to us now, at this level of our time threat, accompanying us down its extension into our future, then vanishing from our stream and circling back to the point where it appeared? Can't you imagine that?

I thought I could. I thought it was a paradox—no more —as simple to explain as ever was. I was wrong, of course, and they are right.

The knife old Walter Toynbee brought back from the museum built in his honor, to house his knife, was perfect—worn, dirty, but perfect. A little notch was sawed in the back of its translucent blue blade—sawed with a diamond saw, to provide the chemist and the physicists with the samples they needed to test its properties. That notch is still in its blade as it lies out there in the museum case— it will be there for the next three hundred years, or until the raids come and the museum falls in ruins. Until an old man comes out of the past to find it—

The knife old Walter Toynbee will find there in our future will have that notch. The knife he brought back to me thirty years ago had no notch in it. Somewhere the circle must have a beginning. Somewhere it must have an end—but where, and how? How was this knife created, out of a strange blue metal, and a strange, black, indurated wood, when its existence has no beginning or end? How can the circle be broken? I wish I knew. I might not dream of murder then. I might find logic and purpose in the future instead of chaos—instead of impossible worlds that never were.

QUIETUS / by Ross Rocklynne

Quietly, inexorably, the earth moves forward through the centuries toward inevitable change. Even now, astronomers have mapped out such changes and can predict a reasonably accurate picture of the globe's geography and climate as far in the future as forty thousand years. Predicated on such theory, "Quietus" is a story of heartbreak and disaster. One might well conclude that the essentially tragic significance of this tale is its brilliant portrayal of the historical struggle of the feminine mind to cope with logic a priori.

THE CREATURES from Alcon saw from the first that Earth, as a planet, was practically dead; dead in the sense that it had given birth to life, and was responsible, indirectly, for its almost complete extinction.

"This type of planet is the most distressing," said Tark, absently smoothing down the brilliantly colored feathers of his left wing. "I can stand the dark, barren worlds which never have, and probably never will, hold life. But these that have been killed by some celestial catastrophe! Think of what great things might have come from their inhabitants."

As he spoke thus to his mate, Vascar, he was marking down in a book the position of this planet, its general appearance from space, and the number and kind of satellites it supported.

Vascar, sitting at the controls, both her claws and her vestigial hands at work, guided the spherical ship at slowly decreasing speed toward the planet Earth. A thousand miles above it, she set the craft into an orbital motion, and then proceeded to study the planet, Tark setting the account into his book, for later insertion into the Astronomical Archives of Alcon.

"Evidently," mused Vascar, her brilliant, unblinking eyes

looking at the planet through a transparent section above the control board, "some large meteor, or an errant asteroid—that seems most likely—must have struck this specimen a terrible blow. Look at those great, gaping cracks that run from pole to pole, Tark. It looks as if volcanic eruptions are still taking place, too. At any rate, the whole planet seems entirely denuded—except for that single, short strip of green we saw as we came in."

Tark nodded. He was truly a bird, for in the evolutionary race on his planet, distant uncounted lights years, his stock had won out over the others. His wings were short, true, and in another thousand years would be too short for flight, save in a dense atmosphere; but his head was large, and his eyes, red, small, set close together, showed intelligence and a kind benevolence. He and Vascar had left Alcon, their planet, a good many years ago; but they were on their way back now. Their outward-bound trip had taken them many light-years north of the Solar System; but on the way back, they had decided to make it one of the stop-off points in their zigzag course. Probably their greatest interest in all this long cruise was in the discovery of planets—they were indeed few. And that pleasure might even be secondary to the discovery of life. To find a planet that had almost entirely died was, conversely, distressing. Their interest in the planet Earth was, because of this, a wistful one.

The ship made the slow circuit of Earth—the planet was a hodge-podge of tumbled, churned mountains; of abysmal, frightfully long cracks exuding unholy vapors; of volcanoes that threw their fires and hot liquid rocks far into the sky; of vast oceans disturbed from the ocean bed by cataclysmic eruptions. And of life they saw nothing save a single strip of green perhaps a thousand miles long, a hundred wide, in the Western Hesmisphere.

"I don't think we'll find intelligent life, though," Tark said pessimistically. "This planet was given a terrific blow—I wouldn't be surprised if her rotation period was cut down considerably in a single instant. Such a charge would be unsupportable. Whole cities would literally be snapped away from their foundations—churned, ground to dust. The intelligent creatures who built them would die by the millions—the billions—in that holocaust; and whatever destruction was left incomplete would be finished up by the appearance of volcanoes and faults in the crust of the planet."

Vascar reminded him, "Remember, where there's vegetation, even as little as evidenced by that single strip down there, there must be some kind of animal life."

Tark ruffled his wings in a shrug. "I doubt it. The plants would get all the carbon dioxide they needed from volcanoes —animal life wouldn't have to exist. Still, let's take a look. Don't worry, I'm hoping there's intelligent life, too. If there is, it will doubtless need some help if it is to survive. Which ties in with our aims, for that is our principal purpose on this expedition—to discover intelligent life, and, wherever possible, to give it what help we can, if it needs help."

Vascar's vestigial hands worked the controls, and the ship dropped leisurely downward toward the green strip.

A rabbit darted out of the underbrush—Tommy leaped at it with the speed and dexterity of a thoroughly wild animal. His powerful hands wrapped around the creature—its struggles ceased as its vertebra was snapped. Tommy squatted, tore the skin off the creature, and proceeded to eat great mouthfuls of the still warm flesh.

Blacky cawed harshly, squawked, and his untidy form came flashing down through the air to land precariously on Tommy's shoulder. Tommy went on eating, while the crow fluttered its wings, smoothed them out, and settled down to a restless somnolence. The quiet of the scrub forest, save for the cries and sounds of movement of birds and small animals moving through the forest, settled down about Tommy as he ate. "Tommy" was what he called himself. A long time ago, he remembered, there used to be a great many people in the world—perhaps a hundred—many of whom, and particularly two people whom he had called Mom and Pop, had called him by that name. They were gone now, and the others with them. Exactly where they went, Tommy did not know. But the world had rocked one night—it was the night Tommy ran away from home, with Blacky riding on his shoulder— and when Tommy came out of the cave where he had been sleeping, all was in flames, and the city on the horizon had fallen so that it was nothing but a huge pile of dust—but in the end it had not mattered to Tommy. Of course, he was lonesome, terrified, at first, but he got over that. He continued to live, eating, drinking, sleeping, walking endlessly; and Blacky, his talking crow, was good company. Blacky was smart. He could speak every word that Tommy knew, and a good many others that he didn't. Tommy was not Blacky's first owner.

But though he had been happy, the last year had brought the recurrence of a strange feeling that had plagued him off and on, but never so strongly as now. A strange, terrible hunger was settling on him. Hunger? He knew this sensation. He had forthwith slain a wild dog, and eaten of the meat. He saw then that it was not a hunger of the belly. It was a hunger of the mind, and it was all the worse because he could not know what it was. He had come to his feet, restless, looking into the tangled depths of the second growth forest.

"Hungry," he had said, and his shoulders shook and tears coursed out of his eyes, and he sat down on the ground and sobbed without trying to stop himself, for he had never been told that to weep was unmanly. What was it he wanted?

He had everything there was all to himself. Southward in winter, northward in summer, eating of berries and small animals as he went, and Blacky to talk to and Blacky to talk the same words back at him. This was the natural life—he had lived it ever since the world went bang. But still he cried, and felt a panic growing in his stomach, and he didn't know what it was he was afraid of, or longed for, whichever it was. He was twenty-one years old. Tears were natural to him, to be indulged in whenever he felt like it. Before the world went bang—there were some things he remembered—the creature whom he called Mom generally put her arms around him and merely said, "It's all right, Tommy, it's all right."

So on that occasion, he arose from the ground and said, "It's all right, Tommy, it's all right."

Blacky, he with the split tongue, said harshly, as was his wont, "It's all right, Tommy, it's all right! I tell you, the price of wheat is going down!"

Blacky, the smartest crow anybody had—why did he say that? There wasn't anybody else, and there weren't any more crows—helped a lot. He not only knew all the words and sentences that Tommy knew, but he knew others that Tommy could never understand because he didn't know where they came from, or what they referred to. And in addition to all that, Blacky had the ability to anticipate what Tommy said, and frequently took whole words and sentences right out of Tommy's mouth.

Tommy finished eating his rabbit, and threw the skin aside, and sat quite still, a peculiarly blank look in his eyes. The strange hunger was on him again. He looked off across the lush plain of grasses that stretched away, searching into the distance, toward where the Sun was setting. He looked to left and right. He drew himself softly to his feet, and peered into the shadows of the forest behind him. His heavily bearded lips began to tremble, and the tears started from his eyes again. He turned and stumbled from the forest, blinded.

Blacky clutched at Tommy's broad shoulder, and rode him, and a split second before Tommy, said, "It's all right, Tommy, it's all right."

Tommy said the words angrily to himself, and blinked the tears away.

He was a little bit tired. The Sun was setting, and night would soon come. But it wasn't that that made him tired. It was a weariness of the mind, a feeling of futility, for, whatever it was he wanted, he could never, never find it, because he would not know where he should look for it.

His bare foot trampled on something wet—he stopped and looked at the ground. He stooped and picked up the skin of a recently killed rabbit. He turned it over and over in his hands, frowning. This was not an animal he had killed, certainly—the skin had been taken off in a different way. Someone else—no! But his shoulders began to shake with a wild excitement. Someone else? No, it couldn't be! There was no one—there could be no one—could there? The skin dropped from his nerveless fingers as he saw a single footprint not far ahead of him. He stooped over it, examining, and knew again that he had not done this, either. And certainly it could be no other animal than a man!

It was a small footprint at which he stared, as if a child, or an under-sized man might have stepped in the soft humus. Suddenly he raised his head. He had definitely heard the crackling of a twig, not more than forty feet away, certainly. His eyes stared ahead through the gathering dusk. Something looking back at him? Yes! Something there in the bushes that was not an animal!

"No noise, Blacky," he whispered, and forgot Blacky's general response to that command.

"No noise, Blacky!" the big, ugly bird blasted out. "No noise, Blacky! Well, fer cryin' out loud!"

Blacky uttered a scared squawk as Tommy leaped ahead,

a snarl contorting his features, and flapped from his master's shoulder. For several minutes Tommy ran after the vanishing figure, with all the strength and agility of his singularly powerful legs. But whoever—or whatever—it was that fled him, outdistanced him easily, and Tommy had to stop at last, panting. Then he stooped, and picked up a handful of pebbles and hurled them at the squawking bird. A single tail feather fell to earth as Blacky swooped away.

"Told you not to make noise," Tommy snarled, and the tears started to run again. The hunger was starting up in his mind again, too! He sat down on a log, and put his chin in his palms, while his tears flowed. Blacky came flapping through the air, almost like a shadow—it was getting dark. The bird tentatively settled on his shoulder, cautiously flapped away again and then came back.

Tommy turned his head and looked at it bitterly, and then turned away, and groaned.

"It's all your fault, Blacky!"

"It's all your fault," the bird said. "Oh, Tommy, I could spank you! I get so exasperated!"

Sitting there, Tommy tried to learn exactly what he had seen. He had been sure it was a human figure, just like himself, only different. Different! It had been smaller, had seemed to possess a slender grace—it was impossible! Every time he thought of it, the hunger in his mind raged!

He jumped to his feet, his fists clenched. his hunger had been in him too long! He must find out wh i caused it—he must find her—why did the word her come to his mind? Suddenly, he was flooded with a host of childhood remembrances.

"It was a girl!" he gasped. "Oh, Tommy must want a girl!"

The thought was so utterly new that it left him stunned; but the thought grew. He must find her, if it took him all the rest of his life! His chest deepened, his muscles swelled, and a new light came into his blue eyes. Southward in winter, northward in summer—eating—sleeping—truly, there was nothing in such a life. Now he felt the strength of a purpose swelling up in him. He threw himself to the ground and slept; and Blacky flapped to the limb of a tree, inserted his head beneath a wing, and slept also. Perhaps, in the last ten or fifteen years, he also had wanted a mate, but probably he had long ago given up hope—for, it seemed, there were no more crows left in the world. Anyway, Blacky was very old, perhaps twice as old as Tommy; he was merely content to live.

Tark and Vascar sent their spherical ship lightly plummeting above the green strip—it proved to be vegetation, just as they had supposed. Either one or the other kept constant watch of the ground below—they discovered nothing that might conceivably be classed as intelligent life. Insects they found, and decided that they worked entirely by instinct; small animals, rabbits, squirrels, rats, raccoons, otters, opossums, and large animals, deer, horses, sheep, cattle, pigs, dogs, they found to be just that—animals, and nothing more.

"Looks as if it was all killed off, Vascar," said Tark, "and not so long ago at that, judging by the fact that this forest must have grown entirely in the last few years."

Vascar agreed; she suggested they put the ship down for a few days and rest.

"It would be wonderful if we could find intelligent life after all," she said wistfully. "Think what a great triumph it would be if we were the ones to start the last members of that race on the upward trail again. Anyway," she added, "I think this atmosphere is dense enough for us to fly in."

He laughed—a trilling sound. "You've been looking for such an atmosphere for years. But I think you're right about this one. Put the ship down there, Vascar—looks like a good spot."

For five days Tommy followed the trail of the girl with a grim determination. He knew now that it was a woman; perhaps—indeed, very probably—the only one left alive. He had only the vaguest of ideas of why he wanted her—he thought it was for human companionship, that alone. At any rate, he felt that this terrible hunger in him—he could give it no other word—would be allayed when he caught up with her.

She was fleeing him, and staying just near enough to him to make him continue the chase, he knew that with a fierce exultation. And somehow her actions seemed right and proper. Twice had had seen her, once on the crest of a ridge, once as she swam a river. Both times she had easily outdistanced him. But by cross-hatching, he picked up her trail again—a bent twig or weed, a footprint, the skin of a dead rabbit.

Once, at night, he had the impression that she crept up

close, and looked at him curiously, perhaps with the same great longing that he felt. He could not be sure. But he knew that very soon now she would be his—and perhaps she would be glad of it.

Once he heard a terrible moaning, high up in the air. He looked upward. Blacky uttered a surprised squawk. A large, spherical thing was darting overhead.

"I wonder what that is," Blacky squawked.

"I wonder what that is," said Tommy, feeling a faint fear. "There ain't nothin' like that in the yard."

He watched as the spaceship disappeared from sight. Then, with the unquestioning attitude of the savage, he dismissed the matter from his mind, and took up his tantalizing trail again.

"Better watch out, Tommy," the bird cawed.

"Better watch out, Tommy," Tommy muttered to himself. He only vaguely heard Blacky—Blacky always anticipated what Tommy was going to say, because he had known Tommy so long.

The river was wide, swirling, muddy, primeval in its surge of resistless strength. Tommy stood on the bank, and looked out over the waters—suddenly his breath soughed from his lungs.

"It's her!" he gasped. "It's her, Blacky! She's drownin'!"

No time to waste in thought—a figure truly struggled against the push of the treacherous waters, seemingly went under. Tommy dived cleanly, and Blacky spread his wings at the last instant and escaped a bath. He saw his master disappear beneath the swirling waters, saw him emerge, strike out with singularly powerful arms, slightly upstream, fighting every inch of the way. Blacky hoved over the waters, cawing frantically, and screaming.

"Tommy, I could spank you! I could spank you! I get so exasperated! You wait till your father comes home!"

A log was coming downstream. Tommy saw it coming, but knew he'd escape it. He struck out, paid no more attention to it. The log came down with a rush, and would have missed him had it not suddenly swung broadside on. It clipped the swimming man on the side of the head. Tommy went under, threshing feebly, barely conscious, his limbs like leaden bars. That seemed to go on for a very long time. He seemed to be breathing water. Then something grabbed hold of his long black hair—

When he awoke, he was lying on his back, and he was staring into her eyes. Something in Tommy's stomach fell out—perhaps the hunger was going. He came to his feet, staring at her, his eyes glazing. She stood only about twenty feet away from him. There was something pleasing about her, the slimness of her arms, the roundness of her hips, the strangeness of her body, her large, startled, timid eyes, the mass of ebon hair that fell below her hips. He started toward her. She gazed at him as if in a trance.

Blacky came flapping mournfully across the river. He was making no sound, but the girl must have been frightened as he landed on Tommy's shoulder. She tensed, and was away like a rabbit. Tommy went after her in long, loping bounds, but his foot caught in a tangle of dead grass, and he plummeted head foremost to the ground.

The other vanished over a rise of ground.

He arose again, and knew no disappointment that he had again lost her. He knew now that it was only her timidity, the timidity of a wild creature, that made her flee him. He started off again, for now that he knew what the hunger was, it seemed worse than ever.

The air of this planet was deliciously breathable, and was the nearest thing to their own atmosphere that Tark and Vascar had encountered.

Vascar ruffled her brilliant plumage, and spread her wings, flapping them. Tark watched her, as she laughed at him in her own way, and then made a few short, running jumps and took off. She spiraled, called down to him.

"Come on up. The air's fine, Tark."

Tark considered. "All right," he conceded, "but wait until I get a couple of guns."

"I can't imagine why," Vascar called down; but nevertheless, as they rose higher and higher above the second growth forest, each had a belt strapped loosely around the neck, carrying a weapon similar to a pistol.

"I can't help but hope we run into some kind of intelligent life," said Vascar. "This is really a lovely planet. In time the volcanoes will die down, and vegetation will spread all over. It's a shame that the planet has to go to waste."

"We could stay and colonize it," Tark suggested rakishly.

"Oh, not I. I like Alcon too well for that, and the sooner we get back there, the better— Look! Tark! Down there!"

Tark looked, caught sight of a medium large animal moving through the underbrush. He dropped a little lower. And then rose again.

"It's nothing," he said. "An animal, somewhat larger than the majority we've seen, probably the last of its kind. From the looks of it, I'd say it wasn't particularly pleasant on the eyes. Its skin shows— Oh, now I see what you mean, Vascar!"

This time he was really interested as he dropped lower, and a strange excitement throbbed through his veins. Could it be that they were going to discover intelligent life after all —perhaps the last of its kind?

It was indeed an exciting sight the two bird-creatures from another planet saw. They flapped slowly above and a number of yards behind the unsuspecting upright beast, that moved swiftly through the forest, a black creature not unlike themselves in general structure riding its shoulder.

"It must mean intelligence!" Vascar whispered excitedly, her brilliant red eyes glowing with interest. "One of the first requisites of intelligent creatures is to put animals lower in the scale of evoluton to work as beasts of burden and transportation."

"Wait awhile," cautioned Tark, "before you make any irrational conclusions. After all, there are creatures of different species which live together in friendship. Perhaps the creature which looks so much like us keeps the other's skin and hair free of vermin. And perhaps the other way around, too."

"I don't think so," insisted his mate. "Tark, the bird-creature is riding the shoulder of the beast. Perhaps that means its race is so old, and has used this means of transportation so long, that its wing have atrophied. That would almost certainly mean intelligence. It's talking now—you can hear it. It's probably telling its beast to stop—there, it has stopped!"

"Its voice is not so melodious," said Tark dryly.

She looked at him reprovingly; the tips of their flapping wings were almost touching.

"That isn't like you, Tark. You know very well that one of our rules is not to place intelligence on creatures who seem like ourselves, and neglect others while we do so. Its harsh voice proves nothing—to one of its race, if there are any left, its voice may be pleasing in the extreme. At any rate, it ordered the large beast of burden to stop—you saw that."

"Well, perhaps," conceded Tark.

They continued to wing their slow way after the perplexing duo, following slightly behind, skimming the tops of
trees. They saw the white beast stop, and place its paws on its
hips. Vascar, listening very closely, because she was anxious
to gain proof of her contention, heard the bird-creature say,
"Now what, Blacky?" and also the featherless beast repeat
the same words: "Now what, Blacky?"

"There's your proof," said Vascar excitedly. "Evidently
the white beast is highly imitative. Did you hear it repeat
what its master said?"

Tark said uneasily, "I wouldn't jump to conclusions, just
from a hasty survey like this. I admit, so far, all the proof
points to the bird. It seems truly intelligent; or at least more
intelligent than the other. But you must bear in mind that we
are naturally prejudiced in favor of the bird—it may not be
intelligent at all. As I said, they may merely be friends in the
sense that animals of different species are friends."

Vascar made a scornful sound.

"Well, let's get goin', Blacky," she heard the bird say; and
heard the white, upright beast repeat the strange, alien words.
The white beast started off again, traveling very stealthily,
making not the least amount of noise. Again Vascar called
this quality to the attention of her skeptical mate—such stealth
was the mark of the animal, certainly not of the intelligent
creature.

"We should be certain of it now," she insisted. "I think
we ought to get in touch with the bird. Remember, Tark,
that our primary purpose on this expedition is to give what
help we can to the intelligent races of the planets we visit.
What creature could be more in need of help than the bird-
creature down there? It is evidently the last of its kind. At
least, we could make the effort of saving it from a life of sheer
boredom; it would probably leap at the chance to hold con-
verse with intelligent creatures. Certainly it gets no pleasure
from the company of dumb beasts."

But Tark shook his handsome, red-plumed head worriedly.

"I would prefer," he said uneasily, "first to investigate the
creature you are so sure is a beast of burden. There is a
chance—though, I admit, a far-fetched one—that it is the
intelligent creature, and not the other."

But Vascar did not hear him. All her feminine instincts

had gone out in pity to the seemingly intelligent bird that rode Tommy's broad shoulder. And so intent were she and Tark on the duo, that they did not see, less than a hundred yards ahead, that another creature, smaller in form, more graceful, but indubitably the same species as the white-skinned, unfeathered beast, was slinking softly through the underbrush, now and anon casting indecisive glances behind her toward him who pursued her. He was out of sight, but she could hear—

Tommy slunk ahead, his breath coming fast; for the trail was very strong, and his keen ears picked up the sounds of footsteps ahead. The chase was surely over—his terrible hunger about to end! He felt wildly exhilarated. Instincts were telling him much that his experience could not. He and this girl were the last of mankind. Something told him that now mankind would rise again—yet he did not know why. He slunk ahead, Blacky on his shoulder, all unaware of the two brilliantly colored denizens of another planet who followed above and behind him. But Blacky was not so easy of mind. His neck feathers were standing erect. Nervousness made him raise his wings up from his body—perhaps he heard the soft swish of large-winged creatures, beating the air behind, and though all birds of prey had been dead these last fifteen years, the old fear rose up.

Tommy glued himself to a tree, on the edge of a clearing. His breath escaped from his lungs as he caught a glimpse of a white, unclothed figure. It was she! She was looking back at him. She was tired of running. She was ready, glad to give up. Tommy experienced a dizzy elation. He stepped forth into the clearing, and slowly, very slowly, holding her large, dark eyes with his, started toward her. The slightest swift motion, the slightest untoward sound, and she would be gone. Her whole body was poised on the balls of her feet. She was not at all sure whether she should be afraid of him or not.

Behind him, the two feathered creatures from another planet settled slowly into a tree, and watched. Blacky certainly did not hear them come to rest—what he must have noticed was that the beat of wings, nagging at the back of his mind, had disappeared. It was enough.

"No noise, Blacky!" the bird screamed affrightedly, and flung himself into the air and forward, a bundle of ebon feathers with tattered wings outspread, as it darted across the clearing. For the third time, it was Blacky who scared her, for again she was gone, and had lost herself to sight even before Tommy could move.

"Come back!" Tommy shouted ragingly. "I ain't gonna hurt you!" He ran after her full speed, tears streaming down his face, tears of rage and heartbreak at the same time. But already he knew it was useless! He stopped suddenly, on the edge of the clearing, and sobbing to himself, caught sight of Blacky, high above the ground, cawing piercingly, warningly. Tommy stooped and picked up a handful of pebbles. With deadly, murderous intent he threw them at the bird. It soared and swooped in the air—twice it was hit glancingly.

"It's all your fault, Blacky!" Tommy raged. He picked up a rock the size of his fist. He started to throw it, but did not. A tiny, sharp sound bit through the air. Tommy pitched forward. He did not make the slightest twitching motion to show that he had bridged the gap between life and death. He did not know that Blacky swooped down and landed on his chest; and then flung himself upward, crying, "Oh, Tommy, I could spank you!" He did not see the girl come into the clearing and stoop over him; and did not see the tears that began to gush from her eyes, or hear the sobs that racked her body. But Tark saw.

Tark wrested the weapon from Vascar with a trill of rage. "Why did you do that?" he cried. He threw the weapon from him as far as it would go. "You've done a terrible thing, Vascar!"

Vascar looked at him in amazement. "It was only a beast, Tark," she protested. "It was trying to kill its master! Surely, you saw it. It was trying to kill the intelligent bird-creature, the last of its kind on the planet."

But Tark pointed with horror at the two unfeathered beasts, one bent over the body of the other. "But they were mates! You have killed their species! The female is grieving for its mate, Vascar. You have done a terrible thing!"

But Vascar shook her head crossly. "I'm sorry I did it then," she said acidly. "I suppose it was perfectly in keeping with our aim on this expedition to let the dumb beast kill its master! That isn't like you at all, Tark! Come, let us see if the intelligent creature will not make friends with us."

And she flapped away toward the cawing crow. When Blacky saw Vascar coming toward him, he wheeled and darted away.

Tark took one last look at the female bending over the male. He saw her raise her head, and saw the tears in her eyes, and heard the sobs that shook her. Then, in a rising, inchoate series of bewildering emotions, he turned his eyes away, and hurriedly flapped after Vascar. And all that day they pursued Blacky. They circled him, they cornered him; and Vascar tried to speak to him in friendly tones, all to no avail. It only cawed, and darted away, and spoke volumes of disappointingly incomprehensible words.

When dark came, Vascar alighted in a tree beside the strangely quiet Tark.

"I suppose it's no use," she said sadly. "Either it is terribly afraid of us, or it is not as intelligent as we supposed it was, or else it has become mentally deranged in these last years of loneliness. I guess we might as well leave now, Tark; let the poor creature have its planet to itself. Shall we stop by and see if we can help the female beast whose mate we shot?"

Tark slowly looked at her, his red eyes luminous in the gathering dusk. "No," he said briefly. "Let us go, Vascar."

The spaceship of the creatures from Alcon left the dead planet Earth. It darted out into space. Tark sat at the controls. The ship went faster and faster. And still faster. Fled at ever-increasing speed beyond the Solar System and into the wastes of interstellar space. And still farther, until the star that gave heat to Earth was not even visible.

Yet even this terrible velocity was not enough for Tark. Vascar looked at him strangely.

"We're not in that much of a hurry to get home, are we, Tark?"

"No," Tark said in a low, terrible voice; but still she urged the ship to greater and greater speed, though he knew it was useless. He could run away from the thing that had happened on the planet Earth; but he could never, never outrun his mind, though he passionately wished he could.

ROBOT'S RETURN / by Robert Moore Williams

Unhappy victim of disease, environmental changes and his own folly, man may some day perish from the earth. But those who depart always leave something of themselves behind. Then the question is: who will inherit from man? A being of his own devising? Granted these premises, we face the inexorable corollary, will the heirs want their inheritance?

AS THOUGH sustained by the strength of a dream, the ship floated gracefully, easily, a bare hundred feet above the surface of the planet. Overhead, slightly more than ninety million miles away, a sullen sun retreated down the dark blue sky. Its long rays fretted across the planet, washed from the low, brown hills, glinted from the jumbled mounds in the center of the valley.

The ship turned, slanted down toward the mounds, rose over them, circled, found a spot where the litter was nearly level and snuggled down to rest as though returning home after weary years spent between the stars.

Hissing from the pressure of air rushing inward, a forward lock opened.

Nine stood in the lock, staring from never-blinking eyes across the landscape—a fixed, somber gaze. Hungrily, his eyes pried among the jumbled masonry, the great blocks of white stone stained a dirty brown in places, the piles of red clay in which grass was reluctantly growing. Five, perhaps ten miles around, the piles circled, then gradually leveled off toward the low brown hills.

Behind him a voice whispered, asking a question.

"It is the same as all the others," his answer went, though the grim line of the mouth did not move. "Silence, and the wreckage of a mighty city. But nothing lives here now. The inhabitants are gone."

For a second there was silence, and then a third voice whispered. "Just as I said. We are only wasting time here. It is true that once some kind of a race lived on this planet —but certainly they were never intelligent enough to have been our ancestors."

Nine, in the lock, sighed softly. "Seven, you must remember that we have not made a complete investigation. You must also remember that we have absolutely no knowledge of our ancestors—even as to whether or not they actually existed. Our records are complete for eight thousand years, but they do not go back beyond the time when the Original Five awaked, finding themselves lying on the edge of the sea, with no knowledge of how they came to be there. Perhaps they were a special creation, for they possessed great intelligence, speedily adapting the planet to their needs, forging and constructing others to help them. Perhaps they had come there, in a ship that had sunk in the sea, from some other planet. But we have never been able to solve the problem."

Eight, silent after his first question, pressed forward, stared over Nine's shoulder.

"I am perfectly familiar with the history of our race." The edge of Seven's thinking was clear over the radio beam. "The point I make is that the little life we have seen on this planet—and little enough we have seen—has been organic, a mess of chemicals. Animals, eating each other, eating grass—Pah! I want no ancestors like that."

Slowly, Eight shook his head, the ripple of interwoven metal strands winking in the light. As if he had not heard the bickering of Seven and Nine he spoke. "For a minute, as I stood here, it seemed to me that I had been on this spot before. The low hills circling a city— Only the city has changed, and over there"—he pointed toward the east— "it seems there should be a lake, or an inlet from the ocean. But no—no—I must be mistaken." He paused, and the fixed gleam in his eyes held a touch of awe. "I spoke —I used the vocal apparatus— Now I wonder why I did that?"

"So do I," Seven's answer rasped. "You used the vocal apparatus when the radio beam is much better. I have never understood why we should equip ourselves with cumbersome apparatus for making and hearing sounds when we have a much better method of communication."

"Because," Eight answered. "Because we have always had them. The Original Five had them. I do not know why they had them, for they also had the radio beam. Perhaps they had a use for them, though what that use could have been— At any rate, we have retained them. Perhaps, some day, we will discover a use for them."

"Bah!" Seven snorted. "You are one of those inexplicable dreamers. It seems that no matter how carefully we construct the brain substance, we always get a few freaks who are unwilling to face reality, who are not sufficient in themselves, but who hunger for some day that is past —a day that never had existence. I have no sympathy with you, nor any sympathy with the Council that sent us here on this wild exploration."

"But," Nine protested, "the Council could not ignore the evidence of the old star map. The Original Five had that map, but we have never understood it, probably never would have understood it if our newly perfected telescopes had not revealed this system to us—nine planets circling a sun, the third planet a strange double system. Obviously that map is somehow a link with our unknown past."

"Nonsense. I am a realist. I face the future, not the past."

"But the future is built on material taken from the past, and how can we build securely when we do not know what our past has been? It is important to us to know whether we are descended from whatever gods there are, or whether we have evolved from some lower form. Come," Nine spoke.

The cunningly twisted strands of metal writhed and Nine stepped lithely from the lock. Eight followed, and after them came Seven, still grumbling.

Three little metal men four and a half feet tall. Two legs, two arms, two eyes, a nose, a mouth—the last two organs almost valueless survivals. For they did not need food or oxygen. The power of the bursting atom supplied them with energy. Nor did they really need the legs, for their evolution during their eight thousand years had been rapid. Seven touched the ground, glowed slightly, rose into the air and drifted after his companions. Eight and Nine used their legs. Somehow, to Eight the feel of the ground was good.

They stood on a little hill. Eight's eyes went around the horizon. The metal face did not shift or change, no flicker of emotion played over it. But in the myriad of cunning photocells that were the eyes, hungry lights appeared to reflect the thinking that went on in the brain substance behind.

"It's larger—larger than it looked from the air," Nine spoke, his vocal apparatus biting at the words, yet somehow reflecting the awe he felt.

"Yes," Eight answered. "All this litter that we see, all these mounds—and some of them are hundreds of feet high—are all that is left of some mighty city. Miles and miles and miles around, it stretches. How much work must have gone into it? How long must it have taken in the building? Centuries, perhaps hundreds of centuries, some race lived here, dreamed here, and dreaming built of clay and stone and steel and glass. I wonder—if they COULD have been our ancestors, our unknown forebears?"

"Nonsense!" Seven blurted.

Eight stirred, his eyes glinting uneasily as he glanced at Seven. "Perhaps it is not nonsense. I have the feeling, have had it ever since we sighted this system from the void—nine little planets clustering around a mother sun —that this is—home." His voice lingered over the word, caressed it.

"Home!" Seven echoed. "We have no meaning for the word. We are at home anywhere. And as for feeling, we have even less meaning for that word. Feeling is not logic," he finished, as if that settled everything.

"Perhaps logic has no meaning for that word," Eight retorted. "But remember that our minds are constructed according to the ancient pattern—and who knows that feeling was not a part of that pattern, a part that has come down to us?"

"I remember only that we are robots. I do not know or care about our origin. Only the future has meaning, the future in which we shall tread the paths beyond the stars."

"Robots!" Eight answered. "I even wonder where we got that name for ourselves."

"It was the name the Original Five had for themselves, just as they had a language."

"But why, among a myriad of possible sounds, should they have selected that one as their name?"

"Because—" Seven was suddenly silent. Eight felt the perturbed pulse of his thinking. Seven was trying to explain to himself why their name should be what it was. He was having a hard time doing it. The answer, somehow, went beyond the bounds of logic. Or was there no answer? But that was not logical either. There had to be an answer, a reason. Seven stirred uneasily, eyed his companions. Abruptly he lowered himself to the ground, shutting off the power that enabled him to bend gravity, as if he wanted the feel of the ground under his feet. He followed Nine over the rubble, and he used his legs.

Eight said nothing.

"What do you suppose this race looked like?" Seven awkwardly voiced the question.

Eight, gazing at the ruins, voiced the question that had been on his mind. "What happened to them? Could it happen to us?"

Seven and Nine stared at him. Seven's hand went to the heat gun swinging at his belt. Nine twisted his eyes away.

"It couldn't happen to us," Seven said flatly.

"I—hope not," Eight answered. "But something happened to the race that was here, and perhaps—"

"There is work to be done," Nine interrupted. "We must examine every inch of this area. Perhaps we may find the rusted bodies of the former inhabitants. At first, I had hoped we would find them alive, but after seeing all those deserted cities, I am afraid we will find no living intelligence. But it may be we will find records."

Slowly, under the unwinking sun overhead, they pressed forward among the ruins, Nine in the lead, then Eight, then Seven. Around them the air, stirred by the pressure of an unknown force, moved restlessly. A wind went with them, as though it, too, quested among tumbled masonry and piles of brick dust for some friend of the long-gone past. Silently, the wind went among the haunted débris. Eight felt it passing, a force touching him with a thousand invisible fingers, a force that could not be seen but only felt.

Eight stared at the ruins, wondering what manner of creatures had once moved among them. The rusted bones of the steel framework of buildings, steel that crumbled at the touch, casing stones upended, the greenish color of corrosion on copper. He tried to imagine the millions of inhabitants going about this city. He saw their glistening metal bodies moving along the streets, floating upward beside the bulk of the buildings. He saw them bringing stone and forging steel, creating a city under that yellow sun. And at night, he saw them looking up at the stars, at that strange dead satellite hovering in the black sky. He wondered if they had ever visited that satellite. They must have visited it, he decided, if not in reality, then in dreams. And possibly the stars beyond. For the towers of their cities had pointed at the stars.

Little metal men. Slowly Eight's imagination failed him. Somehow he could not populate this silent city with little metal men. He shook his head. H could see the dream, but not the dreamers.

Nine stood in front of a pile of masonry. The rains, the heat of summer, the cold of uncounted winters, had brought down the stones from the top. Nine stared somberly at the dark opening between the tumbled blocks. He spoke. "I'm going in there."

Seven and Eight followed.

Darkness folded in around them—a stirring, whispering darkness. A beam of light flashed from Nine's forehead, smashed against the darkness, illumined the walls of what looked like a tunnel.

Under their feet the dust exploded in little gray clouds. Abruptly the tunnel widened into a circle with three other arteries branching out. Broad doors opened in the arteries, doors that now were closed. Staring, Nine pushed against one of the doors, and it crumbled with the pressure, opened into a small room that was totally bare. Nine stepped into it, and the floor crumbled. He shot down into gloom, but instantly his descent slowed as he flicked on the device that bent gravity. He hesitated, then allowed himself to float down into the darkness. His voice whispered over the radio beam and Seven and Eight followed him.

Nine looked up at them as they came down. "That little room was used to carry the former inhabitants up into the building. See, there is the mechanism. Whoever they were, they did not know how to control gravity or they would not have needed this device."

Neither Eight nor Seven answered, and Nine poked forward into the gloom, the bright beam from his light splashing from dozens of sturdy columns that supported the bulk above. His voice called and Seven and Eight moved toward him.

"Here is a machine," Nine spoke. "Or is it—one of our early life-forms?"

Eight stared at the rust-flecked wheels, the crumbling, corroded bulk of the motor housings, the gears falling away into ruin. This, a robot—! He rebelled at the thought. Yet it was hard to know where mechanism left off and robot began. The dividing line was thin. You took inanimate metal and the pressure of exploding force; you worked the metal into a thousand different parts and you confined the force; you added a brain that was in itself a force-field capable of receiving and retaining impressions—and you had a robot. You left out the brain—and you had a machine.

Seven, prying among the mechanism, whispered. "It *is* one of our primitive life-forms—one of the early upward steps. All the fundamentals of robot construction are here. Wheels turn, work is done."

"No," Eight shook his head. "A robot is more than that. This—this is only a machine, unintelligently carrying out reactions its nature set for it. I don't know what those reactions could have been, but I am certain it was not a robot. It was fixed in this place, for one thing, and, for another, I see no signs of brain control."

"A robot is a machine," Seven answered. "A logical machine. There is no doubt about it. Perhaps the control was in some other part of the building."

Nine stirred protestingly. "I—I am inclined to agree with Eight. See, this was only a pump, designed to force water, or some other liquid, through the building. Here is the pressure chamber, and this, I think, was a crude electric motor. But it was only a machine."

"We, ourselves, are only highly developed machines," Seven persisted. "Our operation can be explained purely in terms of mechanics. When you attempt to make us more than machines, you become illogical. True, this is a machine. It is also a primitive robot form, for the two terms mean the same thing. There are many links missing between it and us, but perhaps we may find those links—"

"But how?" Eight asked. "In the beginning how could lifeless, dead metal build itself into the first machine?"

Seven started to answer, hesitated, stared at Eight and

then his gaze wandered off into the gloom of this cavern. His light smashed into the darkness, drove a clean channel through the murk, yet always the darkness crept in around the edges of the beam, and always, when the light moved, the darkness came back.

"I—I don't know the answer to that," Seven spoke. "Perhaps the Universe was different millions of years ago. But I don't know. Nobody knows. However, we have found one link in the chain. Maybe we will find others."

Eight kept his thinking to himself. There was little to be gained in disputing Seven. And, after all, Eight saw that Seven was right. Or partly right. Robots were machines, fundamentally. Yet they were something more than machines. Machines could not dream. In Eight's mind was the wild wonder—where had robots acquired their ability to dream? To what did that ability point?

Eight did not speak. He followed Seven and Nine. He watched, and thought.

They went out of the basement, went back to the floor where they had entered, forced their way up through the silent building. Dust, and furniture that became dust when they touched it, and corroded metal, were in the rooms above, but of the race that had lived there they found no sign.

On through the city they went. Seven crowed exultantly over the wreck of a huge bulk that had turned on its side. An engine, with eight huge driving wheels, and Seven, digging in the dust, uncovered the remnants of the track on which the wheels had run.

"Another link," Seven gloated. "A higher form, possessing the ability to move."

"But not to think," Nine still protested. "It ran on a track. There must have been another, separate intelligence guiding it."

"What of it? Perhaps so—perhaps not. Perhaps the intelligence that guided it was the final robot form." Again Seven suddenly ceased talking, and again Eight could feel the pulse of his troubled thinking. Final robot form—

"There was another, totally different life-form, here," Eight spoke slowly, marshalling his vague thoughts. "A life-form that created and used these machines. But that life has vanished, utterly, leaving no trace of itself, except the ruins of its cities, the wreckage of its machines."

"But what?" Nine gulped.

"What could have destroyed it? I have no idea. Only vaguely can I sense its existence, through the evidence that it once shaped a world to meet its needs. I have seen nothing that will give me a clue to its nature—or its death. Perhaps a new form of corrosion developed, destroying it. Perhaps— But I can't see the answer."

They moved on through the ruins. The slow sun dropped down toward the horizon. The silent wind, searching among the haunted ruins, went with them.

"Look!" Nine called.

They stood in an open space in front of a squat metallic structure that had resisted the rain and the snow. But Nine was not pointing at the building. He moved forward, bent over an object half buried in the mound.

Seven gasped. "A robot. Almost an exact model of us. Here, at last, is final proof!"

Eagerly they bent down, scraping away the soil. Quickly, they uncovered the figure. Perhaps ten feet tall, it was more than twice their size. Eight saw it was a robot. Seven had been right, after all, and here was proof. Those machines had somehow managed to develop intelligence and to evolve into sentient beings.

Somehow the crude ore had shaped and forged itself.

And yet this figure differed from the true robot form. Eight saw the difference as they uncovered it. The hopes rising in his mind failed.

"No— it isn't one of us. It's only a statue."

Cast of solid metal, covered by a thin film of corrosion, the statue lay, its feet still attached to a part of the pedestal that had served as a base from which, in some long-gone time, it had toppled. Eight stared at it, not heeding Seven's thinking which came over the radio beam. Seven was insisting that even if it was a statue—a lifeless thing— the form showed that robots had developed here. Otherwise they would not have made a statue in this shape.

Eight recognized the logic of Seven's statement, but the sight of the statue stirred again those vague rebellious thoughts, and in his mind was the feeling that the statue represented something more, that it was more than a replica of form—that it was the embodiment of an idea. But what that idea was, he could not grasp. Slender and graceful, yet with the suggestion of strength, it lay on the ground, a fallen god with head uplifted and arm outstretched. Eight's thinking became clearer. Yes, it was a fallen god, or the representation of a fallen god, and his mind went back to the builder, the designer, the artist who had dreamed of this figure and had then created in metal a figure adequate to his dreaming. The artist was gone, the statue had fallen. Eight wondered about the dream—

His turgid thinking burst into clarity like a jet of suddenly spouting water. Ever since he had seen this world from afar, especially since he had seen the wreckage of all those mighty cities, he had wondered about the dream of the face that had lived and built here. The fate of the race had never saddened him: all things rusted into ruin eventually, all material things, all logical things. Only a dream might achieve immortality, only a dream could start in slime and go onward to the end of Time. But the dream of this race—whatever that dream had been—appeared to have died. Some catastrophe had overtaken them before they had grown strong enough to forge their dream into an immortal shape. Eight sighed, and the phota-cells that were his eyes lost luster.

Ht did not notice that Seven and Nine had left him, were forcing an entrance into the building, until Nine's sharp call brought him to his feet.

There was only one large room, Eight saw. It had been a laboratory or a workshop. Benches, machinery, tools, were crumbling, just as everything else on this planet was crumbling, just as the dream of the race had crumbled——

Nine's voice, heavy with awe, echoed through the room. "I—I can read it! It's our language!"

The written language of the robots, here on this forgotten planet circling an insignificant sun in a lost corner of the Universe! Eight felt the trembling pulse of currents flowing in his mind. They had found their past; they had found their ancestors. All the other evidence could be explained away, but not this.

Ancestors, forebears, those who had gone before, those who had labored to build for the benefit of some unknown

descendant. Had the machine, the lever and the wheel somehow been their forebears? Or had there been an alien
form preceding the machine?

A metal plate, inches thick, supported on heavy metal
pillars. A tough metal, almost completely rust-resistant.

Now Man dies. A mutant bacteriophage, vicious, beyond imagination, is attacking, eating, destroying all
living cells, even to dead animal matter.

There is no hope of escape on Earth. The only
hope is to flee from Earth. Tomorrow we blast our
first rocket ship off for Mars, ourselves in suspended
animation to withstand the acceleration, the ship
manned by Thoradson's robots.

It may be we shall live again. It may be we shall
die.

We go, and may God go with us.

Thus the record ended. Nine's raspy voice faded, and
for a second the echoes came back from the dark corners
of the room. Then there was silence. Seven shifted his
feet.

"Man," he spoke. "Man. That is a word for which we
have no meaning."

"Perhaps," Eight spoke softly, "perhaps it was the name
of the life-form that created us."

Seven did not answer, and Nine, too, was silent. A wind
came into the room, moved restlessly, and went out again.
The silence held. Seven stared at the metal plate, picking
out the words one by one.

"It must be you are right," he said. "See, they use the
word—robot." Wonder grew in his voice, and then disgust
mingled with the wonder. "An organism—an animal——
Yet obviously they must have created us, used us as slaves.
They manned their ship with robots."

Eight stirred but said nothing. There was nothing to say.

"That," Nine whispered, "is why we are unable to find
a link between the machine and us. *They* developed the
machine, used it. *They* provided the intelligence. Finally
they built machines with some kind of intelligence. It must
have been late in their history, and they built very few of
them. Perhaps they were afraid. There are so many links

missing it is hard to know. But certainly, in a sense, they were our ancestors——"

"Yes," Eight agreed. "In a sense that seems——"

"But they started for a near-by planet," Seven protested. "Our sun is light-years distant. How did they ever get there?"

"They may have missed their aim. Or perhaps the robots rebelled and took the ship elsewhere, and, in landing smashed it, only five of them managing to escape."

"I don't believe that," Seven said. "You have no proof of it."

"No," Eight admitted. "No. We don't even know what happened to the men on the ship."

They stood again outside the building, three little metal men. Out yonder in the west the sun was dipping below the horizon. A soft dusk was coming down, hiding the barren world, and still the lonely wind was stirring in the shadows.

Eight saw the statue lying on the ground and vague thoughts stirred within his mind. "They may have eaten grass," he said. "They may have eaten the flesh of other animals; they may have been weaklings; they may have arisen out of slime, but somehow I think there was something fine about them. For they dreamed, and even if they died——"

The robot bent over. Tiny, ageless, atom-fed motors within him surged with endless power. The robot lifted the dream of an age-dead man and set the statue back on its feet.

The three returned to their ship, and it lifted, following its path out to the stars. The proud, blind eyes of a forgotten statue seemed to follow it.

FAREWELL TO THE MASTER / by Harry Bates

"Farewell to the Master" represents the only occasion on which the editors reached unanimity of agreement on a story—a rare achievement for collaborators! It is our mutual, considered opinion that this is one of the finest stories we have ever read. Mr. Bates has depicted the inevitable tragedy of man confronting a situation beyond his present understanding. The reader is almost overwhelmed by the full realization of humanity's limitations. The utter foolishness of the world's reception of Gnut, visitor from outer space, will be a blow to our pride; yet, the final attempts at understanding and expiation will be a stimulus to our humility and wisdom.

FROM HIS perch high on the ladder above the museum floor, Cliff Sutherland studied carefully each line and shadow of the great robot, then turned and looked thoughtfully down at the rush of visitors come from all over the Solar System to see Gnut and the traveler for themselves and to hear once again their amazing, tragic story.

He himself had come to feel an almost proprietary interest in the exhibit, and with some reason. He had been the only free-lance picture reporter on the Capitol grounds when the visitors from the Unknown had arrived, and had obtained the first professional shots of the ship. He had witnessed at close hand every event of the next mad few days. He had thereafter photographed many times the eight-foot robot, the ship, and the beautiful slain ambassador, Klaatu, and his imposing tomb out in the center of the Tidal Basin, and, such was the continuing news value of the event to the billions of persons throughout habitable space, he was there now once more to get still other shots and, if possible, at a new "angle."

This time he was after a picture which showed Gnut as

142

weird and menacing. The shots he had taken the day before had not given quite the effect he wanted, and he hoped to get it today; but the light was not yet right and he had to wait for the afternoon to wane a little.

The last of the crowd admitted in the present group hurried in, exclaiming at the great pure green curves of the mysterious time-space traveler, then completely forgetting the ship at sight of the awesome figure and great head of the giant Gnut. Hinged robots of crude man-like appearance were familiar enough, but never had Earthling eyes lain on one like this. For Gnut had almost exactly the shape of a man—a giant, but a man—with greenish metal for man's covering flesh, and greenish metal for man's bulging muscles. Except for a loin cloth, he was nude. He stood like the powerful god of the machine of some undreamed-of scientific civilization, on his face a look of sullen, brooding thought. Those who looked at him did not make jests or idle remarks, and those nearest him usually did not speak at all. His strange, internally illuminated red eyes were so set that every observer felt they were fixed on himself alone, and he engendered a feeling that he might at any moment step forward in anger and perform unimaginable deeds.

A slight rustling sound came from speakers hidden in the ceiling above, and at once the noises of the crowd lessened. The recorded lecture was about to be given. Cliff sighed. He knew the thing by heart; had even been present when the recording was made, and met the speaker, a young chap named Stillwell.

"Ladies and gentlemen," began a clear and well-modulated voice—but Cliff was no longer attending. The shadows in the hollows of Gnut's face and figure were deeper; it was almost time for his shot. He picked up and examined the proofs of the pictures he had taken the day before and compared them critically with the subject.

As he looked a wrinkle came to his brow. He had not noticed it before, but now, suddenly, he had the feeling that since yesterday something about Gnut was changed. The pose before him was the identical one in the photographs, every detail on comparison seemed the same, but nevertheless the feeling persisted. He took up his viewing glass and more carefully compared subject and photographs, line by line. And then he saw that there was a difference.

With sudden excitement, Cliff snapped two pictures at

different exposures. He knew he should wait a little and take others, but he was so sure he had stumbled on an important mystery that he had to get going, and quickly folding his accessory equipment he descended the ladder and made his way out. Twenty minutes later, consumed with curiosity, he was developing the new shots in his hotel bedroom.

What Cliff saw when he compared the negatives taken yesterday and today caused his scalp to tingle. Here was a slant indeed! And apparently no one but he knew! Still, what he had discovered, though it would have made the front page of every paper in the Solar System, was after all only a lead. The story, what really had happened, he knew no better than anyone else. It must be his job to find out.

And that meant he would have to secrete himself in the building and stay there all night. That very night; there was still time for him to get back before closing. He would take a small, very fast infrared camera that could see in the dark, and he would get the real picture and the story.

He snatched up the little camera, grabbed an aircab and hurried back to the museum. The place was filled with another section of the ever-present queue, and the lecture was just ending. He thanked Heaven that his arrangement with the museum permitted him to go in and out at will.

He had already decided what to do. First he made his way to the "floating" guard and asked a single question, and anticipation broadened on his face as he heard the expected answer. The second thing was to find a spot where he would be safe from the eyes of the men who would close the floor for the night. There was only one possible place, the laboratory set up behind the ship. Boldly he showed his press credentials to the second guard, stationed at the partitioned passageway leading to it, stating that he had come to interview the scientists; and in a moment was at the laboratory door.

He had been there a number of times and knew the room well. It was a large area roughly partitioned off for the work of the scientists engaged in breaking their way into the ship, and full of a confusion of massive and heavy objects—electric and hot-air ovens, carboys of chemicals, asbestos sheeting, compressors, basins, ladles, a microscope, and a great deal of smaller equipment common to a metallurgical laboratory. Three white-smocked men were deeply engrossed in an experiment at the far end. Cliff, waiting a good moment, slipped inside and hid himself under a table half buried with supplies. He felt reasonably safe from detection there. Very soon now the scientists would be going home for the night.

From beyond the ship he could hear another section of the waiting queue filing in—the last, he hoped, of the day. He settled himself as comfortably as he could. In a moment the lecture would begin. He had to smile when he thought of one thing the recording would say.

Then there it was again—the clear, trained voice of the chap Stillwell. The foot scrapings and whispers of the crowd died away, and Cliff would hear every word in spite of the great bulk of the ship lying interposed.

"Ladies and gentlemen," began the familiar words, "the Smithsonian Institution welcomes you to its new Interplanetary Wing and to the marvelous exhibits at this moment before you."

A slight pause. "All of you must know by now something of what happened here three months ago, if indeed you did not see it for yourself in the telescreen," the voice went on. "The few facts are briefly told. A little after 5:00 p.m. on September 16th, visitors to Washington thronged the grounds outside this building in their usual numbers and no doubt with their usual thoughts. The day was warm and fair. A stream of people was leaving the main entrance of the museum, just outside in the direction you are facing. This wing, of course, was not here at that time. Everyone was homeward bound, tired no doubt from hours on their feet, seeing the exhibits of the museum and visiting the many buildings on the grounds nearby. And then it happened.

"On the area just to your right, just as it is now, appeared the time-space traveler. It appeared in the blink of an eye. It did not come down from the sky; dozens of witnesses swear to that; it just appeared. One moment it was not here, the next it was. It appeared on the very spot it now rests on.

"The people nearest the ship were stricken with panic and ran back with cries and screams. Excitement spread out over Washington in a tidal wave. Radio, television, and newspapermen rushed here at once. Police formed a wide cordon around the ship, and army units appeared and trained guns and ray projectors on it. The direst calamity was feared.

"For it was recognized from the very beginning that this

was no spaceship from anywhere in the Solar System. Every child knew that only two spaceships had ever been built on Earth, and none at all on any of the other planets and satellites; and of those two, one had been destroyed when it was pulled into the Sun, and the other had just been reported safely arrived on Mars. Then, the ones made here had a shell of a strong aluminum alloy, while this one, as you see, is of an unknown greenish metal.

"The ship appeared and just sat here. No one emerged, and there was no sign that it contained life of any kind. That, as much as any single thing, caused excitement to sky-rocket. Who, or what, was inside? Were the vistors hostile or friendly? Where did the ship come from? How did it arrive so suddenly right on this spot without dropping from the sky?

"For two days the ship rested here, just as you now see it, without motion or sign that it contained life. Long before the end of that time the scientists had explained that it was not so much a spaceship as a space-time traveler, because only such a ship could arrive as this one did—materialize. They pointed out that such a traveler, while theoretically understandable to us Earthmen, was far beyond attempt at our present state of knowledge, and that this one, activated by relativity principles, might well have come from the far corner of the Universe, from a distance which light itself would require millions of years to cross.

"When this opinion was disseminated, public tension grew until it was almost intolerable. Where had the traveler come from? Who were its occupants? Why had they come to Earth? Above all, why did they now show themselves? Were they perhaps preparing some terrible weapon of destruction?

"And where was the ship's entrance port? Men who dared go look reported that none could be found. No slightest break or crack marred the perfect smoothness of the ship's curving ovoid surface. And a delegation of high-ranking officials who visited the ship could not, by knocking, elicit from its occupants any sign that they had been heard.

"At last, after exactly two days, in full view of tens of thousands of persons assembled and standing well back, and under the muzzles of scores of the army's most powerful guns and ray projectors, an opening appeared in the wall of the ship, and a ramp slid down, and out stepped a man, god-like in appearance and human in form, closely followed by a giant robot. And when they touched the ground the ramp slid back and the entrance closed as before.

"It was immediately apparent to all the assembled thousands that the stranger was friendly. The first thing he did was to raise his right arm high in the universal gesture of peace; but it was not that which impressed those nearest so much as the expression on his face, which radiated kindness, wisdom, the purest nobility. In his delicately tinted robe he looked like a benign god.

"At once, waiting for this appearance, a large committee of high-ranking government officials and army officers advanced to greet the visitor. With graciousness and dignity the man pointed to himself, then to his robot companion, and said in perfect English with a peculiar accent, 'I am Klaatu,' or a name that sounded like that, 'and this is Gnut.' The names were not well understood at the time, but the sight-and-sound film of the television men caught them and they became known to everyone subsequently.

"And then occurred the thing which shall always be to the shame of the human race. From a treetop a hundred yards away came a wink of violet light and Klaatu fell. The assembled multitude stood for a moment stunned, not comprehending what had happened. Gnut, a little behind his master and to one side, slowly turned his body a little toward him, moved his head twice, and stood still, in exactly the position you now see him.

"Then followed pandemonium. The police pulled the slayer of Klaatu out of the tree. They found him mentally unbalanced; he kept crying that the devil had come to kill every one on Earth. He was taken away, and Klaatu, although obviously dead, was rushed to the nearest hospital to see if anything could be done to revive him. Confused and frightened crowds milled about the Capitol grounds the rest of the afternoon and much of that night. The ship remained as silent and motionless as before. And Gnut, too, never moved from the position he had come to rest in.

"Gnut never moved again. He remained exactly as you see him all that night and for the ensuing days. When the mausoleum in the Tidal Basin was built, Klaatu's burial services took place where you are standing now, attended by the highest functionaries of all the great countries of the world. It was not only the most appropriate but the safest thing to do, for if there should be other living creatures in

the traveler, as seemed possible at that time, they had to be
impressed by the sincere sorrow of us Earthmen at what had
happened. If Gnut was still alive, or perhaps I had better say
functionable, there was no sign. He stood as you see him
during the entire ceremony. He stood so while his master
was floated out to the mausoleum and given to the centuries
with the tragically short sight-and-sound record of his his-
toric visit. And he stood so afterward, day after day, night
after night, in fair weather and in rain, never moving or
showing by any slightest sign that he was aware of what had
gone on.

"After the interment, this wing was built out from the
museum to cover the traveler and Gnut. Nothing else could
very well have been done, it was learned, for both Gnut and
the ship were far too heavy to be moved safely by any
means at hand.

"You have heard about the efforts of our metallurgists
since then to break into the ship, and of their complete
failure. Behind the ship now, as you can see from either
end, a partitioned workroom has been set up where the
attempt still goes on. So far its wonderful greenish metal has
proved inviolable. Not only are they unable to get in, but
they cannot even find the exact place from which Klaatu and
Gnut emerged. The chalk marks you see are the best ap-
proximation.

"Many people have feared that Gnut was only temporarily
deranged, and that on return to function might be dangerous,
so the scientists have completely destroyed all chance of
that. The greenish metal of which he is made seemed to be
the same as that of the ship and could no more be attacked,
they found, nor could they find any way to penetrate to his
internals; but they had other means. They sent electrical
currents of tremendous voltages and amperages through him.
They applied terrific heat to all parts of his metal shell.
They immersed him for days in gases and acids and strongly
corroding solutions, and they have bombarded him with every
known kind of ray. You need have no fear of him now. He
cannot possibly have retained the ability to function in any
way.

"But—a word of caution. The officials of the government
know that visitors will not show any disrespect in this building. It may be that the unknown and unthinkably powerful

civilization from which Klaatu and Gnut came may send other emissaries to see what happened to them. Whether or not they do, not one of us must be found amiss in our attitude. None of us could very well anticipate what happened, and we all are immeasurably sorry, but we are still in a sense responsible, and must do what we can to avoid possible retaliations.

"You will be allowed to remain five minutes longer, and then, when the gong sounds, you will please leave promptly. The robot attendants along the wall will answer any questions you may have.

"Look well, for before you stand stark symbols of the achievement, mystery, and frailty of the human race."

The recorded voice ceased speaking. Cliff, carefully moving his cramped limbs, broke out in a wide smile. If they knew what he knew!

For his photographs told a slightly different story from that of the lecturer. In yesterday's a line of the figured floor showed clearly at the outer edge of the robot's near foot; in today's, *that line was covered*. Gnut had moved!

Or been moved, though this was very unlikely. Where was the derrick and other evidence of such activity? It could hardly have been done in one night, and all signs so quickly concealed. And why should it be done at all?

Still, to make sure, he had asked the guard. He could almost remember verbatim his answer:

"No, Gnut has neither moved nor been moved since the death of his master. A special point was made of keeping him in the position he assumed at Klaatu's death. The floor was built under him, and the scientists who completed his derangement erected their apparatus around him, just as he stands. You need have no fears."

Cliff smiled again. He did not have any fears.

Not yet.

II

A moment later the big gong above the entrance doors rang the closing hour, and immediately following it a voice from the speakers called out, "Five o'clock, ladies and gentlemen. Closing time, ladies and gentlemen."

The three scientists, as if surprised it was so late, hurriedly washed their hands, changed to their street clothes

and disappeared down the partitioned corridor, oblivious of
the young picture man hidden under the table. The slide and
scrape of the feet on the exhibition floor rapidly dwindled,
until at last there were only the steps of the two guards walking from one point to another, making sure everything was
all right for the night. For just a moment one of them
glanced in the doorway of the laboratory, then he joined the
other at the entrance. Then the great metal doors clanged to,
and there was silence.

Cliff waited several minutes, then carefully poked his
way out from under the table. As he straightened up, a faint
tinkling crash sounded at the floor by his feet. Carefully
stooping, he found the shattered remains of a thin glass
pipette. He had knocked it off the table.

That caused him to realize something he had not thought
of before: A Gnut who had moved might be a Gnut who
could see and hear—and really be dangerous. He would
have to be very careful.

He looked about him. The room was bounded at the ends
by two fiber partitions which at the inner ends followed
close under the curving bottom of the ship. The inner side
of the room was the ship itself, and the outer was the
southern wall of the wing. There were four large high windows. The only entrance was by way of the passage.

Without moving, from his knowledge of the building,
he made his plan. The wing was connected with the western
end of the museum by a doorway, never used, and extended westward toward the Washington Monument. The
ship lay nearest the southern wall, and Gnut stood out in
front of it, not far from the northeast corner and at the
opposite end of the room from the entrance of the building and the passageway leading to the laboratory. By re-
tracing his steps he would come out on the floor at the
point farthest removed from the robot. This was just what
he wanted, for on the other side of the entrance, on a low
platform, stood a paneled table containing the lecture apparatus, and this table was the only object in the room
which afforded a place for him to lie concealed while watching what might go on. The only other objects on the floor
were the six manlike robot attendants in fixed stations along
the northern wall, placed there to answer visitors' questions.
He would have to gain the table.

He turned and began cautiously tiptoeing out of the

laboratory and down the passageway. It was already dark there, for what light still entered the exhibition hall was shut off by the great bulk of the ship. He reached the end of the room without making a sound. Very carefully he edged forward and peered around the bottom of the ship at Gnut.

He had a momentary shock. The robot's eyes were right on him!—or so it seemed. Was that only the effect of the set of his eyes, he wondered, or was he already discovered? The position of Gnut's head did not seem to have changed, at any rate. Probably everything was all right, but he wished he did not have to cross that end of the room with the feeling that the robot's eyes were following him.

He drew back and sat down and waited. It would have to be totally dark before he essayed the trip to the table.

He waited a full hour, until the faint beams from the lamps on the grounds outside began to make the room seem to grow lighter; then he got up and peeped around the ship once more. The robot's eyes seemed to pierce right at him as before, only now, due no doubt to the darkness, the strange internal illumination seemed much brighter. This was a chilling thing. Did Gnut know he was there? What were the thoughts of the robot? What *could* be the thoughts of a man-made machine, even so wonderful a one as Gnut?

It was time for the cross, so Cliff slung his camera around on his back, went down on his hands and knees, and carefully moved to the edge of the entrance wall. There he fitted himself as closely as he could into the angle made by it with the floor and started inching ahead. Never pausing, not risking a glance at Gnut's unnerving red eyes, moving an inch at a time, he snaked along. He took ten minutes to cross the space of a hundred feet, and he was wet with perspiration when his fingers at last touched the one-foot rise of the platform on which the table stood. Still slowly, silently as a shadow, he made his way over the edge and melted behind the protection of the table. At last he was there.

He relaxed for a moment, then, anxious to know whether he had been seen, carefully turned and looked around the side of the table.

Gnut's eyes were now full on him! Or so it seemed. Against the general darkness, the robot loomed a mysterious and still darker shadow that, for all his being a hundred and fifty feet away, seemed to dominate the room. Cliff could not tell whether the position of his body was changed or not.

But if Gnut were looking at him, he at least did nothing else. Not by the slightest motion that Cliff could discern did he appear to move. His position was the one he had maintained these last three months, in the darkness, in the rain, and this last week in the museum.

Cliff made up his mind not to give away to fear. He became conscious of his own body. The cautious trip had taken something out of him—his knees and elbows burned and his trousers were no doubt ruined. But these were little things if what he hoped for came to pass. If Gnut so much as moved, and he could catch him with his infrared camera, he would have a story that would buy him fifty suits of clothes. And if on top of that he could learn the purpose of Gnut's moving—provided there was a purpose—that would be a story that would set the world on its ears.

He settled down to a period of waiting; there was no telling when Gnut would move, if indeed he would move that night. Cliff's eyes had long been adjusted to the dark and he could make out the larger objects well enough. From time to time he peered out at the robot—peered long and hard, till his outlines wavered and he seemed to move, and he had to blink and rest his eyes to be sure it was only his imagination.

Again the minute hand of his watch crept around the dial. The inactivity made Cliff careless, and for longer and longer periods he kept his head back out of sight behind the table. And so it was that when Gnut did move he was scared almost out of his wits. Dull and a little bored, he suddenly found the robot out on the floor, halfway in his direction.

But that was not the most frightening thing. It was that when he did see Gnut he did not catch him moving! He was stopped as still as a cat in the middle of stalking a mouse. His eyes were now much brighter, and there was no remaining doubt about their direction: he was looking right at Cliff!

Scarcely breathing, half hypnotized, Cliff looked back. His thoughts tumbled. What was the robot's intention? Why had he stopped so still? Was he being stalked? How could he move with such silence?

In the heavy darkness Gnut's eyes moved nearer. Slowly but in perfect rhythm the almost imperceptible sound of his footsteps beat on Cliff's ears. Cliff, usually resourceful enough, was this time caught flatfooted. Frozen with fear, utterly incapable of fleeing, he lay where he was while the metal monster with the fiery eyes came on.

For a moment Cliff all but fainted, and when he recovered, there was Gnut towering over him, legs almost within reach. He was bending slightly, burning his terrible eyes right into his own!

Too late to try to think of running now. Trembling like any cornered mouse, Cliff waited for the blow that would crush him. For an eternity, it seemed, Gnut scrutinized him without moving. For each second of that eternity Cliff expected annihilation, sudden, quick, complete. And then suddenly and unexpectedly it was over. Gnut's body straightened and he stepped back. He turned. And then, with the almost jerkless rhythm which only he among robots possessed, he started back toward the place from which he came.

Cliff could hardly believe he had been spared. Gnut could have crushed him like a worm—and he had only turned around and gone back. Why? It could not be supposed that a robot was capable of human considerations.

Gnut went straight to the other end of the traveler. At a certain place he stopped and made a curious succession of sounds. At once Cliff saw an opening, blacker than the gloom of the building, appear in the ship's side, and it was followed by a slight sliding sound as a ramp slid out and met the floor. Gnut walked up the ramp and, stooping a little, disappeared inside the ship.

Then, for the first time, Cliff remembered the picture he had come to get. Gnut had moved, but he had not caught him! But at least now, whatever opportunities there might be later, he could get the shot of the ramp connecting with the opened door; so he twisted his camera into position, set it for the proper exposure, and took a shot.

A long time passed and Gnut did not come out. What could he be doing inside? Cliff wondered. Some of his courage returned to him and he toyed with the idea of creeping forward and peeing through the port, but he found he had not the courage for that. Gnut had spared him, at least for the time, but there was no telling how far his tolerance would go.

An hour passed, then another. Gnut was doing something inside the ship, but what, Cliff could not imagine. If the

robot had been a human being, he knew he would have
sneaked a look, but as it was, he was too much of an unknown
quantity. Even the simplest of Earth's robots under certain
circumstances were inexplicable things; what, then, of this
one, come from an unknown and even unthinkable civilization, by far the most wonderful construction ever seen—
what superhuman powers might he not possess? All that the
scientists of Earth could do had not served to derange him.
Acid, heat, rays, terrific crushing blows—he had withstood
them all; even his finish had been unmarred. He might be
able to see perfectly in the dark. And right where he was,
he might be able to hear or in some way sense the least
change in Cliff's position.

More time passed, and then, some time after two o'clock in
the morning, a simple homely thing happened, but a thing
so unexpected that for a moment it quite destroyed Cliff's
equilibrium. Suddenly, through the dark and silent building,
there was a faint whir of wings, soon followed by a piercing, sweet voice of a bird. A mocking bird. Somewhere in the
gloom above his head. Clear and full throated were its notes;
a dozen little songs it sang, one after the other without pause
between—short insistent calls—twirrings, coaxings, cooings—
the spring love song of perhaps the finest singer in the world.
Then, as suddenly as it began, the voice was silent.

If an invading army had poured out of the traveler, Cliff
would have been less surprised. The month was December;
even in Florida the mocking birds had not yet begun their
song. How had one gotten into that tight gloomy museum?
How and why was it singing there?

He waited, full of curiosity. Then suddenly he was aware
of Gnut, standing just outside the port of the ship. He stood
quite still, his glowing eyes turned squarely in Cliff's direction. For a moment the hush in the museum seemed to
deepen; then it was broken by a soft thud on the floor near
where Cliff was lying.

He wondered. The light in Gnut's eyes changed, and he
started his almost jerkless walk in Cliff's direction. When only
a little away, the robot stopped, bent over, and picked something from the floor. For some time he stood without motion and looked at a little object he held in his hand. Cliff
knew, though he could not see, that it was the mocking bird.
Its body, for he was sure that it had lost its song forever.

Gnut then turned, and without a glance at Cliff, walked back
to the ship and again went inside.

Hours passed while Cliff waited for some sequel to this
surprising happening. Perhaps it was because of his curiosity
that his fear of the robot began to lessen. Surely if the
mechanism was unfriendly, if he intended him any harm, he
would have finished him before, when he had such a perfect
opportunity. Cliff began to nerve himself for a quick look inside the port. And a picture; he must remember the picture.
He kept forgetting the very reason he was there.

It was in the deeper darkness of the false dawn when he got
sufficient courage and made the start. He took off his shoes,
and in his stockinged feet, his shoes tied together and slung
over his shoulder, he moved stiffly but rapidly to a position
behind the nearest of the six robot attendants stationed along
the wall, then paused for some sign which might indicate
that Gnut knew he had moved. Hearing none, he slipped
along behind the next robot attendant and paused again.
Bolder now, he made in one spurt all the distance to the
farthest one, the sixth, fixed just opposite the port of the
ship. There he met with a disappointment. No light that he
could detect was visible within; there was only darkness and
the all-permeating silence. Still, he had better get the picture.
He raised his camera, focused it on the dark opening, and
gave the film a comparatively long exposure. Then he stood
there, at a loss what to do next.

As he paused, a peculiar series of muffled noises reached
his ears, apparently from within the ship. Animal noises—
first scrapings and pantings, punctuated by several sharp
clicks, then deep, rough snarls, interrupted by more scrapings and pantings, as if a struggle of some kind were going
on. Then suddenly, before Cliff could even decide to run
back to the table, a low, wide, dark shape bounded out of the
port and immediately turned and grew to the height of a
man. A terrible fear swept over Cliff, even before he knew
what the shape was.

In the next second Gnut appeared in the port and stepped
unhesitatingly down the ramp toward the shape. As he advanced it backed slowly away for a few feet; but then it stood
its ground, and thick arms rose from its side and began a
loud drumming on its chest, while from its throat came a

deep roar of defiance. Only one creature in the world beat its chest and made a sound like that. The shape was a gorilla!

And a huge one!

Gnut kept advancing, and when close, charged forward and grappled with the beast. Cliff would not have guessed that Gnut could move so fast. In the darkness he could not see the details of what happened; all he knew was that the two great shapes, the titanic metal Gnut and the squat but ter- rifically strong gorilla, merged for a moment with silence on the robot's part and terrible, deep, indescribable roars on the other's; then the two separated, and it was as if the gorilla had been flung back and away.

The animal at once rose to its full height and roared deafeningly. Gnut advanced. They closed again, and the sep- aration of before was repeated. The robot continued in- exorably, and now the gorilla began to fall back down the building. Suddenly, the beast darted at a man-like shape against the wall, and with one rapid side movement dashed the fifth robot attendant to the floor and decapitated it.

Tense with fear, Cliff crouched behind his own robot attendant. He thanked Heaven that Gnut was between him and the gorilla and was continuing his advance. The gorilla backed farther, darted suddenly at the next robot in the row, and with strength almost unbelievable picked it from its roots and hurled it at Gnut. With a sharp metallic clang, robot hit robot, and the one of Earth bounced off to one side and rolled to a stop.

Cliff cursed himself for it afterward, but again he com- pletely forgot the picture. The gorilla kept falling back down the building, demolishing with terrific bursts of rage every robot attendant that he passed and throwing the pieces at the implacable Gnut. Soon they arrived opposite the table, and Cliff now thanked his stars he had come away. There followed a brief silence. Cliff could not make out what was going on, but he imagined that the gorilla had at last reached the corner of the wing and was trapped.

If he was, it was only for a moment. The silence was suddenly shattered by a terrific roar, and the thick, squat shape of the animal came bounding toward Cliff. He came all the way back and turned just between Cliff and the port of the ship. Cliff prayed frantically for Gnut to come back quickly, for there was now only the last remaining robot attendant between him and the madly dangerous brute. Out of the dimness Gnut did appear. The gorilla rose to its full height and again beat its chest and roared its challenge.

And then occurred a curious thing. It fell on all fours and slowly rolled over on its side, as if weak or hurt. Then panting, making frightening noises, it forced itself again to its feet and faced the oncoming Gnut. As it waited, its eye was caught by the last robot attendant and perhaps Cliff, shrunk close behind it. With a surge of terrible destructive rage, the gorilla waddled sideward toward Cliff but this time, even through his panic, he saw that the animal moved with difficulty, again apparently sick or severely wounded. He jumped back just in time; the gorilla pulled out the last robot attendant and hurled it violently at Gnut, missing him narrowly.

That was its last effort. The weakness caught it again; it dropped heavily on one side, rocked back and forth a few times, and fell to twitching. Then it lay still and did not move again.

The first faint pale light of the dawn was seeping into the room. From the corner where he had taken refuge, Cliff watched closely the great robot. It seemed to him that he behaved very queerly. He stood over the dead gorilla, looking down at him with what in a human would be called sadness. Cliff saw this clearly; Gnut's heavy greenish features bore a thoughtful, grieving expression new to his experience. For some moments he stood so, then as might a father with his sick child, he leaned over, lifted the great animal in his metal arms and carried it tenderly within the ship.

Cliff flew back to the table, suddenly fearful of yet other dangerous and inexplicable happenings. It struck him that he might be safer in the laboratory, and with trembling knees he made his way there and hid in one of the ovens. He prayed for full daylight. His thoughts were chaos. Rapidly, one after another, his mind churned up the amazing events of the night, but all was mystery; it seemed there could be no rational explanation for them. That mocking bird. The gorilla. Gnut's sad expression and his tenderness. What could account for a fantastic melange like that!

Gradually full daylight did come. A long time passed. At last he began to believe he might yet get out of that place of mystery and danger alive. At 8:30 there were noises at the

entrance, and the good sound of human voices came to his
ears. He stepped out of the oven and tiptoed to the passageway.

The noises stopped suddenly and there was a frightened
exclamation and then the sound of running feet, and then
silence. Stealthily Cliff sneaked down the narrow way and
peeped fearfully around the ship.

There Gnut was in his accustomed place, in the identical
pose he had taken at the death of his master, brooding sul-
lenly and alone over a space traveler once again closed tight
and a room that was a shambles. The entrance doors stood
open and, heart in his mouth, Cliff ran out.

A few minutes later, safe in his hotel room, completely
done in, he sat down for a second and almost at once fell
asleep. Later, still in his clothes and still asleep, he staggered
over to the bed. He did not wake up till midafternoon.

III

Cliff awoke slowly, at first not realizing that the images
tumbling in his head were real memories and not a fantastic
dream. It was recollection of the pictures which brought him
to his feet. Hastily he set about developing the film in his
camera.

Then in his hands was proof that the events of the night
were real. Both shots turned out well. The first showed clearly
the ramp leading up to the port as he had dimly discerned it
from his position behind the table. The second, of the open
port as snapped from in front, was a disappointment, for a
blank wall just back of the opening cut off all view of the
interior. That would account for the fact that no light had
escaped from the ship while Gnut was inside. Assuming Gnut
required light for whatever he did.

Cliff looked at the negatives and was ashamed of himself.
What a rotten picture man he was to come back with two
ridiculous shots like these! He had had a score of opportunities to get real ones—shots of Gnut in action—Gnut's
fight with the gorilla—even Gnut holding the mocking bird—
spine-chilling stuff!—and all he had brought back was two
stills of a doorway. Oh, sure, they were valuable, but he was a
Grade A ass.

And to top his brilliant performance, he had fallen asleep!

Well, he'd better get out on the street and find out what was doing.

Quickly he showered, shaved, and changed his clothes, and soon was entering a nearby restaurant patronized by other picture and newsmen. Sitting alone at the lunch bar, he spotted a friend and competitor.

"Well, what do you think?" asked his friend when he took the stool at his side.

"I don't think anything until I've had breakfast," Cliff answered.

"Then haven't you heard?"

"Heard what?" fended Cliff, who knew very well what was coming.

"You're a fine picture man," was the other's remark. "When something really big happens, you are asleep in bed." But then he told him what had been discovered that morning in the museum, and of the world-wide excitement at the news. Cliff did three things at once, successfully—gobbled a substantial breakfast, kept thanking his stars that nothing new had transpired, and showed continuous surprise. Still chewing, he got up and hurried over to the building.

Outside, balked at the door, was a large crowd of the curious, but Cliff had no trouble gaining admittance when he showed his press credentials. Gnut and the ship stood just as he had left them, but the floor had been cleaned up and the pieces of the demolished robot attendants were lined up in one place along the wall. Several other competitor friends of his were there.

"I was away; missed the whole thing," he said to one of them—Gus. "What's supposed to be the explanation for what happened?"

"Ask something easy," was the answer. "Nobody knows. It's thought maybe something came out of the ship, maybe another robot like Gnut. Say—where have you been?"

"Asleep."

"Better catch up. Several billion bipeds are scared stiff. Revenge for the death of Klaatu. Earth about to be invaded."

"But that's—"

"Oh, I know it's all crazy, but that's the story they're being fed; it sells news. But there's a new angle just turned up, very surprising. Come here."

He led Cliff to the table where a knot of people looking

with great interest at several objects guarded by a technician. Gus pointed to a long slide on which were mounted a number of short dark-brown hairs.

"Those hairs came off a large male gorilla," Gus said with a certain hard-boiled casualness. "Most of them were found among the sweepings of the floor this morning. The rest were found on the robot attendants."

Cliff tried to look astounded. Gus pointed to a test tube partly filled with a light amber fluid.

"And that's blood, diluted—gorilla blood. It was found on Gnut's arms."

"Good Heaven!" Cliff managed to exclaim. "And there's no explanation?"

"Not even a theory. It's your big chance, wonder boy."

Cliff broke away from Gus, unable to maintain his act any longer. He couldn't decide what to do about his story. The press services would bid heavily for it—with all his pictures—but that would take further action out of his hands. In the back of his mind he wanted to stay in the wing again that night, but—well, he simply was afraid. He'd had a pretty stiff dose, and he wanted very much to remain alive.

He walked over and looked a long time at Gnut. No one would ever have guessed that he had moved, or that there had rested on his greenish metal face a look of sadness. Those weird eyes! Cliff wondered if they were really looking at him, as they seemed, recognizing him as the bold intruder of last night. Of what unknown stuff were they made—those materials placed in his eye sockets by one branch of the race of man which all the science of his own could not even serve to disfunction? What was Gnut thinking? What could be the thoughts of a robot—a mechanism of metal poured out of man's clay crucibles, Was he angry at him? Cliff thought not. Gnut had had him at his mercy—and had walked away.

Dared he stay again?

Cliff thought perhaps he did.

He walked about the room, thinking it over. He felt sure Gnut would move again. A Mikton ran gun would protect him from another gorilla—or fifty of them. He did not yet have the real story. He had come back with two miserable architectural stills!

He might have known from the first that he would stay. At dusk that night, armed with his camera and a small Mikton gun, he lay once more under the table of supplies in the

laboratory and heard the metal doors of the wing clang to
for the night.

This time he would get the story—and the pictures.

If only no guard was posted inside!

IV

Cliff listened hard for a long time for any sound which
might tell him that a guard had been left, but the silence
within the wing remained unbroken. He was thankful for
that—but not quite completely. The gathering darkness and
the realization that he was now irrevocably committed made
the thought of a companion not altogether unpleasant.

About an hour after it reached maximum darkness he took
off his shoes, tied them together and slung them around his
neck, down his back, and stole quietly down the passageway
to where it opened into the exhibition area. All seemed as
it had been the preceding night. Gnut looked an ominous,
indistinct shadow at the far end of the room, his glowing
red eyes again seemingly right on the spot from which Cliff
peeped out. As on the previous night, but even more carefully, Cliff went down on his stomach in the angle of the
wall and slowly snaked across to the low platform on which
stood the table. Once in its shelter, he fixed his shoes so that
they straddled one shoulder, and brought his camera and
gun holster around, ready on his breast. This time, he told
himself, he would get pictures.

He settled down to wait, keeping Gnut in full sight every
minute. His vision reached maximum adjustment to the darkness. Eventually he began to feel lonely and a little afraid.
Gnut's red-glowing eyes were getting on his nerves; he had
to keep assuring himself that the robot would not harm him.
He had little doubt but that he himself was being watched.

Hours slowly passed. From time to time he heard slight
noises at the entrance, on the outside—a guard, perhaps, or
maybe curious visitors.

At about nine o'clock he saw Gnut move. First his head
alone; it turned so that the eyes burned stronger in the direction where Cliff lay. For a moment that was all; then the
dark metal form stirred slightly and began moving forward
—straight toward himself. Cliff had thought he would not
be afraid—much—but now his heart stood still. What would
happen this time?

With amazing silence, Gnut drew nearer, until he towered an ominous shadow over the spot where Cliff lay. For a long time his red eyes burned down on the prone man. Cliff trembled all over; this was worse than the first time. Without having planned it, he found himself speaking to the creature.

"You would not hurt me," he pleaded. "I was only curious to see what's going on. It's my job. Can you understand me? I would not harm or bother you. I . . . I couldn't if I wanted to! Please!"

The robot never moved, and Cliff could not guess whether his words had been understood or even heard. When he felt he could not bear the suspense any longer, Gnut reached out and took something from a drawer of the table, or perhaps he put something back in; then he stepped back, turned, and retraced his steps. Cliff was safe! Again the robot had spared him!

Beginning then, Cliff lost much of his fear. He felt sure now that this Gnut would do him no harm. Twice he had had him in his power, and each time he had only looked and quietly moved away. Cliff could not imagine what Gnut had done in the drawer of the table. He watched with the greatest curiosity to see what would happen next.

As on the night before, the robot went straight to the end of the ship and made the peculiar sequence of sounds that opened the port, and when the ramp slid out he went inside. After that Cliff was alone in the darkness for a very long time, probably two hours. Not a sound came from the ship.

Cliff knew he should sneak up to the port and peep inside, but he could not quite bring himself to do it. With his gun he could handle another gorilla, but if Gnut caught him it might be the end. Momentarily he expected something fantastic to happen—he knew not what; maybe the mocking bird's sweet song again, maybe a gorilla, maybe—anything. What did at last happen once more caught him with complete surprise.

He heard a sudden muffled sound, then words—human words—every one familiar.

"Gentlemen," was the first, and then there was a very slight pause. "The Smithsonian Institution welcomes you to its new Interplanetary Wing and to the marvelous exhibits at this moment before you."

It was the recorded voice of Stillwell! But it was not coming through the speakers overhead, but much muted, from within the ship.

After a slight pause it went on:—

"All of you must . . . must—" Here it stammered and came to a stop. Cliff's hair bristled. That stammering was not in the lecture!

For just a moment there was silence; then came a scream, a hoarse man's scream, muffled, from somewhere within the heart of the ship; and it was followed by muted gasps and cries, as of a man in great fright or distress.

Every nerve tight, Cliff watched the port. He heard a thudding noise within the ship, then out the door flew the shadow of what was surely a human being. Gasping and half stumbling, he ran straight down the room in Cliff's direction. When twenty feet away, the great shadow of Gnut followed him out of the port.

Cliff watched, breathless. The man—it was Stillwell, he saw now—came straight for the table behind which Cliff himself lay, as if to get behind it, but when only a few feet away, his knees buckled and he fell to the floor. Suddenly Gnut was standing over him, but Stillwell did not seem to be aware of it. He appeared very ill, but kept making spasmodic futile effort to creep on to the protection of the table.

Gnut did not move, so Cliff was emboldened to speak.

"What's the matter, Stillwell?" he asked. "Can I help? Don't be afraid. I'm Cliff Sutherland; you know, the picture man."

Without showing the least surprise at finding Cliff there, and clutching at his presence like a drowning man would a straw, Stillwell gasped out:

"Help me! Gnut . . . Gnut—" He seemed unable to go on.

"Gnut what?" asked Cliff. Very conscious of the fire-eyed robot looming above, and afraid even to move out to the man, Cliff added reassuringly: "Gnut won't hurt you. I'm sure he won't. He doesn't hurt me. What's the matter? What can I do?"

With a sudden accession of energy, Stillwell rose on his elbows.

"Where am I?" he asked.

"In the Interplanetary Wing," Cliff answered. "Don't you know?"

Only Stillwell's hard breathing was heard for a moment. Then hoarsely, weakly, he asked:

"How did I get here?"

"I don't know," said Cliff.

"I was making a lecture recording," Stillwell said, "when suddenly I found myself here . . . or I mean in there—"

He broke off and showed a return of his terror.

"Then what?" asked Cliff gently.

"I was in that box—and there, above me, was Gnut, the robot. Gnut! But they made Gnut harmless! He's never moved!"

"Steady, now," said Cliff. "I don't think Gnut will hurt you."

Stillwell fell back on the floor.

"I'm very weak," he gasped. "Something— Will you get a doctor?"

He was utterly unaware that towering above him, eyes boring down at him through the darkness, was the robot he feared so greatly.

As Cliff hesitated, at a loss what to do, the man's breath began coming in short gasps, as regular as the ticking of a clock. Cliff dared to move out to him, but no act on his part could have helped the man now. His gasps weakened and became spasmodic, then suddenly he was completely silent and still. Cliff felt for his heart, then looked up to the eyes in the shadow above.

"He is dead," he whispered.

The robot seemed to understand, or at least to hear. He bent forward and regarded the still figure.

"What is it, Gnut?" Cliff asked the robot suddenly. "What are you doing? Can I help you in any way? Somehow I don't believe you are unfriendly, and I don't believe you killed this man. But what happened? Can you understand me? Can you speak? What is it you're trying to do?"

Gnut made no sound or motion, but only looked at the still figure at his feet. In the robot's face, now so close, Cliff saw the look of sad contemplation.

Gnut stood so several minutes; then he bent lower, took the limp form carefully—even gently, Cliff thought—in his mighty arms, and carried him to the place along the wall where lay the dismembered pieces of the robot attendants. Carefully he laid him by their side. Then he went back into the ship.

Without fear now, Cliff stole along the wall of the room. He had gotten almost as far as the shattered figures on the floor when he suddenly stopped motionless. Gnut was emerging again.

He was bearing a shape that looked like another body, a larger one. He held it in one arm and placed it carefully by the body of Stillwell. In the hand of his other arm he held something that Cliff could not make out, and this he placed at the side of the body he had just put down. Then he went to the ship and returned once more with a shape which he laid gently by the others; and when this last trip was over he looked down at them all for a moment, then turned slowly back to the ship and stood motionless, as if in deep thought, by the ramp.

Cliff restrained his curiosity as long as he could, then slipped forward and bent over the objects Gnut had placed there. First in the row was the body of Stillwell, as he expected, and next was the great shapeless furry mass of a dead gorilla—the one of last night. By the gorilla lay the object the robot had carried in his free hand—the little body of the mocking bird. These last two had remained in the ship all night, and Gnut, for all his surprising gentleness in handling them, was only cleaning house. But there was a fourth body whose history he did not know. He moved closer and bent very low to look.

What he saw made him catch his breath. Impossible!— he thought; there was some confusion in his directions; he brought his face back, close to the first body. Then his blood ran cold. The first body was that of Stillwell, but the last in the row was Stillwell, too; there were two bodies of Stillwell, both exactly alike, both dead.

Cliff backed away with a cry, and then panic took him and he ran down the room away from Gnut and yelled and beat wildly on the door. There was a noise on the outside.

"Let me out!" he yelled in terror. "Let me out! Let me out! Oh, hurry!"

A crack opened between the two doors and he forced his way through like a wild animal and ran far out on the lawn. A belated couple on a nearby path stared at him with amazement, and this brought some sense to his head and he slowed down and came to a stop. Back at the building, everything looked as usual, and in spite of his terror, Gnut was not chasing him.

He was still in his stockinged feet. Breathing heavily, he sat down on the wet grass and put on his shoes; then he stood and looked at the building, trying to pull himself together. What an incredible melange! The dead Stillwell, the dead gorilla, and the dead mocking bird—all dying before his eyes. And then that last frightening thing, the second dead Stillwell whom he had not seen die. And Gnut's strange gentleness, and the sad expression he had twice seen on his face.

As he looked, the grounds about the building came to life. Several people collected at the door of the wing, above sounded the siren of a police copter, then in the distance another, and from all sides people came running, a few at first, then more and more. The police planes landed on the lawn just outside the door of the wing, and he thought he could see the officers peeping inside. Then suddenly the lights of the wing flooded on. In control of himself now, Cliff went back.

He entered. He had left Gnut standing in thought at the side of the ramp, but now he was again in his old familiar pose in the usual place, as if he had never moved. The ship's door was closed, and the ramp gone. But the bodies, the four strangely assorted bodies, were still lying by the demolished robot attendants where he had left them in the dark.

He was startled by a cry behind his back. A uniformed museum guard was pointing at him.

"This is the man!" the guard shouted. "When I opened the door this man forced his way out and ran like the devil!"

The police officers converged on Cliff.

"Who are you? What is all this?" one of them asked him roughly.

"I'm Cliff Sutherland, picture reporter," Cliff answered calmly. "And I was the one who was inside here and ran away, as the guard says."

"What were you doing?" the officer asked, eyeing him, "And where did these bodies come from?"

"Gentlemen, I'd tell you gladly—only business first," Cliff answered. "There's been some fantastic goings on in this room, and I saw them and have the story, but"—he smiled —"I must decline to answer without advice of counsel until

I've sold my story to one of the news syndicates. You know how it is. If you'll allow me the use of the radio in your plane—just for a moment, gentlemen—you'll have the whole story right afterward—say in half an hour, when the television men broadcast it. Meanwhile, believe me, there's nothing for you to do, and there'll be no loss by the delay."

The officer who had asked the questions blinked, and one of the others, quicker to react and certainly not a gentleman, stepped toward Cliff with clenched fists. Cliff disarmed him by handing him his press credentials. He glanced at them rapidly and put them in his pocket.

By now half a hundred people were there, and among them were two members of a syndicate crew whom he knew, arrived by copter. The police growled, but they let him whisper in their ear and then go out under escort to the crew's plane. There, by radio, in five minutes, Cliff made a deal which would bring him more money than he had ever before earned in a year. After that he turned over all his pictures and negatives to the crew and gave them the story, and they lost not one second in spinning back to their office with the flash.

More and more people arrived, and the police cleared the building. Ten minutes later a big crew of radio and television men forced their way in, sent there by a syndicate with which he had dealt. And then a few minutes later, under the glaring lights set up by the operators and standing close by the ship and not far from Gnut—he refused to stand underneath him—Cliff gave his story to the cameras and microphones, which in a fraction of a second shot it to every corner of the Solar System.

Immediately afterward the police took him to jail. On general principles and because they were pretty blooming mad.

V

Cliff stayed in jail all that night—until eight o'clock the next morning, when the syndicate finally succeeded in digging up a lawyer and got him out. And then, when at last he was leaving, a Federal man caught him by the wrist.

"You're wanted for further questioning over at the Continental Bureau of Investigation," the agent told him. Cliff went along willingly.

Fully thirty-five high-ranking Federal officials and "big

names" were waiting for him in an imposing conference room—one of the president's secretaries, the undersecretary of state, the underminister of defense, scientists, a colonel, executives, department heads, and ranking "C" men. Old gray-mustached Sanders, chief of the CBI, was presiding.

They made him tell his story all over again, and then, in parts, all over once more—not because they did not believe him, but because they kept hoping to elicit some fact which would cast significant light on the mystery of Gnut's behavior and the happenings of the last three nights. Patiently Cliff racked his brains for every detail.

Chief Sanders asked most of the questions. After more than an hour, when Cliff thought they had finished, Sanders asked him several more, all involving his personal opinions of what had transpired.

"Do you think Gnut was deranged in any way by the acids, rays, heat, and so forth applied to him by the scientists?"

"I saw no evidence of it."

"Do you think he can see?"

"I'm sure he can see, or else has other powers which are equivalent."

"Do you think he can hear?"

"Yes, sir. That time when I whispered to him that Stillwell was dead, he bent lower, as if to see for himself. I would not be surprised if he also understood what I said."

"At no time did he speak, except those sounds he made to open the ship?"

"Not one word, in English or any other language. Not one sound with his mouth."

"In your opinion, has his strength been impaired in any way by our treatment?" asked one of the scientists.

"I have told you how easily he handled the gorilla. He attacked the animal and threw it back, after which it retreated all the way down the building, afraid of him."

"How would you explain the fact that our autopsies disclosed no mortal wound, no cause of death, in any of the bodies—gorilla, mocking bird, or the two identical Stillwells?" —this from a medical officer.

"I can't."

"You think Gnut is dangerous?"—from Sanders.

"Potentially very dangerous."

"Yet you say you have the feeling he is not hostile."

"To me, I meant. I do have that feeling, and I'm afraid that I can't give any good reason for it, except the way he spared me twice when he had me in his power. I think maybe the gentle way he handled the bodies had something to do with it, and maybe the sad, thoughtful look I twice caught on his face."

"Would you risk staying in the building alone another night?"

"Not for anything." There were smiles.

"Did you get any pictures of what happened last night?"

"No, sir." Cliff, with an effort, held on to his composure, but he was swept by a wave of shame. A man hitherto silent rescued him by saying:

"A while ago you used the word 'purposive' in connection with Gnut's actions. Can you explain that a little?"

"Yes, that was one of the things that struck me: Gnut never seems to waste a motion. He can move with surprising speed when he wants to; I saw that when he attacked the gorilla; but most other times he walks around as if methodically completing some simple task. And that reminds me of a peculiar thing: at times he gets into one position, any position, maybe half bent over, and stays there for minutes at a time. It's as if his scale of time values was eccentric, compared to ours; some things he does surprisingly fast, and others surprisingly slow. This might account for his long periods of immobility."

"That's very interesting," said one of the scientists. "How would you account for the fact that he recently moves only at night?"

"I think he's doing something he wants no one to see, and the night is the only time he is alone."

"But he went ahead even after finding you there."

"I know But I have no other explanation, unless he considered me harmless or unable to stop him—which was certainly the case."

"Before you arrived, we were considering incasing him in a large block of glasstex. Do you think he would permit it?"

"I don't know. Probably he would; he stood for the acids and rays and heat. But it had better be done in the daytime; night seems to be the time he moves."

"But he moved in the daytime when he emerged from the traveler with Klaatu."

"I know."

That seemed to be all they could think of to ask him. Sanders slapped his hand on the table.

"Well, I guess that's all, Mr. Sutherland," he said. "Thank you for your help, and let me congratulate you for a very foolish, stubborn, brave young man—young businessman." He smiled very faintly. "You are free to go now, but it may be that I'll have to call you back later. We'll see."

"May I remain while you decide about that glasstex?" Cliff asked. "As long as I'm here I'd like to have the tip."

"The decision has already been made—the tip's yours. The pouring will be started at once."

"Thank you, sir," said Cliff—and calmly asked more: "And will you be so kind as to authorize me to be present outside the building tonight? Just outside. I've a feeling something's going to happen."

"You want still another scoop, I see," said Sanders not unkindly, "then you'll let the police wait while you transact your business."

"Not again, sir. If anything happens, they'll get it at once."

The chief hesitated. "I don't know," he said. "I'll tell you what. All the news services will want men there, and we can't have that; but if you can arrange to represent them all yourself, it's a go. Nothing's going to happen, but your reports will help calm the hysterical ones. Let me know."

Cliff thanked him and hurried out and phoned his syndicate the tip—free—then told them Sanders' proposal. Ten minutes later they called him back, said all was arranged, and told him to catch some sleep. They would cover the pouring. With light heart, Cliff hurried over to the museum. The place was surrounded by thousands of the curious, held far back by a strong cordon of police. For once he could not get through; he was recognized, and the police were still sore. But he did not care much; he suddenly felt very tired and needed that nap. He went back to his hotel, left a call, and went to bed.

He had been asleep only a few minutes when his phone rang. Eyes shut, he answered it. It was one of the boys at the syndicate, with peculiar news. Stillwell had just reported, very much alive—the real Stillwell. The two dead ones were some kind of copies; he couldn't imagine how to explain them. He had no brothers.

For a moment Cliff came fully awake, then he went back to bed. Nothing was fantastic any more.

VI

At four o'clock, much refreshed and with an infrared viewing magnifier slung over his shoulder, Cliff passed through the cordon and entered the door of the wing. He had been expected and there was no trouble. As his eyes fell on Gnut, an odd feeling went through him, and for some obscure reason he was almost sorry for the giant robot.

Gnut stood exactly as he had always stood, the right foot advanced a little, and the same brooding expression on his face; but now there was something more. He was solidly encased in a huge block of transparent glasstex. From the floor on which he stood to the top of his full eight feet, and from there on up for an equal distance, and for about eight feet to the left, right, back, and front, he was immured in a water-clear prison which confined every inch of his surface and would prevent the slightest twitch of even his amazing muscles.

It was absurd, no doubt, to feel sorry for a robot, a man-made mechanism, but Cliff had come to think of him as being really alive, as a human is alive. He showed purpose and will; he performed complicated and resourceful acts; his face had twice clearly shown the emotion of sadness, and several times what appeared to be deep thought; he had been ruthless with the gorilla, and gentle with the mocking bird and the other two bodies, and he had twice refrained from crushing Cliff when there seemed every reason that he might. Cliff did not doubt for a minute that he was still alive, whatever that "alive" might mean.

But outside were waiting the radio and television men; he had work to do. He turned and went to them and all got busy.

An hour later Cliff sat alone about fifteen feet above the ground in a big tree which, located just across the walk from the building, commanded through a window a clear view of the upper part of Gnut's body. Strapped to the limbs above him were three instruments—his infrared viewing magnifier, a radio mike, and an infrared television eye with sound pickup. The first, the viewing magnifier, would allow him to see in the dark with his own eyes, as if by daylight, a magnified image of the robot, and the others would pick up any sights and sounds, including his own remarks, and transmit them to the several broadcast studios which would fling them millions of miles in all directions through space. Never before had a picture man had such an important assignment, probably—certainly not one who forgot to take pictures. But now that was forgotten, and Cliff was quite proud, and ready.

Far back in a great circle stood a multitude of the curious —and the fearful. Would the plastic glasstex hold Gnut? If it did not, would he come out thirsting for revenge? Would unimaginable beings come out of the traveler and release him, and perhaps exact revenge? Millions at their receivers were jittery; those in the distance hoped nothing awful would happen, yet they hoped something would, and they were prepared to run.

In carefully selected spots not far from Cliff on all sides were mobile ray batteries manned by army units, and in a hollow in back of him, well to his right, there was stationed a huge tank with a large gun. Every weapon was trained on the door of the wing. A row of smaller, faster tanks stood ready fifty yards directly north. Their ray projectors were aimed at the door, but not their guns. The grounds about the building contained only one spot—the hollow where the great tank was—where, by close calculation, a shell directed at the doorway would not cause damage and loss of life to some part of the sprawling capital.

Dusk fell; out streamed the last of the army officers, politicians and other privileged ones; the great metal doors of the wing clanged to and were locked for the night. Soon Cliff was alone, except for the watchers at their weapons scattered around him.

Hours passed. The moon came out. From time to time Cliff reported to the studio crew that all was quiet. His unaided eyes could now see nothing of Gnut but the two faint red points of his eyes, but through the magnifier he stood out as clearly as if in daylight from an apparent distance of only ten feet. Except for his eyes there was no evidence that he was anything but dead and unfunctionable metal.

Another hour passed. Now and again Cliff thumbed the levels of his tiny radio-television watch—only a few seconds at a time because of its limited battery. The air was full of Gnut and his own face and his own name, and once the tiny screen showed the tree in which he was then sitting and even, minutely, himself. Powerful infrared long-distance television pickups were even then focused on him from nearby points of vantage. It gave him a funny feeling.

Then, suddenly, Cliff saw something and quickly bent his eye to the viewing magnifier. Gnut's eyes were moving; at least the intensity of the light emanating from them varied. It was as if two tiny red flashlights were turned from side to side, their beams at each motion crossing Cliff's eyes.

Thrilling, Cliff signaled the studios, cut in his pickups, and described the phenomenon. Millions resonated to the excitement in his voice. Could Gnut conceivably break out of that terrible prison?

Minutes passed, the eye flashes continued, but Cliff could discern no movement or attempted movement of the robot's body. In brief snatches he described what he saw. Gnut was clearly alive; there could be no doubt he was straining against the transparent prison in which he had at last been locked fast; but unless he could crack it, no motion should show.

Cliff took his eye from the magnifier—and started. His unaided eye, looking at Gnut shrouded in darkness, saw an astonishing thing not yet visible through his instrument. A faint red glow was spreading over the robot's body. With trembling fingers he readjusted the lens of the television eye, but even as he did so the glow grew in intensity. It looked as if Gnut's body was being heated to incandescence!

He described it in excited fragments, for it took most of his attention to keep correcting the lens. Gnut passed from a figure of dull red to one brighter and brighter, clearly glowing now even through the magnifier. And then he moved! Unmistakably he moved!

He had within himself somehow the means to raise his own body temperature, and was exploiting the one limitation of the plastic in which he was locked. For glass-tex, Cliff now remembered, was a thermoplastic material, one that set by cooling and conversely would soften again with heat. Gnut was melting his way out!

In three-word snatches, Cliff described this. The robot became cherry-red, the sharp edges of the icelike block rounded, and the whole structure began to sag. The process accelerated. The robot's body moved more widely. The plastic lowered to the crown of his head, then to his neck, then his waist, which was as far as Cliff could see. His body was free! And then, still cherry-red, he moved forward out of sight!

Cliff strained eyes and ears, but caught nothing but the distant roar of the watchers beyond the police lines and a few low, sharp commands from the batteries posted around him. They, too, had heard, and perhaps seen by telescreen, and were waiting.

Several minutes passed. There was a sharp, ringing crack; the great metal doors of the wing flew open, and out stepped the metal giant, glowing no longer. He stood stock-still, and his red eyes pierced from side to side through the darkness.

Voices out in the dark barked orders and in a twinkling Gnut was bathed in narrow crisscrossing rays of sizzling, colored light. Behind him the metal doors began to melt, but his great green body showed no change at all. Then the world seemed to come to an end; there was a deafening roar, everything before Cliff seemed to explode in smoke and chaos, his tree whipped to one side so that he was nearly thrown out. Pieces of debris rained down. The tank gun had spoken, and Gnut, he was sure, had been hit.

Cliff held on tight and peered into the haze. As it cleared he made out a stirring among the debris at the door, and then dimly but unmistakably he saw the great form of Gnut rise to his feet. He got up slowly, turned toward the tank, and suddenly darted toward it in a wide arc. The big gun swung in an attempt to cover him, but the robot side-stepped and then was upon it. As the crew scattered, he destroyed its breech with one blow of his fist, and then he turned and looked right at Cliff.

He moved toward him, and in a moment was under the tree. Cliff climbed higher. Gnut put his two arms around the tree and gave a lifting push, and the tree tore out at the roots and fell crushing to its side. Before Cliff could scramble away, the robot had lifted him in his metal hands.

Cliff thought his time had come, but strange things were yet in store for him that night. Gnut did not hurt him. He looked at him from arm's length for a moment, then lifted him to a sitting position on his shoulders, legs straddling his neck. Then, holding one ankle, he turned and without hesitation started down the path which led westward away from the building.

Cliff rode helpless. Out over the lawns he saw the muzzles of the scattered field pieces move as he moved, Gnut—and himself—their one focus. But they did not fire. Gnut, by placing him on his shoulders, had secured himself against that—Cliff hoped.

The robot bore straight toward the Tidal Basin. Most of the field throbbed slowly after. Far back, Cliff saw a dark tide of confusion roll into the cleared area—the police lines had broken. Ahead, the ring thinned rapidly off to the sides; then, from all directions but the front, the tide rolled in until individual shouts and cries could be made out. It came to a stop about fifty yards off, and few people ventured nearer.

Gnut paid them no attention, and he no more noticed his burden than he might a fly. His neck and shoulders made Cliff a seat hard as steel, but with the difference that their underlying muscles with each movement flexed, just as would those of a human being. To Cliff, this metal musculature became a vivid wonder.

Straight as the flight of a bee, over paths, across lawns and through thin rows of trees Gnut bore the young man, the roar of thousands of people following close. Above droned copters and darting planes, among them police cars with their nerve-shattering sirens. Just ahead lay the still waters of the Tidal Basin, and in its midst the simple marble tomb of the slain ambassador, Klaatu, gleaming black and cold in the light of the dozen searchlights always trained on it at night. Was this a rendezvous with the dead?

Without an instant's hesitation, Gnut strode down the bank and entered the water. It rose to his knees, then waist, until Cliff's feet were under. Straight through the dark waters for the tomb of Klaatu the robot made his inevitable way.

The dark square mass of gleaming marble rose higher as they neared it. Gnut's body began emerging from the water as the bottom shelved upward, until his dripping feet took the first of the rising pyramid of steps. In a moment they were at the top, on the narrow platform in the middle of which rested the simple oblong tomb.

Stark in the blinding searchlights, the giant robot walked around it, then, bending, he braced himself and gave a mighty push against the top. The marble cracked; the thick cover slipped askew and broke with a loud noise on the far side. Gnut went to his knees and looked within, bringing Cliff well up over the edge.

Inside, in sharp shadow against the converging light beams, lay a transparent plastic coffin, thick walled and sealed against the centuries, and containing all that was mortal of Klaatu, unspoken visitor from the great Unknown. He lay as if asleep, on his face the look of godlike nobility that had caused some of the ignorant to believe him divine. He wore the robe he had arrived in. There were no faded flowers, no jewelry, no ornaments; they would have seemed profane. At the foot of the coffin lay the small sealed box, also of transparent plastic, which contained all of Earth's records of his visit—a description of the events attending his arrival, pictures of Gnut and the traveler, and the little roll of sight-and-sound film which had caught for all time his few brief motions and words.

Cliff sat very still, wishing he could see the face of the robot. Gnut, too, did not move from his position of reverent contemplation—not for a long time. There on the brilliantly lighted pyramid, under the eyes of a fearful, tumultuous multitude, Gnut paid final respect to his beautiful and adored master.

Suddenly, then, it was over. Gnut reached out and took the little box of records, rose to his feet and started down the steps.

Back through the water, straight back to the building, across lawns and paths as before, he made his irresistible way. Before him the chaotic ring of people melted away, behind they followed as close as they dared, trampling each other in their efforts to keep him in sight. There are no television records of his return. Every pickup was damaged on the way to the tomb.

As they drew near the building, Cliff saw that the tank's projectile had made a hole twenty feet wide extending from the roof to the ground. The door still stood open, and Gnut, hardly varying his almost jerkless rhythm, made his way over the debris and went straight for the port end of the ship. Cliff wondered if he would be set free.

He was. The robot set him down and pointed toward the

door; then, turning, he made the sounds that opened the ship. The ramp slid down and he entered.

Then Cliff did the mad, courageous thing which made him famous for a generation. Just as the ramp started sliding back in he skipped over it and himself entered the ship. The port closed.

VII

It was pitch dark, and the silence was absolute. Cliff did not move. He felt that Gnut was close, just ahead, and it was so.

His hard metal hand took him by the waist, pulled him against his cold side, and carried him somewhere ahead. Hidden lamps suddenly bathed the surroundings with bluish light.

He set Cliff down and stood looking at him. The young man already regretted his rash action, but the robot, except for his always unfathomable eyes, did not seem angry. He pointed to a stool in one corner of the room. Cliff quickly obeyed this time and sat meekly, for a while not even venturing to look around.

He saw he was in a small laboratory of some kind. Complicated metal and plastic apparatus lined the walls and filled several small tables; he could not recognize or guess the function of a single piece. Dominating the center of the room was a long metal table on whose top lay a large box, much like a coffin on the outside, connected by many wires to a complicated apparatus at the far end. From close above spread a cone of bright light from a many-tubed lamp.

One thing, half covered on a near-by table, did look familiar—and very much out of place. From where he sat it seemed to be a brief case—an ordinary Earthman's brief case. He wondered.

Gnut paid him no attention, but at once, with the narrow edge of a thick tool, sliced the lid off the little box of records. He lifted out the strip of sight-and-sound film and spent fully half an hour adjusting it within the apparatus at the end of the big table. Cliff watched, fascinated, wondering at the skill with which the robot used his tough metal fingers. This done, Gnut worked for a long time over some accessory aparatus on an adjoining table. Then he paused thoughtfully a moment and pushed inward a long rod.

A voice came out of the coffinlike box—the voice of the slain ambassador.

"I am Klaatu," it said, "and this is Gnut."

From the recording!—flashed through Cliff's mind. The first and only words the ambassador had spoken. But, then, in the very next second he saw that it was not so. There was a man in the box! The man stirred and sat up, and Cliff saw the living face of Klaatu!

Klaatu appeared somewhat surprised and spoke quickly in an unknown tongue to Gnut—and Gnut, for the first time in Cliff's experience, spoke himself in answer. The robot's syllables tumbled out as if born of human emotion, and the expression on Klaatu's face changed from surprise to wonder. They talked for several minutes. Klaatu, apparently fatigued, then began to lie down, but stopped midway, for he saw Cliff. Gnut spoke again, at length. Klaatu beckoned Cliff with his hand, and he went to him.

"Gnut has told me everything," he said in a low, gentle voice, then looked at Cliff for a moment in silence, on his face a faint, tired smile.

Cliff had a hundred questions to ask, but for a moment hardly dared open his mouth.

"But you," he began at last—very respectfully, but with an escaping excitement—"you are not the Klaatu that was in the tomb?"

The man's smile faded and he shook his head.

"No." He turned to the towering Gnut and said something in his own tongue, and at his words the metal features of the robot twisted as if with pain. Then he turned back to Cliff. "I am dying," he announced simply, as if repeating his words for the Earthman. Again to his face came the faint, tired smile.

Cliff's tongue was locked. He just stared, hoping for light. Klaatu seemed to read his mind.

"I see you don't understand," he said. "Although unlike us, Gnut has great powers. When the wing was built and the lectures began, there came to him a striking inspiration. Acting on it at once, in the night, he assembled this apparatus . . . and now he has made me again, from my voice, as recorded by your people. As you must know, a given body makes a characteristic sound. He constructed an apparatus which reversed the recording process, and from the given sound made the characteristic body."

Cliff gasped. So that was it!

"But you needn't die!" Cliff exclaimed, eagerly. "Your voice recording was taken when you stepped out of the ship, while you were well! You must let me take you to a hospital! Our doctors are very skillful!"

Hardly perceptibly, Klaatu shook his head.

"You still don't understand," he said slowly and more faintly. "Your recording had imperfections. Perhaps very slight ones, but they doom the product. All of Gnut's experiments died in a few minutes, he tells me . . . and so must I."

Suddenly, then, Cliff understood the origin of the "experiments." He remembered that on the day the wing was opened a Smithsonian official had lost a brief case containing film strips recording the speech of various world fauna. There, on that table, was a brief case! And the Stillwells must have been made from strips kept in the table drawer!

But his heart was heavy. He did not want this stranger to die. Slowly there dawned on him an important idea. He explained it with growing excitement.

"You say the recording was imperfect, and of course it was. But the cause of that lay in the use of an imperfect recording apparatus. So if Gnut, in his reversal of the process, had used exactly the same pieces of apparatus that your voice was recorded with, the imperfections could be studied, canceled out, and you'd live, and not die!"

As the last words left his lips, Gnut whipped around like a cat and gripped him tight. A truly human excitement was shining in the metal muscles of his face.

"Get me that apparatus!" he ordered—in clear and perfect English! He started pushing Cliff toward the door, but Klaatu raised his hand.

"There is no hurry," Klaatu said gently; "it is too late for me. What is your name, young man?"

Cliff told him.

"Stay with me to the end," he asked. Klaatu closed his eyes and rested; then, smiling just a little, but not opening his eyes, he added: "And don't be sad, for I shall now perhaps live again . . . and it will be due to you. There is no pain—" His voice was rapidly growing weaker. Cliff, for all the questions he had, could only look on, dumb. Again Klaatu seemed to be aware of his thoughts.

"I know," he said feebly, "I know. We have so much to ask each other. About your civilization . . . and Gnut's—"

"And yours," said Cliff.

"And Gnut's," said the gentle voice again. "Perhaps . . . some day . . . perhaps I will be back—"

He lay without moving. He lay so for a long time, and at last Cliff knew that he was dead. Tears came to his eyes; in only these few minutes he had come to love this man. He looked at Gnut. The robot knew, too, that he was dead, but no tears filled his red-lighted eyes; they were fixed on Cliff, and for once the young man knew what was in his mind.

"Gnut," he announced earnestly, as if taking a sacred oath, "I'll get the original apparatus. I'll get it. Every piece of it, the exact same things."

Without a word, Gnut conducted him to the port. He made the sounds that unlocked it. As it opened, a noisy crowd of Earthmen outside trampled each other in a sudden scramble to get out of the building. The wing was lighted. Cliff stepped down the ramp.

The next two hours always in Cliff's memory had a dreamlike quality. It was as if that mysterious laboratory with the peacefully sleeping dead man was the real and central part of his life, and his scene with the noisy men with whom he talked a gross and barbaric interlude. He stood not far from the ramp. He told only part of his story. He was believed. He waited quietly while all the pressure which the highest officials in the land could exact was directed toward obtaining for him the apparatus the robot had demanded.

When it arrived, he carried it to the floor of the little vestibule behind the port. Gnut was there, as if waiting. In his arms he held the slender body of the second Klaatu. Tenderly he passed him out to Cliff, who took him without a word, as if all this had been arranged. It seemed to be the parting.

Of all the things Cliff had wanted to say to Klaatu, one remained imperatively present in his mind. Now, as the green metal robot stood framed in the great green ship, he seized his chance.

"Gnut," he said earnestly, holding carefully the limp body in his arms, "you must do one thing for me. Listen carefully. I want you to tell your master—the master yet to come—that what happened to the first Klaatu was an accident, for which all Earth is immeasurably sorry. Will you do that?"

"I have known it," the robot answered gently.

"But will you promise to tell your master—just those words—as soon as he is arrived?"

"You misunderstand," said Gnut, still gently, and quietly spoke four more words. As Cliff heard them a mist passed over his eyes and his body went numb.

As he recovered and his eyes came back to focus he saw the great ship disappear. It just suddenly was not there any more. He fell back a step or two. In his ears, like great bells, rang Gnut's last words. Never, never was he to disclose them till the day he came to die.

"You misunderstand," the mighty robot had said. "I am the master."

THE TWILIGHT ZONE

Rod Serling, one of America's exciting writers, has fashioned amazing excursions into the fifth dimension — the world of imagination. Here are three brilliant collections of fantastic stories written expressly for Bantam, based upon the suspense-filled CBS television series. Discover, for yourself, the fascinating world of Rod Serling in:

STORIES FROM THE TWILIGHT ZONE 45¢

MORE STORIES FROM THE TWILIGHT ZONE 45

NEW STORIES FROM THE TWILIGHT ZONE 45¢

 Bantam Books

Buy them wherever paperbacks are sold.